Woven In Dreams

Tapestry of Fated Dreams
Book 1

Kristen Tassin

ISBN 978-1-7374589-8-2 eBook

ISBN 978-1-7374589-7-5 Paperback (Kaye Rae Edition)

ISBN 978-1-7374589-9-9 Paperback Kristen Tassin

Developmental Editor- Jodi Henly

Editor- Patty MacFarlane

Cover Design- KTK Design

Map Design- Arvin AI App and Canva

Sensitivity Warning: This is an NA (New Adult) romantic fantasy novel that has depictions of panic and anxiety attacks, self-harm, abuse, references to drugs and alcohol, and closed-door sex scenes.

WOVEN IN DREAMS

TAPESTRY OF FATED
DREAMS
BOOK ONE

Woven In Dreams

*To all of you who doubt you can— stop it!
You can and you will.*

NOD
REALM OF ERÉBUS
TARTARUS

REALM OF DREAMS
EARTH
HADES

"My only love sprung from my only hate,
Too early seen unknown and known too late!
Prodigious birth of love is it to me,
That I must love a loathed enemy."— Juliet

Romeo and Juliet
William Shakespeare

Chapter One

Despite the whirring fan and flimsy sheet, the oppressive heat clung to me like a second skin. Even the pre-dawn darkness offered no solace. A sliver of moonlight peeked through my window, illuminating the room I'd transformed into a desperate sanctuary. Sunshine yellow walls pulsed with a feverish warmth, a mockery of the open fields I craved. My gaze drifted to the sky-blue ceiling, dotted with glow-in-the-dark stars, a feeble attempt to recapture the vast, star-studded nights I used to cherish.

Pushing back the covers, I tentatively touched the cool, grass-green shag carpet, the texture a distant memory of long summer days spent barefoot in the meadow behind our old house. A wave of panic surged through me, the phantom sensation of rough asphalt scraping my skin, and the cacophony of the city threatening to drown me. My breath hitched, a strangled gasp escaping my lips. The walls seemed to constrict, the air thick and suffocating. "No," I rasped, clawing at my chest for a single, clean breath, and jumped back into bed as if the monster under the bed was about to grab my ankles.

My heart sped up when my door creaked open. "Don't shoot the messenger, but this was just delivered." Aurora, my best friend and roommate, pushed her hand around my door.

She held a chocolate cupcake with way too many candles. I swallowed my anxiety, covering it up with a perfectly acceptable groan that Aurora would understand. She knew I hated my birthday, and so did Aunt Marie, but for some reason, Aunt Marie thought I would somehow be okay three days after the big day, and I wouldn't think celebrating my birthday would be dreadful.

Ignoring the cake, I leaned up on one elbow. "You're awake early!"

Aurora stepped into the room. "Go on," she said, waving it at me. "It's your big two-one, go ahead, make a wish, and blow them out."

I took a deep, whooping breath and crawled back under the sheets, pulling them up over my head. "No! "I'm going back to sleep."

Aurora's Dr. Martens made shuffling noises on the carpet. She blew out the candles and set the cupcake on my nightstand. "I need fresh air. Want to come with?"

The churning in my gut anytime she mentioned leaving my safe space always happened. I was grateful she never gave up on me, but at the same time, I wished she'd just stop.

She was waiting for me to say something in return, but I didn't. I hid under my covers with my fingers knotted in the sheets like I was afraid she'd rip them off and leave me exposed. "Sleep well," she finally said.

She always waited a long time, which made me feel even worse.

I was grateful that she accepted my rejection, but I couldn't help wondering how I got so lucky to have such a patient best friend. She was the only person I could still be myself with; she understood me and never pressured me to leave my safe space. Maybe she worried about me being safe and was secretly glad I didn't leave. Or at least that is what I hoped.

I kicked my sheets off once I heard her leave. The weight of the approaching date settled on me like a suffocating blanket. Not only had my birthday failed to pass unnoticed, but Séverin would soon be getting out of prison. I rolled to my side, opened my tablet to the latest dream drawing I was working on, and sighed, hugging the image to my chest.

Felix, the ever-present purring machine, hopped up beside me. He always seemed to know when I thought about drawing. He loved chasing my pen. This time, he lay next to the tablet, pushing it deeper into my chest with his body. It didn't take long before his rhythmic rumble pulled me back into my dreams.

The air crackled, and static ran through my body as I heard my name being called. The world dissolved around me, replaced by a shadowy forest path damp and slick beneath my bare feet. Moonlight filtered through the dense canopy, casting long, skeletal shadows that danced with my panicked breaths. Tears streamed down my cheeks, blurring the already indistinct path ahead.

"Delphine!" The voice echoed through the trees, filled with a frantic urgency that mirrored my own. I tripped, my dress snagging on a gnarled branch. Ignoring the rip, I yanked free and continued running, the heavy thud of my heart a relentless drumbeat.

As I rounded a bend, a figure emerged from the darkness. Relief flooded me – it was Cyprien! His normally warm, inviting smile seemed strained in the pale moonlight, but I didn't care. He was here, and that was all that mattered. I launched myself into his arms, seeking the comfort of his familiar embrace. His touch, usually grounding and calming, felt...off. A flicker of unease snaked through me, but I pushed it down.

Suddenly, the darkness writhed, swirling around us in a menacing mist. Cyprien started to pull away, but I clung to him desperately. "No! Don't leave me!" His voice, once a soothing melody, now held a chilling edge. "You belong to my brother. You are stronger than you think. You'll survive."

Visions assaulted me – the screech of tires, the blood-curdling scream ripped from my throat the night of the accident, the overwhelming grief of losing my parents. My past, dark and hungry, rose from its grave, threatening to consume me. Panic seized me, a primal urge to break free from the suffocating darkness.

"Please," I gasped, clinging to him with all my might. Each breath felt like a struggle for survival. He felt like a manifestation of my deepest fears, his touch a conduit to the relentless magic that threatened to pull me under.

As his hands slid down my arms, a chilling transformation occurred. His strong, familiar touch morphed into Séverin's cold, bruising embrace. The screeching sound of screams and crashing metal faded into an unsettling silence.

Séverin's voice echoed in my mind, a twisted justification for his horrific actions. "You know I had to do it. They wanted you to leave me."

A surge of defiance ignited within me. "No!" I screamed, twisting away from his grasp. "Where is Cyprien?"

A chilling smile played on Séverin's lips. "He doesn't exist here. You are mine."

"No, this can't be happening," I muttered, the world blurring around me. The shadowy forest morphed into Magic Brew Café and then back again. Black threads of smoke swirled around me, constricting and suffocating.

Before the shadows completely took me over again, a bright figure wrapped in golden light emerged, a beacon of hope in the darkness. Cyprien, steadfast and resolute, stepped forward. "Delphine?"

He grabbed my arm, and asked, "What is going on? The second my back was turned, you appeared out of thin air."

His voice sounded off. "Cyprien?"

He shook my arm, "Phin!" His touch and voice were all wrong.

With a desperate cry, I tore myself awake.

The room trembled around me, voices washed in and out like white noise—French, English, the clatter of cups and hiss of the espresso machine. Somebody laughed, and abruptly, it smelled like blood. I couldn't remember how I got there. I wrapped my arms around me and dropped to the floor, hyperventilating.

Cyprien and the golden light were gone, and I was on the floor in the middle of Magic Brew Café. Bev squatted next to me with her hand on my arm. "Phin, do you need me to take you home?"

I curled around myself, shivering. Bev tried to help me up, but I flinched out of her arms and scrambled back. "No!" I choked out.

Bev's concerned gaze looked at me with pity. I hated that look. It reminded me how weak and afraid I was of living. But in circumstances like this, fear was a familiar companion. It was as if my nightmare leaked into reality, which freaked me out because this was the first time I had sleepwalked.

I scrambled to my feet. Bev reached out to help me as I swayed. She grabbed my wrist, dragging me to a table. The words tumbled out before I could stop them, a desperate plea, "Don't touch me."

My wrist throbbed, bruised in the shape of Séverin's hand that grabbed me in my dream. It was his fault I didn't like to be touched; he poisoned me, leaving me raw, exposed, and untouchable.

Unable to bear the thought of anyone else touching me, I pulled my sleeve down, hiding the evidence. Bev's gaze lingered on my wrist, a flicker of concern morphing into something else entirely. It was a look I couldn't decipher, a mixture of worry and...curiosity. Bev generally respected my boundaries and backed away, but she held her ground this time.

"Sorry, shug, but you looked like you were in a trance

or something." Bev seemed to have a bright glow around her that I'd never seen before.

A shiver ran down my spine, and I wondered, not for the first time since my birthday, that bizarre occurrences had happened, and I started to think I might be slowly going insane. Maybe it was my birthday on Monday, the constant nagging fear in the back of my mind that Séverin's release from prison was imminent. Our five years were up – his in jail, and my self-imposed confinement fueled by isolation, fear, and anxiety. But what good was all this self-imposed torture if I couldn't even protect myself in a dream?

"Sorry," I muttered, curling into myself like a frightened animal seeking a safe haven. "I think I was sleepwalking." It was Thursday, and I had been so exhausted that I could barely stay awake since Monday. Each night, the dreams felt more vivid, more real, like fragmented memories from a life I never lived. Tears welled in my eyes, a mixture of grief for Cyprien and betrayal for choosing not to run away with me to escape Séverin.

"Well," Bev said, her voice laced with a concern that felt off. You're awake now. Let me make you a relaxation brew."

I recoiled. "No! Your relaxation brew is disgusting. Sour lemons and lavender in espresso?" Just the thought made me gag. "Seriously, who even developed that? It's beyond gross, Bev."

Bev's laugh had a sharp edge, and for a fleeting moment, I could have sworn I saw a glint of something otherworldly in her eyes. Was it my imagination, or was the strange glow around her intensifying?

"I add the sour only when I can sense anxiety bubbling up," she said, her gaze lingering on me a beat too long. "The sour helps the human brain stop thinking so hard."

"I'm not anxious," I lied, unconvincing.

She raised an eyebrow, a silent challenge in her eyes. "I'll believe that when you stop flinching, every time someone tries to touch you."

Bev had known me before my parents died. Back then, she wasn't just the cafe manager—she was a good friend. She remembered when I was a normal person—an average teen with lots of friends and a hot college boyfriend who was completely obsessed with me. My friends had been so jealous of my luck, and I'd been so cocky about it in return. Now, things were different. Bev's loyalty seemed to lie primarily with Aunt Marie, co-owner of Magic Brew, and my roommate Aurora's mother.

Marie wasn't really my aunt, but her bond with my parents had run so deep she'd become part of our family. My parent's death meant I received an income from the cafe and apartments, making me financially independent. Bev, in turn, became more like a distant relative, a constant fixture managing the cafe.

A sudden burst of steam from the espresso machine made me jump. Bev cursed under her breath at the almost ten-year-old machine. As I watched her rush to fix it, I realized that I had missed that friendship. I picked up the notebook I must have brought and crossed the room to my favorite table, trying to remember the last time I thought of Bev as a friend.

It was five years ago when Bev came to Séverin's hearing with me. She glared daggers at him from the courtroom bench, passed me tissues, and muttered fierce obscenities under her breath. We almost got kicked out when she told the judge the sentence was a joke—a reckless outburst fueled by anger and fierce protectiveness.

The worst part was that even knowing his crimes, the sight of him sent a tremor through me. Across the crowded courtroom, through the murmurs and shuffling of feet, I heard his voice, laced with promise. "See you later, Phin." He'd laughed as he was escorted out in handcuffs.

Technically, it wasn't a threat, but the look in his eyes, that smile—I knew he burned with hatred. Bev had vowed to call the police if he ever dared come near me, once his sentence was over, but nobody could be with me 24/7. The thought sent a fresh wave of panic crashing over me.

I sat at the table and rubbed my finger over the etched carvings people made over the years. Its worn surface spoke of a long history and character and always made me feel connected. It was pressed against the window overlooking Royal Street. I took a seat and face-planted on the table, hands over my head, trying to tune out my thoughts. I turned my head to the side to get a breath of fresh air, but the inside of the cafe wasn't much of an improvement from the muggy air of the city.

My chin sank into my hand as I rested my elbow on the table, glaring at the door. It never quite fit in the frame. Still, it felt good to be here. Despite my emotions running rampant like wild dogs, I felt grounded here.

Over the last five years, staring out the window had filled the hole inside me and kept me feeling like I was still a part of society. Until Cyprien appeared in my dreams, I hadn't realized the depth of my longing for connection. I was never lonely in my dream world. I was loved, cherished, and, for the most part, happy and free. One detail about the dream lingered in my mind – his name, Cyprien. It was a name I'd never encountered before, yet it felt oddly familiar as if it resonated deep within my subconscious.

I've always been drawn to archaic names like mine— Delphine, a name I shared with no one else I knew. I remember when I met my ex and told my parents his name was Séverin Moreau; they thought it was cute that I also met a boy with an old-sounding name.

Ugh, why did he keep worming his way into my thoughts? It's like he and the dream were all intertwined. I had to keep reminding myself and focus on the reality of who he was— a monster. This is just another reminder of why I shouldn't leave my apartment.

Falling in love again and the thought of giving someone that much power over me, attaching every part of me to them, and watching helplessly as they destroy what's left of me was terrifying. I knew myself too well. I'm powerless against my romantic tendencies and fell for another man like Séverin. It would kill me.

Unless Séverin found me first and took his vengeance out on me, then I wouldn't have to worry anymore.

Trembling, I opened my tablet to the sketches I'd been working on – portraits of Cyprien. He bore an uncanny resemblance to the drawing of Paul Victor

Grandhomme by Raphaël Collin, with his strong jawline and kind eyes. For the first time in ages, I stayed away from my usual rainy-day drawings of the hauntingly beautiful world hidden within New Orleans and opted to begin a light and airy fairytale series using Cy as my model.

With the sketches complete, all that was left were the details and colors. The thought of bringing Cyprien to life on the page, even in this fantastical form, sparked a flicker of excitement within me. I pushed away the absurdity of the notion. What was wrong with me? I hoped drawing my dreams, woven with threads of fear and longing, into art would help stop me from thinking about love and loss. But a nagging worry crept in – could these dreams be my subconscious yearning for Séverin, buried beneath the layers of fear?

The truth was, I couldn't escape his memory. It creeps its way back in because it knows the way, and I end up longing for him next to me. I shivered as the memory of his touch – both tender and cruel – washed over me. No, I wouldn't go there. The cost was far too high.

Bev came out from behind the counter, a steaming mug in hand. "Here you go, shug. Milk and espresso."

I reached for my card and swatted my hand away. "It's on me. When are you gonna graduate from this kiddie drink?" Her thick New Orleans accent rolled over the words like molasses, leaving little room to interject.

A grimace twisted her features, deepening the wrinkles around her mouth. Her nose crinkled in a theatrical display of disapproval. She slid the cup on the table around my iPad and closer to my hand. It all seemed a bit dramatic. "It's just strong coffee milk," I mumbled, the familiar warmth radiating through the mug. A small comfort that held a sacred place in my memories. It was my usual Saturday morning treat, one of the small but treasured routines my parents never failed to maintain until they died. It's a bittersweet reminder of the last interaction I had with my parents before their tragic demise.

We had been in an argument fueled by their disapproval of Séverin. They saw the darkness beneath his charm, a darkness I was completely blind to. I dropped my head in my arms. Bev's talking faded into the background. She was probably used to it. After all, I did work here for a while, right after I quit school. Back then, I was slowly becoming more of a recluse. Because of my rapid mood changes, she usually had me work in the back, behind the scenes, rather than with the public.

Bev tutted as she walked away. I was so tired of being afraid, tired of pushing people away. I know my parents wouldn't want me like this, but for some reason, I still felt trapped within my naive sixteen-year-old self. Our relationship developed so fast, fueled by a shared passion for art back then, and the fact that Séverin was four years older and otherworldly than my immature self captivated me. It felt like fate, a cosmic alignment that brought the love of my life into my orbit. My parents, however, weren't convinced, and our age difference troubled them. I refused to listen to them, and Séverin changed, turned to drugs, and blamed me for ruining his life, taking him away from his family, and trapping him in this forsaken city. He was right. I begged him to forgive me and stay with me. I was stupid.

A tear leaked out of the corner of my eye, and I regretted that I hadn't listened. If only I had listened, we would all be sitting here together, drinking coffee milk. I sniffed and wiped my eyes on my sleeve. Maybe it *was* time to change my drink. I cradled the warm cup in my cold hands and stared into the milky liquid.

A loud clatter yanked me from my reverie. Bev was on the phone, her voice hushed, a conspiratorial glint in her eyes as she glanced my way. She and Aunt Marie, practically inseparable, were like two peas in a pod, both concerned about my every move. Aunt Marie appointed Bev as my guardian angel when she wasn't near; Bev always constantly watched me and was sure to share it with Aunt Marie. At first, it annoyed me, but now I didn't even care.

I rubbed my arms, goosebumps prickling my skin despite the app's insistence it was still the seventies. The frosted window mocked the digital display. New Orleans weather was notoriously fickle, but a drop of this magnitude in such a short time felt...off. Pushing aside the unsettling thought, I marched to the thermostat. Set at a comfortable seventy, the air sensor displayed a chilling fifty-three. I clicked on the heater, and a few minutes later, the unmistakable scent of dust burning on the furnace that clearly had not been used —was it really that cold in here? A few customers shouted their thanks to me as I went to the door to investigate the outside air.

My brows furrowed in confusion as I opened the door, and a wall of heat and humidity slammed into me. How strange, it wasn't cold at all. As I turned to go back in, a flash of movement from across the street caught my eye. A glimpse of familiar blonde hair, disappearing into the alley by the old news station. I jumped back, slamming my back into the door of the café. My breath caught in my throat, and my heart thundered as cold sweat coated my entire body. "Séverin?" The word escaped in a choked scream.

Panic urged me to run back inside. I rushed into the bathroom, locked the door, and slid to the floor, panting, the rank smell of fear oozing from my pores. Why did I call for him? I tried to take a deep breath and settle my shaking. Just as I started to regulate my breathing, a knock on the door made me jump.

A woman called out from the other side, "You almost done in there?"

"Sorry," I croaked, forcing myself to my feet and letting the woman in. The dreams were a warning — Séverin was free.

Before returning to my table, I took a moment to peek around the corner, offering a silent prayer to the universe that Séverin hadn't heard me call out to him. The cafe was mostly empty, save for a lone woman at a table with two cups, no doubt the companion to the woman who had just forced me from my refuge.

Bev, oblivious to my distress, hummed as she wiped down tables.

Scanning the area again, I confirmed I was in the all-clear. I made my way back to the table, my eyes drawn to the unfinished drawing. It was part of my dream where I was kissing the man– the back of his head still uncolored, and, for a horrifying moment, Séverin's face replaced my dream love. My foot wouldn't stop bouncing, so I had to put my hand over my knee to prevent the table from rattling.

With trembling hands, I slammed the tablet shut. I would not let him win. I could not let him destroy me again after I finally was ready to heal. Taking a deep breath, I wiped the sweat from my brow. I wouldn't be a prisoner of fear any longer.

Rain pelted the window in front of me, and I found myself transfixed by the fat drops beating upon the glass. Aurora would freak out if she knew I'd seen him. I needed to calm down before she came to work. She'd be angry if she found out I called out to him. Little did she know, I'd do anything within my power to stay away from him. If revenge was his game, I wouldn't be an easy target. Never again.

I opened my phone contacts and scrolled, looking at the very few numbers I kept when I got a new phone. Besides family, only Goldie, a mutual friend of mine and Aurora's, remained. She'd gotten my new number after pestering Aurora. The good thing about Goldie is she respects my need for space. She mostly sent texts like "thinking of you" or random updates. I desperately needed friends around me now, and Goldie was always willing to go the extra mile to stay in touch.

The urge to bang my head on the table when I realized how out of touch I was with the real world battled with the fear that if Bev saw me, she'd be sure to tattle on my behavior to my aunt, and they might want to commit me. I couldn't believe I completely lost contact with everyone.

"Phin?" Bev's voice, laced with concern, cut through my thoughts.

I shifted uncomfortably. "I'm okay," I mumbled, forcing a lightness I didn't feel. "Just trying to figure out how to color the next part of the drawing."

Bev raised an eyebrow, skepticism etched on her face. "Girl, you talented!" she conceded, though her hand hovering near her apron pocket, likely feeling for her phone. Her compliment may have been sincere, but I wasn't convinced.

"Really, Bev, I'm cool. I've been working all day, I'm tired, and I came down because I needed coffee in a major way." I forced a smile. She looked as if she were going to argue with me or ask me twenty questions. I blew out a breath I didn't realize I was holding. It made a wisp of hair near my eye flutter.

Bev studied me, her brow furrowed. "I guess that makes sense, but since you're obviously tired, you better get some sleep." Her words held a hint of skepticism, and my breath hitched in my throat. Elaborating would only draw more attention, so I pushed my chair back with unnecessary force, scraping it against the floor.

Just as I rose to escape the conversation, Bev's hand darted out, her touch sending a jolt through me. My body recoiled like a spring before I snapped my arm back, nearly smacking her away. Shame flooded me as I realized my reaction to what was presumably an affectionate touch.

"Sorry, shug," Bev offered, a pained smile pulling at her lips. "I forgot."

My eyes darted to the door, my muscles were rigid, and I gripped my toes inside my Converse; I wouldn't run away from her. This was pitiful. This wasn't just about isolation anymore. I had to learn to trust touch again, even the most casual kind. My gaze darted to the door once more, the need to flee warring with the knowledge of how pathetic that would appear.

"No, Bev, I'm so sorry!" I Forced myself to uncross my arms to seem less tense.

Bev's gaze held mine for a long moment, her eyes searching mine. I met her stare, willing her to see the lie I was trying to project – the lie that I was okay. The silence stretched thick with unspoken emotions. Finally, Bev offered a single, hesitant nod. Relief washed over me, so intense it left me weak. "Shug, why don't ya go?" she suggested gently."I'll put ya cup away." Her hand reached out to take the mug.

"No!" I said louder than I intended. Heads swiveled in our direction. I gave them an apologetic smile.

"I can get it," I stammered, my voice regaining some semblance of control. "You're the only one here, plus someone could walk in any minute."

"Phin, if you won't go home to bed, at least try to relax."

A wave of relief washed over me as a group of boisterous tourists, their clothes dripping from the downpour, flooded into the cafe. They huddled together, chattering in a language I didn't understand, before making their way towards the counter.

Bev cast me a final, scrutinizing look before turning to greet the new customers.

Chapter Two

The bell on the door jingled again, and a gust of wind whooshed in as Aurora entered. She wrestled with her umbrella, finally shoving it into a corner with a muttered curse. Ignoring the tourists clustered near the counter trying to decide what to order, she made a beeline for back, her movements all hurried impatience.

Bev materialized beside her, her voice clipped. "Forty minutes late, Aurora! This can't keep happenin'."

Aurora rolled her shoulders, her smile strained. "You really should come with a storm warning label, Bev," she replied with a hint of defiance in her voice.

They exchanged a look, a silent tension crackling between them. It was clear they weren't on the best of terms.

I felt a pang of sympathy for Aurora. Her mother, Marie, harped on her constantly – college was for finding a husband, not hiding in a lab, and marriage by a certain age was practically a mandate. Thankfully, Marie hadn't subjected me to the same tirade, knowing my aversion to all things romantic.

Aurora, on the other hand, craved love. Beneath her tough exterior, she was a hopeless romantic, clinging to the belief in a fairytale happily ever after. Her mother, however, viewed love as a business transaction, a pragmatic approach that clashed head-on with Aurora's idealistic dreams.

Aurora shrugged off Bev's hand, her voice dripping with mock sweetness. "Sorry for the tardiness, ma'am," she said, addressing Bev with a title that hung heavy with sarcasm. The customers were watching, and creating a scene wasn't the best way to start her shift. She prayed that one of them would defuse the tension before it escalated.

Just as Aurora turned to leave, she pivoted on her heel, a wicked half-smile twisting her lips. It looked like she was going to make a scene, too—double trouble.

I whispered, "Oh shit." I stood frozen in place, watching.

Her voice, deceptively sweet, dripped with sarcasm, "Oh, and while you're dialing Maman with your tattling tales, be sure to mention I was delayed by my new chemistry partner. The one whose father, by pure coincidence, just funded the department's new lab. Speaking of coincidences, I also discovered today that this same gentleman is the new client Justin bragged about at dinner - the one with the million-dollar contract for his firm. So, kindly ask Maman to mind her own beeswax. I'm a busy woman, building my independence."

A young customer, a woman, clapped in amusement.

I returned a smile, relieved they weren't offended. Bev, however, was a different story. Her cheeks burned a furious red, and her eyes looked like they were going to pop out of the sockets.

Aurora, usually bubbly and kind, hadn't had an outburst like this since her battle with migraines as a kid. I hoped she wasn't getting them again. She always acted so differently with them, and I never knew what to do for her. Scanning her face for a hint of pain, I found none.

Bev let it go and turned back to the customers, but she had one hand fidgeting in her apron pocket. I knew she was itching to call Aunt Marie.

As if on cue, Aurora's megawatt smile returned. She dipped into a playful curtsy for her cheering supporter, then turned to me. My smile mirrored hers, widening until her cheek piercings resembled dimples.

"That felt good!" Aurora mouthed, then grabbed an apron. The purple Magic Brew logo was a stark contrast against her goth attire—a beautiful black lace blouse and a flowing pleated skirt. Tall and perfectly proportioned (in my biased opinion), she secured the extra-long apron strings around her waist, a task that wouldn't be quite as cute on my forever-short, curvy self. A sigh escaped my lips.

"Stop that sighing," Aurora swatted, a playful glint in her pale, usually gothically inclined face.

I rolled my eyes. "I wasn't sighing. I was just breathing."

"You were sighing, and you know it."

She glanced at Bev, engrossed in a customer's phone translator. Aurora practically vibrated with an inner light

I hadn't seen since childhood. It was like she was barely contained, bouncing on the balls of her feet. Something had shifted within her, and I was eager to pry it out of her - anything to distract myself from the craziness of the afternoon.

A genuine smile spread across my face. This girl, cloaked in darkness with her jet-black clothes and hair, held a light within that was the one bright spot in my entire life. She was the glue that held me together, and I didn't know what I would do without her.

Aurora grabbed my hand over the counter and started bouncing. She was the only person in my life who could randomly touch me, and I did not flinch.

Reaching across the counter, Aurora grabbed my hand, the only person who could get away with such random contact. Her excitement pulsed through me, threatening to spill the leftover coffee in my hand. Happiness, a foreign visitor lately, bloomed in my chest. Even from her rain-soaked entrance, I'd noticed a spark in her golden eyes, a hint of something bigger than the downpour. And now, those eyes practically glowed.

Releasing my hand, she started doing the Charlie Brown Christmas dance, hopping from side to side, her black hair swishing back to her the music only she could hear. "I have news." She sang along to the internal rhythm.

Laughter bubbled up, and I couldn't help but join in her joy.

Aurora's dance stopped abruptly. A blush crept up her neck as she tucked a stray strand behind her ear, revealing a Hello Kitty gauge. Curiosity gnawed at me.

Shyness wasn't exactly Aurora's forte. "Spill it, girl! What's got you so giddy?"

Leaning across the counter, I set down my coffee as she inhaled deeply.

Words tumbled out of her mouth in a rush, "We got invited to the Vampire Ball next weekend!"

Her grip tightened on my hands as she bounced with barely contained glee. My emotions were a tangled mess. Excitement bubbled up - the Vampire Ball had been a shared dream since we were twelve. But a wave of panic crashed over me, and I broke out in a cold sweat. A ball? Too many people? My breath caught in my lungs, and then an even greater fear surfaced. Séverin was loose. What if he found me there?

Aurora stopped jumping, sensing my withdrawal. Her hand brushed mine, concern replacing the earlier joy. I flinched away, mortified by my fear overshadowed our bucket list wish. Her eyes drooped, her disappointment evident. "Please, Phin. This is huge!" She held her hands as if in prayer. "I know it's sudden, but please break your code of social isolation and come. I can't imagine living this dream without you."

Guilt gnawed at me. My promise to be more social, to not be alone - all overshadowed by the suffocating fear of a crowded ball. My heart hammered a frantic rhythm against my ribs. A lump formed in my throat, threatening to choke back any response. Just months ago, the ball was a fantasy, the tickets a distant dream. My bravado had far exceeded my actual courage.

Aurora's fingers snapped in front of my eyes. "Phin, say something?"

Her joy was replaced with concern. I had to tell her something. Just six months ago, we were imagining going to the ball together, but the tickets were so expensive. I knew it was all just talk, and my bravado had far exceeded my actual courage. "It was...supposed to be just a dream," I choked out.

Aurora raised her brow in question. I tried again. "I thought the tickets were all sold out?"

"They are."

"Then how did you get some?"

Bev called Aurora over to help take orders.

"Work calls!" she chirped, cheeks flushed. "Don't leave. I have even bigger news than the ball!"

Intrigued, I returned to my table. Bigger news than the ball? My cold coffee did little to soothe my troubled mind. Maybe letting go of the past truly was the answer.

Hours passed as I I digitally captured a haunting dream scene: myself, a lifeless sacrifice in the pouring rain. Why? Why would I die for him? Could such a love even exist?

Romeo and Juliet, once a source of teenage disdain for their impulsive demise, now held a strange allure. Their love, reckless and tragic, was undeniably romantic. A confusing knot of emotions tightened in my chest.

Gazing at the painted dream, I mirrored its despair. The emotions felt so real, so raw. My logic screamed at the recklessness of such dependence. No one should hold such power over my happiness. Yet, the love I felt for him, the reasons behind the sacrifice...a part of me whispered I would do it all again.

Elbows on the table, I buried my face in my hands,

frustration warring with a confusing loyalty. What was wrong with me?

Disgusted with myself for indulging in such a morbid fantasy, I shoved away the dream image. Sacrificing myself for some dream guy? This was ridiculous, a product of stress overload. Maybe I did need some of Bev's relaxation brew.

Instead, I flipped the page back to the idyllic image of me and Cyprien kissing. I didn't want to look at my death any longer. But the drawing, a reminder of a love that didn't exist, only fueled more questions. I pushed my iPad to the side, grabbed my phone, and searched the web: "dream interpretation - sacrifice for love."

The first result mocked me: "Martyr complex, self-punishment... forbearance." Perfect. Exactly how I'd spent the last five years. This was messed up, but at least I'd resolved to be social again. Maybe the ball with Aurora was a good idea. Living was the key to hopefully stopping these bizarre dreams.

"Whoa, this is amazing!"

I jumped, sending my pen flying. Aurora's silent approach startled me.

A snicker escaped her lips as she retrieved the pen. "Seriously, Phin, these are intense!" Settling beside me, she scrolled through the images on my iPad. "Very Studio Ghibli vibes. But you and this guy are insanely realistic. I had no idea you drew like this!"

Panic gripped me. I should've hidden the tablet. These images were deeply personal, and the thought of her seeing Cyprien churned my stomach. I clenched my fists, forcing myself not to snatch it away.

I bit my lip and sat on my hands, forcing myself to wait patiently. Aurora, oblivious, devoured the artwork. Her eyes widened with each detail, and she leaned closer for a better look. Her fingers zoomed in, studying specific parts before swiping to the next image. Every breathy "Wow" confirmed her genuine awe. Maybe these could be my next series; the girl didn't have to be me. After all, I remained anonymous online. My avatar – dark hair, brown eyes, fair skin – resembled Snow White's innocence, a stark contrast to my inner turmoil.

Aurora's face flickered with emotions, finally settling on a heartstruck gasp. "Who is this?" she breathed, holding up the portrait of Cyprien. "He's gorgeous!"

I gave her a wobbly grin. "Just someone I dreamed up."

"Well, dream him into reality then! He's perfect for you," Aurora teased.

She wasn't lying. Cyprien was everything I adored: tall, dark-haired, golden skin, mysterious eyes that showed a hint of mischief. And completely, utterly in love with me, flaws and all. Lost in this fantasy, I barely registered Aurora's tightening grip on my wrist.

The playful glint in Aurora's eyes vanished as she glanced at the next image on the iPad. Her voice trembled, "What the hell, Phin?"

The scene depicted Cyprien lying lifeless in a glass coffin, our last kiss still a vibrant stain on his lips. A prince in an old-fashioned costume, forever frozen in death.

"Why would you dream of him dead? That is so sad, especially because y'all looked so happy. This sucks."

She sniffed and started to flip through the last few images. I knew the following images were worse, a chronicle of my self-destruction. Aurora's brow furrowed as she flipped through them, each bite of her lip a silent scream. Then, on the final image, Aurora's breath hitched. Tears welled in her eyes as she glared at me, her voice tight with fury, "Don't you ever, ever, ever consider doing this in real life. I will never forgive you."

The final image on the screen mirrored my internet search: me, lifeless, in a blood-soaked dress. Shame washed over me as I slammed the iPad shut. "No," I whispered, the word heavy with conviction. "I won't do that. I promise. In fact, In fact, I looked it up. The result was pretty accurate, going on about self-punishment and such."

Aurora offered a single nod of understanding. She'd been there through it all: Séverin's attack, his disappearance, the accident that stole my parents. The guilt, a constant weight on my chest.

"I need to let go," I whispered, the words both terrifying and liberating. The fear of moving on screamed like a banshee, but a stronger voice, one tinged with hope, rose above the noise. "I need to live again. Stop being a prisoner of the past."

Aurora's stunned silence spoke volumes.

This wasn't just a decision; it was a declaration of war against the self-destruction that had gripped me. "I want to go to the ball. Tell me how you got the tickets."

A flicker of joy crossed Aurora's face about my decision, but a flicker of concern remained."I'm so relieved," she admitted, then hesitated. "but I have to ask you something. Do you think this... dream... has anything to do with the five-year mark and Sé–"

I cut her off, a hand flying to Aurora's mouth. "Stop! No."

When she lowered my hand, I stammered, "Seriously, I'm okay. I promise. I just... hibernated when I should have been living."

Aurora grasped my hands, her gaze searching. Doubt lingered in her eyes, but I held her stare. Finally, with a sigh, Aurora relented. "Okay. I believe you... for now."

Thank goodness, I thought because I didn't think I could keep the façade much longer. Desperate to change the subject, I feigned excitement. "Hurry up already. I'm dying to know how you got tickets."

Aurora's demeanor transformed. A blush bloomed on her cheeks, and she practically melted into the table. "Okay, brace yourself," she whispered, her voice laced with dreamy excitement.

"Did you know they moved the location last month to the Steamboat Natchez?"

Her question took me off guard. What did the location have to do with getting the tickets? "No," I said. "Why?"

Aurora launched into an explanation, her hands gesturing wildly. "Plumbing problems at the usual venue. Repairs are taking forever, so they had to scramble. The organizers either had to postpone or find a new place. Luckily, they found one fast!"

"Hence the Steamboat Natchez." I reiterated.

"Exactly!" Aurora beamed. "But it gets better."

"How?"

"You know how we got a new chem lab?"

I nodded.

"Well, the same man who invested in our lab is also the investor in the Steam Boat Natchez."

I was so confused. "So, how'd this get you Vampire Ball tickets?"

Aurora's grin stretched wider. "Almost there!" she squealed, then bit her lip dramatically. "Guess who my new chem partner is?"

"What happened to your old partner?"

"She had to drop because she delivered her baby early. But she isn't important. You need to guess who my new partner is!" Aurora was about to burst out of her skin in excitement.

"Spill already!"

Aurora leaned forward, a mischievous glint in her eyes. "The investor's son!"

Aurora's eyes eyes glazed over.

I chuckled. "Hot guy, right?"

Aurora gave me a mock glare.

I laughed, "So, I was right. It was a guy."

Aurora pouted. "Sadly, he's only my temporary partner." She rested her chin on her hand and sighed.

"Why?"

She sat back up and started fiddling with my apple pen. "Because he already graduated. He's a serious genius and is only auditing the class to make sure the equipment is up to the standards his dad expects. So, he's participating like an active student. Being the only one who was partnerless, my professor put us together. I think he's only here for a couple of weeks at the most."

I shoved her knee with my hand. "Bummer. But on a good note, you move fast. You totally must have made an impression on him because he told you all that and invited you to the ball within—" I frowned, trying to remember how long her class was. "What, like fifty minutes?"

Aurora fanned herself. "There's more! You won't believe this, but he is no stranger to us."

I'd nearly forgotten how much Aurora thrived on theatrics. It had been a while since something so exciting happened to her. I wracked my brain, trying to figure out who this mystery classmate could be

Silence stretched between us. Finally, I blurted out, 'Who is he already?'

"I thought you'd never ask."

I rolled my eyes. 'Technically, I did ask before. I just wanted to know his name, not his life story." With a playful groan, I muttered, "Come on, spill it!"

Aurora leaned into my personal space, moved the hair away from my ear, and whispered, "Theo Pantazis!"

"What? We haven't talked about him since middle school!"

"Are you telling me the guy you met is the thick, curly-haired Greek boy you had a crush on in the first grade who moved away, and you cried for nearly a year because you wanted to marry him, Theo Pantazis?"

"The one and the same!"

Suddenly, it all clicked. The blushing, the swooning, the nervous energy—it all made sense. This guy? He was her first-grade crush. Back then, she'd envisioned their entire lives together, a future filled with marriage and a gaggle of kids. She'd held onto that dream, convinced their paths would cross again. Then came eighth grade, and a real boy asked her out. That's when the fairytale faded.

"Does he live up to all your daydreams?"

There were stars in her eyes. "He is just as beautiful as he was in first grade, only now he's all man."

"You mean he's a 'geek' God." I snickered at my own punny joke.

"Just because I find it sexy when a guy is lean and lanky and wears dark-rimmed glasses does not make him a geek. Besides, Theo is beyond hot. He may be lean, but I doubt he's lanky."

I grabbed a napkin, wiping the non-existent drool from the corner of her mouth. Aurora laughed as she swatted my hand away, a playful kick landing on my ankle.

"Ow!" I yelped, surprised by the sting through my leggings. "Hey, boots!"

Aurora immediately knelt, her touch gentle as she rubbed my ankle. "Sorry," she mumbled. It's just...Theo. You know how Maman used to harp on it. That's why I shut down in eighth grade. I couldn't take it anymore."

A flicker of understanding dawned on me. "Is that why you stopped talking about him? I thought you just moved on."

Her gaze turned serious, arms crossed defensively. "Seriously, as if I could forget my soulmate." Her eyes, a mesmerizing swirl of gold and blue, locked on mine, waiting for me to come to the same conclusion.

How had I been so self-absorbed? Aurora's life

seemed meticulously planned from a young age. Science since third grade, a perfect GPA, and even her casual relationships felt like placeholders until Theo reappeared. Meanwhile, I was still navigating the twists and turns of my own life.

I was so not going back there... instead of dwelling on me, I bombarded her with questions. "So, did Theo get better with age? Did y'all recognize each other right away?"

Aurora nodded, a hint of a smile playing on her lips. "Theo spoke to me first. After we reintroduced ourselves, we caught up on everything that went on after Plessy."

"Wow, he recognized you?" I blurted, surprised.

"Somewhat," she chuckled. "He asked about my red hair and where it went."

"Yeah, the black hair and makeup probably threw him off," I agreed. "You look nothing like your childhood self."

"I know, right?" Aurora's smile widened, revealing a dimple in her cheek. Her eyes, those captivating pools of gold and blue, sparkled with amusement. The way the light danced around the unusual irises, creating a mesmerizing golden ring around them, was unlike anything I'd ever seen. They were a window into her emotions, reflecting her current happiness.

"Well, your eyes," I said softly, "they've always been the most beautiful color. A captivating blend of gold and blue."

Aurora's cheeks flushed a rosy pink, and she shyly tucked a strand of hair behind her ear. Despite her attempts to downplay her beauty with dark clothes and dyed hair, the truth was undeniable—Aurora was striking.

Then it hit me! "Hey, you're bare faced today!" I exclaimed, noticing the lack of makeup for the first time.

Aurora's hand flew to her cheek, her hair cascading down like a curtain. "Took you long enough, Sherlock," she teased, a hint of self-consciousness creeping into her voice. "Rain, you know? Washed it all away, and I was already running late."

Her posture shifted, and confidence radiated from her as she leaned forward. "He said the sweetest thing," she confessed, her eyes sparkling. "Theo told me he's dreamt of my red hair since we were kids."

"Aww, that's adorable," I offered, genuinely happy for her.

A wide smile spread on Aurora's face. "Right? I think... if things work out, I'm going to stop coloring it."

"Seriously?" I blurted out, surprised. "He told me he always wondered what happened to me. Isn't it crazy how fate works?"

I nodded, "It is." A bittersweet feeling settled in my gut. The truth was clear, and I could tell that Aurora couldn't wait to see Theo again. "I'm glad y'all found one another again. What are the odds right?"

"Exactly!" She squeezed my hand.

I was glad fate was being good to her because fate had sure been a bitch to me and my love life.

"Too bad we were so shy back then, huh? Maybe he could have hung out with us. If I remember correctly, he was always alone at recess."

A pang of guilt shot through me. Now that she

mentioned it, I vaguely recalled a quiet boy sitting by himself. Maybe if I'd paid more attention, I would have developed my observation skills sooner and possibly not made so many poor decisions in my teens.

"Gosh, we were such dweebs for not helping out another loner," I muttered, kicking my toe against hers. I was still a dweeb because as she was having a dream come true, I was moping about my messed up life.

Aurora placed her hand over her heart. "My poor Theo."

"Hey, stop looking so miserable. We were just kids. Six or seven? No way we could have known Theo would move. Besides, we were busy learning and having fun. That's all that matters at that age, right?"

"True." She nodded and perked back up, straightening her posture. "Anyway, I took this meeting as my opportunity to rectify the past."

"How?"

A mischievous grin spread across Aurora's face. "I told him flat out I had a crush on him for years after he moved away and that when I was in eighth grade and understood what dating was if I ever met him again and was single, I'd ask him out."

My mouth dropped open, and Aurora laughed as she used her forefinger to lift my chin back where it belonged. "What did he say?" Before she could respond I added, "Is he single?"

She squealed loudly, then covered her mouth. "He is. But I only told him all this after he invited me to the Vampire Ball, so technically, he asked me out first."

I laughed. She finally got to the part about how she

got tickets. She ignored my interruption. "He told me he originally didn't want to go. He's kinda like you and not big into crowds. He prefers smaller gatherings and he just moved back into town after living with his uncle most of his life. His dad sort of forced him back to learn about his company. So, when he kept asking me if I enjoyed dancing, I didn't quite get where he was going. Eventually, after I told him yes, he asked me, and Girl—I never nodded my head so fast." She rubbed her neck with a huge smile. "I may have given myself whiplash."

I snickered at her antics. "What happened after that?"

"Class ended. I had no clue what we did in that entire hour because Theo and I talked the entire time. He walked with me to the streetcar, and we kept talking and I missed my ride. He waited with me for the next one to come, and as I finally got on after telling him I was late for work he grabbed my hand and slipped me his phone number." She held her palm in her other one to her heart. Her eyes closed in what looked like bliss for a moment then she opened them her cheeks pink.

"I still feel his hand in mine when I think about it. There is such a powerful pull to him that I am a little worried I am not being realistic about who he is and mixing him up with all my fantasies. It's so strange - it seems he feels the same way about me. I don't know how to explain it."

I pulled her into my arms and hugged her. Then Aurora started to squeal in joy and started bouncing us up and down. I joined in and let her happiness flood into me as we spun circles like little kids knocking down a chair in our exuberance. The few customers inside turned in our direction at the sound, but we didn't care, and both started laughing. This is the first time in ages I felt so light.

Bev came around the bar. "Aurora, your break is over!"

If looks could kill, Bev would have been a goner from Aurora's quick mood change. Her energy changed, and I suddenly felt cold and weighed down again. I hated that something was going on between Aurora and Bev and wished I knew what it was. I didn't want Aurora to have a bad shift after having such an awesome day at school, so I squeezed her hand, trying my hardest to express my gratitude and love for her.

Aurora squeezed back. "I'm so glad you were here today because I didn't think I'd be able to work my entire shift without telling you."

She started back to the counter, and I shouted, "Wait! I know you got invited, but how did I get tickets?"

Aurora pulled out her phone, fiddled with it for a bit, and then showed me her screen. It was a text from 'PC'. I lifted my brow and looked at her for clarity. She mouthed, "Prince Charming," then gave me a beaming smile. I shook my head in laughter as I started to read Theo's messages.

Aurora: This is Aurora Toussaint 😃 I'm so glad to have seen you again, and thank you for the invitation to the Vampire Ball. I am thrilled, but I was wondering if we could meet up sooner than next week to catch up some more and get to know one another. Maybe dinner?

I looked up at Aurora. "Bold. I can't believe the courage that is coming out of you."

Her smile was huge. "Keep reading." She bit her lip and put her hands in the apron pocket while I read the rest of the messages.

PC: I'd love that. Are you free tonight?

I looked up at her, a grin plastered on my face. Aurora nodded her head and urged me to keep reading.

Aurora: 🙁 I have to work until 10.

PC: Where do you work? I can meet you after for a late-night stroll???

I couldn't help but comment. "Oh, my god. Who talks like this these days?"

"I know, right? I love it."

Aurora: Magic Brew Cafe on the corner of Saint Philip and Royal Street.

PC: I will be there. Also, I told my dad I found a date and he just texted me two more tickets to the Vampire Ball. Do you have any friends interested in coming with us?

Aurora: Do you remember Phin, my cousin and bestie from 1st grade? We live together, and I know she would love to come. I'm sure we can find a fourth.

PC: I do remember her. That is perfect. She can invite her boyfriend.

Aurora: Talk later. The streetcar just stopped, and it's raining. Gotta pull out my umbrella.

PC: See you tonight.

"Aurora, I need your help," Bev shouted.

I handed the phone back to a beaming Aurora, who skipped away.

My heart plummeted when the first person I thought of inviting to the Vampire Ball was Séverin. I turned back to my table, a wave of nausea washing over me. Even after five years, after all the damage he'd done, a part of me still felt inexplicably drawn to him. It was as if our connection was twisted, a soulmate bond laced with poison.

The familiar ache in my chest intensified, a stark reminder of the five years that had passed since I last saw him. Five years without his chaos, without the highs and lows that left me feeling hollow and perpetually off-balance.

I squeezed my head, burying my face in my hands. The memory of his last visit surfaced, vivid and horrifying. The slurred words, the reeking haze of alcohol and drugs, the way his temper flared, unpredictable and explosive.

Pushing him out had been a futile effort. He'd shoved me back, a snarl twisting his features. Panic surged as I fumbled for my phone, a desperate attempt to call for help.

But he grabbed my phone, and it flew across the room. His hands found my chest, pushing me back. A sickening crack echoed as it hit the wall, and I stumbled backward, landing hard against the edge of the stairs. The world spun. Séverin spat in my face, "Where's your protection now? You powerless witch." Then, everything faded to black.

But on one horrifying level, he'd been right. I had been powerless.

When I awoke, a concerned police officer stood over me. The front door hung open, barely on its henge.

Disoriented, I found myself strapped to a gurney, the sterile white a stark contrast to the blood stain spread on the wall. The physical injuries paled in comparison to the chilling truth the officers delivered. They had come for a reason, a reason that would forever alter the course of my life.

Chapter Three

Aurora was at the table behind me wiping it down. "Hey, before you leave, I was thinking maybe you can invite Goldie to come with us to the ball. You still like her, right?

I nodded.

Aurora was rambling while she moved on to the next table. "Goldie was just telling me the other day that she had been trying for the last six months to find someone wanting to sell their ticket. Do you want me to ask her?"

I shook my head as I packed up my backpack. "I think maybe it's time I return one of her texts."

Aurora smiled at me. "That would be great."

We knew Goldie when we all worked here in high school together. She was a little older than us, but we always got along well. Since we graduated, Goldie moved around a lot but always found her way back to New Orleans. No matter where she moved or how poor a friend I became, she always kept in contact with me. Even though I think she and Aurora were closer friends.

"Goldie is fun. She misses hanging out with you."

I felt like my smile was forced, but I picked up my phone right then and there and sent Goldie a text so I wouldn't chicken out.

My phone dinged before I could even put it back in my pocket. I glanced at the response then walked over to Aurora and showed her the response.

Phin: Hey, I got an extra ticket to the Vampire Ball. Want to be my plus one?

Goldie: I'm in. I already have a dress. I read my cards last week telling me fortune was headed my way. I had a feeling that I manifested this into existence. Thanks for thinking of me. See you soon.

"She's so intuitive."

"Yeah, she's really interesting," I muttered, my mind shutting down from the intensity of the day. I walked out of the cafe without even saying goodbye.

My brain was fried. Walking back home took a matter of minutes and I was so consumed with the notion that I agreed to go to the ball that I forgot to be afraid that Séverin was free. All I could think of now was that I would be trapped on a boat with hundreds of people. Why did I say yes? Why did Theo ask Aurora when originally he didn't intend to go?

I climbed the stairs and was standing before the French doors leading to my apartment. A little black cat head was poking through the blinds hanging against the interior glass. I could hear Felix meowing.

"Hey buddy, I'm home. Sorry I was gone for so long."

I unlocked the French door and placed my foot in to

keep Felix from running out. I shimmied in while watching him closely. We just adopted Felix a few days ago, and I was still training him that inside was his home now. He looked to be a few years old already, but so far he was adjusting well to being an inside cat.

I dropped my backpack by the door, bent down, and rubbed his head. He meowed a few times at me, and it literally sounded as if he were fussing at me. Hearing him warmed my heart, and I smiled at him.

"I hear you, buddy. It was naughty of me to leave you alone for so long. I get it."

I stood back up and he snaked his body in and out of my ankles as I started walking to our small kitchen and tried not to trip over him. I opened the cabinet over the stove and pulled out a can of his favorite food. He jumped on the counter and chirped when I popped off the lid.

Felix was so utterly adorable as he licked his lips in anticipation. I rubbed his head. "Enjoy!"

I left him to feast on his dinner. I turned the lamp on in the living area next to the sofa for when Aurora would get home later, then went down the hall closing the doors to Aurora's bedroom and our joint bathroom on the way to my room. I flopped down on the rainbow duvet covering my white iron daybed and stared at the pale blue ceiling. It wasn't dark enough for the glow-in-the-dark stars, but I could see them like a promise of starlight. My room was my happy place. It was private and beautiful, and I had two windows that faced Royal St and another on the opposite side of my room that faced the court-yard. It helped me stay sane in my self-induced isolation.

But right now, with the lights out, dusk cast eerie shadows in the room. I rubbed my chest; the memories of my past were too strong today. I sat up and turned on my bedside lamp and scanned my room and noticed that I didn't have any photographs. When had I banished them? I got up and slowly walked over to my closet and pulled out the decorative hat box where I had shoved all of the photos. I placed it on the floor and sat beside it. I hadn't even opened it and already felt the tears wanting to form. Taking a deep breath, I opened the lid. I shivered as the smell of home wafted into my nose. The scent of home and my parents were trapped inside. I wiped tears off my cheeks.

The photo on top had been taken the morning of my seventeenth birthday. The three of us together smiled happily, only that happiness didn't last. Before the day was done, I was cornered in the kitchen by my parents trying to get me not to go out with Sév that night and instead go to dinner with them. Being a stubborn teenager, I'd argued that I'd spent all day with them and really wanted to go out with my boyfriend.

They picked the wrong night to argue. It was supposed to be my day after all, but when they started harping on me that Séverin wasn't the same as when we first met and that they could smell not only the alcohol on him but were disgusted by the subtle jabs and insults he took at me. I didn't want to hear it and ran up to my room locking myself in to get ready for my date.

After a couple of hours, I heard my parents leave. I waited for Séverin to pick me up. I texted asking where he was, and his response was incoherent letters. I cried. He probably forgot again that it was my birthday. He'd been getting worse and worse with his drugs, and I'd been getting more and more frustrated but also scared for him.

I threw the picture back in the box. It was now stained with wet spots. I wiped my eyes with the inside of my shirt collar.

After a few moments of staring at the box, I made myself continue looking through the photos. I found a few of me and my parents over the years and those actually brought a small smile to my face. The first one in years at the memory of them. The next one was a framed five by seven of my parents on their wedding day. I felt something cold on the back and when I flipped it over, I had forgotten I taped their wedding bands to the back. I hugged the photo to my chest, my lip quivered as I fought back the intense feeling of remorse.

I looked at the photo again. My parents gazed into one another's eyes and looked so in love. I remember my mom telling me that when she met my dad, it was like fate placed him right in front of her at the perfect time. They fell in love instantly and were engaged two weeks later.

I picked up the picture, stood up, and placed it on my nightstand. Looking down at my parents' smiling faces – happy and in love was how I wanted to remember them.

I turned around back to the hat box, and Felix had made himself comfortable inside it. He was purring and seemed so content I didn't have the heart to shoo him out of the box.

A knock on the door startled both of us. Felix

popped his head up. His ears twitched and he chirped at me in a soft sort of sound that sounded like a question.

I went ahead and acknowledged him as if it were, "I don't know?"

I got up off the floor and tiptoed down the hall, hoping whoever was at the door couldn't hear me inside. I peeked around the corner of the hall and living room. The blinds were still crooked from where Felix had been looking out earlier. I noticed some patchwork flowing fabric through the small opening and only knew one person who would even consider wearing something of that sort.

I whispered to Felix, "It's gotta be Goldie but her text earlier led me to believe I wouldn't see her until closer to the ball."

I wondered what made her come tonight. Just because I asked her to come with us to the ball didn't give her the invitation to just pop on over anytime.

I sighed and leaned back against the wall, and asked Felix who was sitting upright in the box. "What should I do? I'm peopled out, bud. Should I just pretend I'm not home?"

Felix meowed, jumped out of the hat box, and walked to the door.

"Hey, little man, I really don't want company."

He turned his head back on me, and I could swear he was laughing. He turned back around, ignoring my huff, and scratched the window. I could hear Goldie through our poorly insulated glass French doors.

"Felix, is your companion home?"

He chirped and chittered as though he were talking to her.

"She is, is she? Well in that case maybe I should knock again."

Goldie knocked on the door again. I groaned and whispered, "Traitor." Felix turned his nose up in the air and flicked his tail. He'd obviously heard me and knew what I'd said. I came out from behind the wall and slowly walked to the door. I tried to mentally prepare myself for an unexpected guest. Today was a hard day. As I grabbed the knob, I was a little peeved that Felix seemed excited to have a visitor. I wasn't too happy with him and scolded him.

"Back up dude, or I'll send your company away."

He moved behind me and sat licking his paw. I rolled my eyes at him and opened the door.

Chapter Four

Goldie's waist-length golden blonde hair bounced in perfection as she glided through the door and into the living room. At five-ten, her long patchwork skirt wrapped gracefully around her ankles as it swayed. I had forgotten how tall she was compared to my five foot two inches. The contrast of the navy-blue linen shirt that she had belted at the waist made her skin look sun kissed. She was stunning and I looked pasty, washed out, and dumpy compared to her.

"Delphine," she hugged me.

I flinched back and she ignored it.

"I am so sorry for dropping by unexpectedly. I know how you prefer your alone time, but I was in the neigh-borhood, and when I passed by the cafe without even realizing what I was doing I was heading upstairs and knocking on your door."

Felix head-butted her ankle, and she leaned down and picked Felix up in her arms. He purred happily.

I muttered, "You little turncoat," under my breath, and Goldie chuckled.

"Funny how fate is sometimes, huh."

I rubbed the back of my neck. "Yeah, funny."

Why'd she bring up fate? I didn't like the idea of fate just now. It ruined my life, and now the cat that I'd rescued was all cozy with her.

Goldie glanced up from whispering sweet nothings in my cat's ear. "You doing okay? You seem a little peaked."

She put Felix down and came beside me, patting my shoulders, just like my mom used to when I was crabby. Her hand radiated warmth through my shirt. I felt tears threaten to escape. Why wasn't I moving away from her? I hated being touched, being consoled, I didn't deserve it.

A huge lump in my throat made it hard to swallow.

"Oh Delphine, I'm so sorry I barged in. I didn't mean to make you uncomfortable."

Why wasn't I saying anything? Oh yeah, the lump in my throat.

Thank goodness for Felix because he shot out of the living room like a rocket and all I heard was a crash in my room.

Goldie followed me. "I love what you've done with your room; you have an elemental theme going on. Very nice."

I picked up the photo of my parents that Felix knocked over. Luckily, the glass hadn't shattered, but the rings had come loose. I looked around the room at my decor. I never really thought of it as being elemental.

"Um, thanks, but I didn't choose elemental. It's just

the colors and things that make me feel less claustrophobic."

"Of course, it would. That is very common for elementals." Goldie walked over to the frame I just placed back on my nightstand. She picked it up. "Your parents were lovely, a true fated match."

Goldie was looking at me in an odd sort of hopeful way.

I gave her a half smile. "My mom believed so."

After I spoke, the hope vanished from Goldie's expression, and she sighed as she placed the photo down. "Theirs was meant to be."

She turned back to me. "Your parents passed away when you were seventeen, right?" She looked at me but didn't wait for me to confirm before she started walking around my room.

"Did you ever mention to your parents that you leaned toward elemental magic?"

I was so confused. Just because I liked earthy decor didn't mean I was magic. "I'm not magical," I told her.

She stopped pacing and tapped her finger to her natural pink lips. "I certainly feel something powerful in this room. I mean I do understand if you prefer to keep it hush-hush. Not everyone is accepting."

Exhausted, I sat on the edge of my bed. "You've totally lost me."

She sat next to me and pointed at all the different things in my room. "The elements are calling to you. You were subconsciously listening. Your green shag rug is earth, the blue ceiling is air, the candles on your desk are fire, and the overhead light in the shape of the sun represents the source of your light of course, but look over there where you have that hat box."

I turned toward the box.

"It is cast in shadows, as is true to every magical being. We all have a bit of darkness in our souls. What is yours hiding?"

Goldie had always been odd. Maybe this was her way of letting me know she was glad I'd texted her.

"The only thing you seem to be missing is the actual magic," she said.

The fakest of laughs erupted from my lips, and I struggled to think of what to say and only came up with this because of her unique sense of humor. "You had me!" I hadn't socialized for so long I'd forgotten how people joked. "That is funny. I'm sorry I didn't get the joke at first."

She was about to say something when Felix jumped in the box again and started tearing into it. I hurriedly ran to shoo him away before he destroyed all my memories.

"Stop that, Felix!" I tried grabbing him to pull him out. He was hissing, and his fur was standing on end. I started to shush him in a soothing manner as if he were a crying baby. He calmed and curled into me, but his paw was entangled in the strings of a small leather pouch with dark stains on it that almost looked like blood.

Goldie came over to us and grabbed the pouch off his paw. "Ooh, what do we have here?" She opened the bag and whooped with joy. "Good boy." She pet his head, then looked at me shaking the bag. "We have magic."

I grabbed the pouch and poured the six stones and a ring into my palm. "This isn't magic, this is just some pretty stones and a ring. It probably belonged to my mom."

"No, those are magical. I knew I was supposed to come here for a reason, and this is it. It is finally time."

Goldie was giddy. I started to wonder once more if she was high on something because tonight she was odder than remembered.

"Goldie, I really don't understand what you are trying to say. I mean, I know we haven't talked in ages, and I know you are into all sorts of mystical things, but I'm not, and to me, these are just stones."

I opened the pouch to put them back inside and noticed a small, folded piece of paper. I pulled it out. The paper was so fragile and yellowed with age the ink had practically faded, but the script was still legible.

Goldie came beside me and leaned over to read, "It's in Greek."

"It is?"

"Yes, it says seven dwarves of the elementals."

She took the bag and poured the stones back into my hand. They were warm, and I could feel the energy sending little currents into my palm.

She picked up the ring. "This ring, along with those stones, are the seven dwarfs. The source of your elemental magic. Created from dwarf stars beyond our galaxy."

"Have you lost your mind?"

Goldie looked at me as if I were slow. "This is malachite-earth, labradorite-air, carnelian-fire, opal-water, diamond-light, onyx-shadow, and this ring is hematite which activates the magic in the stones." She looked at me. "You, Delphine, are an Elemental. The stones found you, like I knew they would. Wake up and embrace your magic!"

I sat down on my bed. I didn't know if I should laugh or not because Goldie seemed so serious, as if what she was saying was true. And, here I was worried about my social skills being rusty.

A news alert blared over my phone, and seconds later, Goldie's phone beeped. I picked my phone up off my bed and glanced at the app.

Live report coming from the banks of the Mississippi: A glass coffin of a man floated up in the river. The burning question is the coffin appears hundreds of years old so how is his body so well preserved.

"Goldie! Did you get this too?" I held my phone out to her, but she barely glanced up before she looked back down at her phone.

"I'm looking at it right now," she said.

I ran into the living area and turned the TV on to the local station. The reporter had his back turned to the camera. The cameraman focused on a Cruise ship that had delayed off-boarding. The people lined the deck watching everything unfold. The flashing lights of a police boat pulled up to the dock.

News Reporter: Earlier this evening, our station started getting a ton of social media messages and photos of a glass coffin floating in the Mississippi River.

A video that someone shared was now on the screen. A coffin looked to be made of some sort of glass as it bobbed up and down.

Goldie patted my back. "Girl, you all right?"

"Yeah, just swallowed wrong."

"Things are really changing…" Goldie murmured to herself.

I had no idea what she meant, and before I could ask the door opened, making me jump a mile high. Aurora stood half in and half out the door.

"I thought you were going on a date," I said, once my heart slowed down.

She glanced outside. "I am," her voice cracked, "but I, we," her cheeks flushed and she closed her eyes as if trying to think, finally she spit out why she was home. "Got the news report, and I just got off and thought that our first date could be watching the news?"

I held in a laugh. Poor Theo. That was not a first date.

Aurora ignored me to wave at Goldie. "Hey, Goldie, I didn't know you would be here."

Goldie waved back. "I was just in the neighborhood, so I stopped by to thank you both for the invite."

I pointed to the door. "Is you-know-who out there?"

Aurora's cheeks grew flushed, and she nodded. "Is it okay if he comes in and watches the news with us?"

"Definitely, stop dawdling and bring him in."

Although I said that with enthusiasm, I was so not in the mood for more company. Today was emotionally exhausting, and seeing the news also reminded me of my dream and Goldie's weird behavior. I was burnt out.

Just because I decided to become social didn't mean I wanted the universe to throw everything at me at once.

I put on a smile, ready to greet Theo as Aurora opened the door. The smile changed as my mouth dropped open. Aurora was tall, but next to Theo she looked short. He ducked to get in the door. Holy hotcakes! Now I knew why she was practically drooling all day. I swear a human Greek statue literally just walked into our apartment. There was no geek about him.

Theo had to be one of the best-looking guys I had ever seen in my whole life, or at least the tallest of the few I knew. But no matter how incredibly attractive he was, my heart only pounded for Séverin and now Cyprien. But now I knew why Aurora couldn't help but fall all over him. His black hair reached his shoulders, and my goodness, his full curls were layered, glossy, and gorgeous. Envy messed with my head as I wished my frizzy waves looked half as good. Then I noticed his eyes.

Okay, now I think I was drooling. Next to his bronzed skin, his eyes popped; they were the palest blue and looked like some type of crystal. I didn't remember his eyes being that enthralling when he was a kid.

I turned to Aurora, and she was standing tall and beaming. Theo was definitely not a nerd and Aurora knew it.

Goldie jumped off the couch and stood in front of me. "Pantazis."

I stood up, and Goldie threw her arm out preventing me from moving.

Theo shifted in front of Aurora, doing the same. "Spinner."

Now that was weird. Aurora and I both leaned around them and gave each other what the hell eyes.

Aurora spoke first "Um, you two know each other?"

Theo made a rumbling sound in his chest that eerily

sounded like a growl. Then he cleared his throat. His voice was rough. "Not personally, but Spinner is not welcome near my family."

Goldie huffed. "I'm surprised a soul-shifting dog like yourself actually disobeyed his pack." Her hand waved over to Aurora. "What's the meaning of mixing company with my alchemist?"

Aurora and I gave each other a 'What the F' look.

"From what I understand, your father is into collecting souls. And your extended family isn't much better." Goldie turned to me, "You better stay close to Aurora, or she will disappear like my sister did when she went to his family for help."

"I am neither my family nor my father," Theo growled, and with clenched teeth, finished his thought in the lowest, almost inaudible voice. "Don't you ever compare me to that monster again!"

Aurora was hanging on to his hand as if she would die if she let go, and Goldie gave him an assessing look. "You better not be. I guarantee if you hurt these girls, I will have your head."

She shoved past Theo knocking into him. He fell into Aurora, knocking her off balance. He caught her gracefully, and Goldie gave Aurora a small apologetic smile and then walked herself to the door.

"Sorry girls, I don't play well with dogs. See you next week."

She left and slammed the door hard, making the glass rattle.

Theo still had a death grip on Aurora's hand, but his other hand was rubbing the back of his neck. Aurora was embarrassed. She tended to bite the inside of her cheek piercing when she was uncomfortable or anxious. She was biting it so hard that I was concerned she might accidentally swallow it. I hated that it was up to me to break the silence when all I wanted to do was turn around and go lock myself in my room, but instead I helped my cousin out.

I turned to Theo. "Well, that was an interesting way to make a reintroduction." I tried to laugh, but to me, it sounded shrill and fake. "Anyway, it's really nice to see you again."

Neither of them said anything.

"You, uh, grew. I don't remember you being this tall last time we met." God, I was so out of practice with small talk. Still, no one said anything. "Of course, you were only in first grade, so you would have to have been short."

Theo stared at me.

"Ha! That's funny. I do think Theo may have always been tall." Aurora took his hand and led him to the sofa.

Theo gave her a half smile and lifted his shoulders. "May have been. I can't remember."

He sat on the floor beside Aurora. She ran her fingers through his wavy dark hair, and he leaned into her palm. His eyes closed, and he reminded me of a contented dog for a second.

Aurora's hand stopped moving, and Theo looked up at her as if she had called his name or something, then she spoke to him. "I have to admit that was weird. What in the world was Goldie going on about?"

Theo folded his arms over his chest. His body tensed,

and I could see the veins on his forearms bulge. "Nothing. It's just bad blood between the families."

Nothing sure didn't seem like nothing from his reaction, and Goldie's accusations were serious. Maybe his dad was into human trafficking and used his business as a cover.

I shook my head. No, that can't be real. Goldie messed up. She'd even thought I was magical.

Aurora turned her head toward me while Theo was staring at the TV. She kept tilting her head to the side as if using it to point to Theo.

I mouthed, "What?"

She started mouthing something, and I had no clue what she was trying to ask. She finally pulled out her phone and texted me. My phone vibrated in the pocket of my leggings.

"Tell him Goldie is your date."

I shook my head and texted her. "No. You."

She shook her head.

I turned to the TV and stubbornly crossed my arms. We had missed the rest of the news, but I didn't care. I wouldn't tell him, and we would just sit here until Aurora told him instead. I buried myself further into the back of the sofa. The day I finally decided to step out of my isolation bubble, my life suddenly turned to hell in a handbasket. Theo and Aurora were the ones who got me into this mess of going to the ball and inviting Goldie. How was I supposed to know she and his family were in a feud? A pretty bad one at the rate Goldie was talking.

Honestly, it wasn't Theo I needed to tell; it was Goldie. She was the one I invited as my date, and she was looking forward to it. I picked up my phone and texted her.

Phin: I'm sorry tonight ended the way it did, but I couldn't let the night continue if I didn't let you know Theo is the one who gave us the tickets.

I sent the message, then thought about it for a second and added—

Phin: I totally understand if you want to back out from coming with me because of the bad blood between your families.

The second I sent that message, the three little dots indicating she was typing back appeared.

Goldie: 😠 His family is so annoying, but I can ignore him for one night. I don't want to miss the ball. Thanks for letting me know. I apologize for my rude behavior and hope you can forgive me. I want to finish our conversation. I work tomorrow. Maybe you can come to visit me at the new shop I opened Underground Sorcery and Co.

I responded with an affirmative as the news report came back on screen breaking through the TV program.

News Reporter: We are back. The Coast Guard has towed the coffin in, and it has been confirmed by the police chief that this is no hoax. There is a young man inside, fully preserved. Now we need information as to what happened and figure out who he is and find his family. If you recognize this coffin, call 1-800-tips to help this young man return to his final resting place.

Aurora jumped forward, practically falling over Theo to look closer at the TV. He caught her waist super-fast.

"Oh my god!" Aurora pointed to the screen.

"Phin." The way Aurora whimpered my name made me freeze. It wasn't my imagination. Séverin was out of prison.

I heard Theo say something, and Aurora's frightened response. "That's Séverin, her ex."

There he was in jeans and a long sleeve shirt. He was thinner than he'd been five years ago but still as handsome. My heart thudded heavily in my chest at seeing him again. I still felt the draw to him. His jaw was sharper, and his blond hair was cropped shorter than it had been back then. The coffin had passed right in front of him. Within seconds his expression turned haunted, and he fell to his knees and wept. My heart ached for him. Was he ever reminded of what he did while drunk? Did he regret killing my parents?

I didn't realize I had walked to the TV, when my hand touched his face on the screen static zapped my fingers and he looked up into the camera, into my eyes. Aurora used the remote to power it off. "Phin, it will be all right. I won't let him hurt you ever again. I swear it."

Embarrassed that I got caught, I ran to my bedroom to escape. I climbed into bed and pulled the comforter up over my head.

Aurora pulled it down. "You need to try to rest. Don't think about him tonight and get some sleep. I promise we will figure everything out in the morning."

I pulled the comforter up under my chin and nodded.

She left my room and shut the door.

Suddenly, I was freezing, my teeth chattering as the reality of everything started crashing around me. Séverin was free. I couldn't breathe. I winced when Felix jumped on my bed. Shivering harder, I tried to control my panic. Felix climbed onto my stomach and dropped the pouch with the stones on my chest. Then he lay on top of it and fell asleep.

I didn't have the heart to move him, especially because the rumble of his purrs and the warmth from his body calmed me down.

Chapter Five

Slowly, I began to drift. I smiled and spun around under the sacred willow tree. I was in my favorite place in Nod and waiting for the love of my life. I was early and my heart fluttered in anticipation. A shift in the branches alerted me to the early arrival of Cyprien.

"You beat me," he said. "And here I purposefully left early to surprise you."

I laughed. "And you did! You are early, that means we will have longer to visit today."

He took the last two strides to my side and without hesitation I was in his arms and his lips were on mine.

I shouldn't be this happy to see him. I was to be married to Séverin in less than a week. But over the last three months, the willow tree had become my haven. Cyprien had stumbled upon me crying over something critical my betrothed told me. Cy flat-out told me to leave the scurvy dog. Then he got up on a fallen tree stump and stood as if on the bow of a ship braving the winds, back erect and both fist firm on his waist, his feet spread apart to keep his balance, and shouted, "Yo Ho! There is the mighty beast that must be slayed. No one shall hurt a fair maiden as long as Cyprien is near."

He got out of character, turned to me, winked, and whispered jovially, "That is my name." Then went back into his playful banter and deepened his voice as he fought my invisible groom, aka the beast.

He made me laugh. From that moment on, this became our spot. The first few meetings were all coincidental times. After a few meetings, we ended up making planned dates. He always created some grand adventure for us in our little hidden glen.

I couldn't help but giggle watching him now. He had a tendency to get lost in his own world, and at twenty-two, he behaved very much like a boy. He pranced around using a stick as a sword, fighting off an invisible foe. I shook my head and lifted the weeping willow branches like a curtain and made my way towards him. He was truly something, and over the last few months of summer, I couldn't help but fall in love with this man who lit up my entire world. He seemed so fearless and capable and full of so much joy. I wished I could be more adventurous like him. And the closer my wedding day approached, he pulled me into his arms.

"I wish I could protect you forever. Let's run away together. You and I can travel the entire Land of Nod, and you will never have to face that boorish oaf you are to marry."

I returned the hug. "I wish my life were my own, but I can't. My family is depending on this marriage."

"But they aren't even your real family. You won't

even tell me who your betrothed is. How can I fight for you if I don't know which of these River folk dandies you are marrying? There are five weddings alone planned for next week. My brother is included in that bunch."

"You never told me you had a brother." There was still so much about Cyprien I didn't know, and I wondered if this was just a summer folly.

"We're not as close as we used to be."

I nodded. "Have you seen who he is to marry?'

"Not yet but I hear she is beautiful, and my brother is enthralled by her."

I felt silly asking, but unlike Séverin, one thing I did know about Cyprien was that he would never dismiss my curiosity. "Maybe she is descended from the gods."

"My family sure acts like she is."

"Are you saying the only way to be revered is to be a descendant of the gods?"

He grabbed my hand and kissed my palm. "I couldn't care less who she is, she will never compare to you."

"No, there are definitely some dark, hideous descendants of the gods out there as well; some who are very good at hiding as regular gentry."

He turned to me and tucked a piece of my hair behind my ear. "You, on the other hand, are the most beautiful woman I ever encountered and for all I know, you could be the goddess of love in disguise with the spell you've put me under."

I laughed and playfully pushed him away. "I am no goddess. If I were, I guarantee I would have used my magic to leave this place."

Cyprien squeezed my hand, then I glanced at him

and turned a bit coyish. "Although, I do admit when I first met him, I found him quite attractive."

Cy stepped back and placed his hand on his heart. "My lady, you wound me." He playfully fell back onto the ground. When he didn't get up, I knelt beside him, joining in his game. He opened one eye and then feigned passing out again.

"Well— when I first met you, I did think that you and he were similar. You are both exceedingly tall. Almost as tall as a tiny giant."

He laughed then winked at me. "You found out my secret. I am descended from the ancient giants who once roamed these parts. Thankfully, we have lost our vengeful ways."

I shook my head at his antics. "In that case I am glad. I wouldn't want you upset with me for comparing you to a beast."

I gave him a smirk using the name he always used to make fun of my fiancé.

He placed his hand over his heart and leaned back playfully. "You wound me. Please tell me I have better qualities than the beast."

I gently ran the back of my finger over his cheek. "Your skin is golden like the sun and brings warmth into my soul, and I must tell you the truth that your unruly dark hair is beastly, yet I love that you don't tame it. It shows me your playful side and that you don't live by the rules all of the time.

Cyprien sat up, his grin wide showing off another of his perfect traits: his beautiful straight teeth. "There now, that wasn't so hard."

I knocked his knee with my hand. "Conceited much..."

His smile faded as his body tensed. He shifted to sit with his knees up and his elbows resting on them. His gaze met mine. "Delphine, I have never felt like this before with any woman. I never once wanted to settle down. I have always wanted to travel the world." He grabbed my hand and brought it to his lips kissing my palm. "But this summer, I never expected to meet you. Please don't get married. Run away with me."

He moved quickly and grabbed my hands. "Please?"

I wanted to leave with him, but I couldn't abandon my family and my obligations to Séverin. Cyprien pulled me into an embrace and nuzzled my neck with his lips, kissing his way to my ear. He whispered, "Please" once more. It sounded desperate. My heart pounded heavily, excitement and fear laced my emotions. I was going to do it. "Yes!" I barely got the words out before his mouth was over mine in a fierce kiss.

Felix moved off my stomach, and I rolled over. I felt the pouch of stones roll off my belly and hit the bed. I laid on top of them, and even though it felt like I was lying on hard rock, I couldn't make myself wake up.

The dreams pulled me further in until I was no longer in my bed but standing in a large room with a canopied bed. I had opened the French doors leading out to the balcony to let the fresh air in. Tonight was the night I was to run away with Cyprien. We were leaving after I came home from the first ball of the season. Cy wanted to leave before the ball, but I felt I owed it to my family and my betrothed to at least be there. They spent a lot of money on my new gown, and I felt guilty if they didn't at least get to see me in it once. I spun around, looking at myself in the mirror. My dark hair was twisted in a simple knot at the nape of my neck, and my lips were ruby red from the lip concoction Aurora had gifted me. I had to admit I felt beautiful. The pale blue gown had a sweetheart neckline and flowed like a moving spring. Cyprien and I planned to elope on the ship we were to catch. I wanted to make myself as beautiful as possible because tonight would be my real wedding night with the man I chose.

Aurora and her friend Goldie came in. Aurora caught my hand. "You look stunning tonight."

Goldie looked at me assessing and said nothing. I couldn't figure out why Aurora's friend always seemed to be watching me. I couldn't tell if she liked me or not, and tried for the longest time to be extra kind to her. None of that seemed to matter because she still looked at me as if she were assessing if I was worthy to be her friend, but I honestly didn't care anymore. After tonight I would never see her again. I would miss Aurora; though she was not my blood sister she had been my chosen sister and best friend.

I would miss her greatly. I vowed that I would write to her once Cyprien and I were married and long gone and explain my hasty departure. She would understand.

Aurora, Goldie, and I walked into the receiving line

together. Aunt Marie, as she liked to be called, came in with her new husband.

My stomach was fluttering with nerves. I needed to act calm with all these witnesses. Hopefully, they would mistake my anxieties for seeing my betrothed because it was now only three days until we were to be married. I was cutting it close, leaving. Séverin would despise me. I just hoped he wouldn't take it out on my family.

The line moved slowly, and we finally made it into the grand Moreau Estate. Cyprien said he was going to a ball tonight as well, and I was so hoping it was this one. I needed to see him to help my fears vanish. I didn't see him in line anywhere behind me, so if he was here, he had to be inside already or coming very late.

The moment I noticed Séverin, my heart dropped. Standing on the other side of him was none other than Cyprien. He was dressed in formal wear and looked like a grand prince. His hair wasn't hanging freely in his face like when we met. He wasn't loose and free with his body or his smiles. He was stiff and tall, and when he turned my way, his eyes lit up until Séverin stepped out of line to greet me.

"Finally," he said gratingly but kindly. I could tell he was agitated that we were late. He dragged me along behind him. We now stood directly in front of Cyprien, who gave me the strangest look as if understanding was finally sinking in.

"This is my elusive brother who would rather be wasting away at sea than at home helping his family. Brother, this is my betrothed. Isn't she everything I said she was?"

Cyprien swallowed hard. I could see his Adam's apple move up and down, and before long, he plastered a smile on his face and brought me into a hug. Whispering, "This changes everything. You lied to me."

He stepped out of the hug and his voice no longer held the joviality I was used to. It was as if we'd never met or fallen in love. He was cold. "Well, sister, I am sorry I was negligent in greeting. Sév, you are correct, she is more beautiful in person than in your words. You are a very lucky man."

I wanted to die. This couldn't be happening. Cyprien already had my luggage on the boat we were to take. It couldn't end this way; he couldn't just let me go. I needed to explain that I didn't lie, and my heart ached for him to fight for me.

I was frozen. Aurora came to my aid and greeted Cyprien. I felt like I was drowning as the music and chatter of everyone became muffled. My legs became wooden, and I couldn't seem to move. Thankfully, Aurora guided me away from my nightmare. Why had I been so adamant about not giving Cyprien my betrothed's name? And why did Cy never mention his family name to me?

I struggled to stay at the dance as long as I could. I danced with Séverin, then once with Cyprien. We fit in each other's arms perfectly. I couldn't look at him without wanting to cry so I kept my focus on the people behind him.

I did, however, defend myself in a whisper. "I didn't lie. I never dreamed you would be his brother. You are nothing alike."

His hand spread wider on my lower back and brought me a bit closer. I hoped that was a sign he'd still run away with me. He whispered, "I'm sorry. I wish we could still leave."

My heart sank. He wasn't going to fight for me. My eyes burned, but I braved a look, praying I wouldn't cry. "Why can't we? Why does this have to change our plan?"

"Because even though my brother may seem bad to you, he isn't. He is a very good man and has always been my best friend. He is passionate about the family farm and about our people. I don't know why he had behaved so poorly to you other than maybe he feels forced into this marriage as much as you do. I cannot just steal you away from him."

I lowered my head and whispered my true feelings for the first time. "But I love you. I choose you."

Before he could return my vows of love, the dance ended, and he walked away, leaving me in the center of the dance floor. I couldn't bear it any longer and went outside on the back porch. I leaned against the rail, looking out into the night. I could hear the wolves howling in the distance, and for some reason, they sounded as if they felt my misery. Without thinking, I took off running. I ran through the garden maze and into the woods that would lead me back home.

My hair came undone, sweat ran down between my breasts, and my beautiful dress was getting all ripped up from the branches of undergrowth that had not been maintained this far off the property.

I stopped running, panting. My hand cupping my side in pain as I tried to catch my breath, but it was difficult. My dress was too tight and sticking to my skin. Although September's evenings were cooler, it wasn't cold enough to keep me from sweating. I found a deer trail, and walked it instead of running, it led me to all places, the glen with the sacred willow, the place where I found solace these last few months.

I opened up the curtain of branches under the weeping willow and started to cry great big heaping sobs.

The sound of a snapping branch made me stifle my tears. The light sound of footsteps alerted me I was no longer alone. Whoever it was, they had a lantern. Maybe Séverin saw me leave and sent someone to bring me back.

I tried to stay quiet, but the curtain of trees opened. The bright light blinded me for a moment. "Thank the gods you are all right."

Of course, Cy was the one who noticed I left. I couldn't stop my tears from returning as I got up and ran into his arms. He immediately brought me in, holding me tight.

I cried into his shoulder. "I don't want to marry your brother. I love you. I should be with you."

He smoothed the back of my head with his hand, and I felt his lips kiss my forehead.

"I wish I never would have gone away. I would have met you first."

I looked up at him. "Please let us go, the boat already has our luggage, please."

He gently pushed me out of his arms. He pulled out a handkerchief, softly wiped my eyes, and then handed it to me. I wiped my nose. He paced around the lantern he had dropped on the ground when he hugged me. It cast strange shadows across his face, and I couldn't tell what he was thinking. He stopped in front of me, grabbed my hand, and brought it to his lips. He kissed the inside of my wrist where my pulse beat rapidly, then lay my palm over his heart, which felt as if it were beating like a drum.

Pain crossed his features. "My heart is telling me to leave with you this instant, but my mind is telling me that we must confront my brother."

"We don't have time. The wedding is in less than two days."

"I'm sorry, Delphine, I just need time to think. Please don't run off until we talk again."

I took a deep breath and nodded. "I will put my faith in you, but if you don't have a solution by tomorrow evening, I may have to run away alone. I cannot tie myself to your brother. Meeting you made that very clear to me."

A conversation I overheard between Aurora and her friend Goldie trickled into my mind. They were discussing alchemy. Why had I been so clueless all these years that my adopted family was magical? I'd been incredibly blind, or they were very good at hiding it from me. Why hadn't they told me outright? It was nothing to be ashamed of. Aurora had been asking Goldie if she knew any other alchemist who could get her some ingredients to help her with a love match.

Goldie held Aurora by the shoulders. "From experience, do not play with the red thread of fate. It can be detrimental to the true match's mental state."

Aurora had argued love should be a choice and that the red threads should be set aside until the couple decided that they wanted to be together, then they could collect their red thread and let it develop naturally and complete the tapestry of fate that way. I had to agree with her now. It should not be predestined because look at where it got me. I was stuck with Séverin who didn't feel like my other half, my sayonee, my soulmate. All those labels were for Cyprien. The man I chose.

Goldie dropped her hands from Aurora's shoulders and sighed. "You are right. The fates need to change. It is time for us to choose." She then told Aurora where to find an elf named Alfrock. Aurora would have to sneak into his home before dusk. As he was sleeping, she would have to remove a red thread magically entangled in his fingers, and once she had it, she would need to return to Goldie for the next instruction.

I needed to have a backup plan, and Goldie seemed to know a lot about witches and fate. I needed to confide in both her and Aurora. I knew they'd be on my side.

"Cy, what if I found a way to change our fate? To change it where you and I were together forever." I told him what I had overheard. He started pacing in and out of the light from the lantern. He stopped and grabbed my hands in his. "We shouldn't play with fate or magic. Nothing good comes from the dark arts. There will always be a high price to pay, and I don't want you to take that chance."

"But..."

"No! I love you. Give me a day to figure something out. If I can't talk Sév out of marrying you, then I don't know what we will do, but I know it will not be done with magic."

I wanted to cry. I knew what would happen. I was a coward with no money to travel alone. Marriage would be my only way to survive. But I had to trust Cy.

He wrapped me in an embrace, his head buried in my neck, and he inhaled deeply. "I love you," he whispered. I turned my face bringing our lips closer, the hunger burned deep in my belly as I opened my mouth letting him in. My hand knotted into his hair pulling him closer to me, pressing his lips harder to mine. I needed more; I needed him more than I needed to breathe. He shifted his mouth from mine, breathing heavily. I didn't want it to be the end; I wanted more, but if he failed, this would be my last kiss with my one true love, and I wanted to remember it for eternity. He pulled away, sweeping the hair from my face.

He handed me the lantern. "Take this and head home. I will find my own way back." Then he was gone.

Chapter Six

As I was walking into the house, Goldie was walking out. "Thank goodness I found you. I was so worried when I saw you run out of the ball. You looked ill. I came here to see if you'd come home."

It was strange that she was being so nice to me, since she never seemed to really take the time to know me before. But in a way, I was glad because maybe it would help me brave it up and ask for help. Tonight, I needed to sleep, but I would figure out a way to ask her tomorrow when Aurora was around. I didn't say anything to her but tried to pass around her to escape into the house.

She grabbed my arm, preventing me from leaving. "What happened to you? Your dress is shredded. Were you attacked by wolves?"

"No. I–" The tears I suppressed for so long couldn't be controlled any longer. Shame at not making it to my room in time filled me, but Goldie didn't seem to care. She came to my side and wrapped her arm around my shoulder. I could hear true sympathy in her words. "I had a feeling that you just discovered your secret rendezvous with your young man turned out to be your betrothed's younger brother."

I gasped. "How did you know?"

"I stumbled upon you and your lover in the glen one afternoon when I was out looking for herbs."

I swallowed. "Do you think anyone else knows? Séverin?"

She patted me on my shoulder as she guided me upstairs.

"No, I do believe you two have been very discreet. It was by pure chance I found my way to that little glen near the willow. Did you know that it is a sacred place? According to legend, the weeping willow only appears when a person is in deep need of escape. The willow tree you hid under is there as a protector for those who are lost. That is why her branches weep. She takes on all the sorrows in hopes of relieving the person of their woes. By taking on your sorrow, she also clears your head and heart to find solutions to your escape."

"That is so sad." My heart ached for the willow tree to have such a heavy burden. "But I must admit I am grateful she let me in. The glen has been a solace for me these last few months and led me to Cyprien."

We entered my room without a word. "Let me help you out of your gown."

I turned for her to unlace the back of my dress.

"I will go back to the ball and tell your family that you had a headache, and I walked you home."

I was stunned by her kindness and her use of the same excuse Cyprien had come up with. I was standing in my chemise. She was already about to exit my room when I decided to be bold and brave. I had to ask her about Alfrock and the red threads.

"Goldie, wait."

She stopped at the door and turned back to me. My throat was dry. I tried to swallow. Then cleared my throat. She waited patiently by the door for me to speak. Eventually, my words tumbled out of my mouth. "I overheard you telling Aurora about how to change her fate. Is it true that there is a red thread of fate? And is it possible to break a thread of fate to someone that I feel is the wrong person?"

Goldie came very close to me, placed her hands on my shoulders, and looked me directly in the eyes. "Delphine, you sweet girl, I am so glad you are asking. I have been hoping for this day, laying hints hoping you would come to me."

"You have? Why?"

"My sister has been very cruel. She has taken to playing games with the love lives of certain people and this time she has gone beyond forgiveness. Aza, my sister, had kept this disaster hidden from me and I wasn't sure you were the one until recently."

"I am confused. Your sister?"

"Aza is the eldest of the three fates. She strayed from the path that we had been given. She's been using her soul shifting to manipulate and alter the threads of fate. She has cut red threads that my other sister and I had already begun and taken them and reconstructed them to ill matched pairs. The ones she separated have cruel and unfulfilling lives."

I stood there with my mouth open.

"You're a Moirae..."

"I am the Spinner of Fate, the alchemist."

The fates were eternal. No wonder why I always thought she was ethereal. It's because she was, she wasn't mortal. I should have guessed from the beginning that she was a goddess or a child of the gods. She had the height, golden hair, and the perfect complexion that always appeared to be glowing from within as if sun kissed.

Her finger lifted my chin and shut my mouth that I had forgotten I opened in awe.

"My sister, Vida, and I are secretly trying to fix the mess Aza has made."

She reached for my hand. "You are right, your red thread was never meant to be Séverin, it was always supposed to be Cyprien. He is your true, destined love, your Sayonee. Séverin's thread has been broken. Because of Aza's meddling, his love for you is obsessive. You are like a drug to him, and now cruelty is his only way to show his distorted love for you."

Stunned, I didn't have words for what Goldie just told me. I wanted to be angry with her. Aurora was right, the fates shouldn't exist. We should all be able to choose who we love and let the red threads form naturally.

"So Cyprien won't succeed in talking to him?"

"No, your ancestry and Aza's soul magic combined are very powerful."

"Then, is there a way I can break my tie to him and bind myself to Cyprien?"

Goldie gave me a sad look. "My sister Vida and I have

been working on a spell in hopes of breaking your tie to Séverin."

She wouldn't look at me and suspicion reared its ugly head. "What kind of spell?"

"Never mind the details," she said. "He will never give you up. I need to ensure breaking your tie to him is something you want."

"The only red thread that will bind souls properly are the ones Aza hasn't touched yet, and tomorrow I will send Aurora to get one for us."

"I can go."

"No, you will need to wait for Cyprien to see how his talk went."

She placed her hands on my shoulders. Her stance demanded attention and I looked up at her. She was serious. "You need to understand something before all of this is done. There are rules to magic, especially dark magic."

"What are they?"

"One thing of great value must be sacrificed."

I interrupted her before she could say more. "I will sacrifice anything to be with Cyprien."

Goldie tutted and petted my head like a child. "Anything is a brave word."

I repeated my words. "I will do anything."

"Aza doesn't want this thread to break."

"Then nothing can be done to change my fate? I thought you were working on something."

"We are. It will be difficult, but I never said it was impossible. We only recently discovered a loophole in this dark magic, and the trouble is not in if it can be broken and mended, but if you are willing to pay the sacrificial price."

"What do I need to do?"

"Die."

"So what? So Séverin can live his life? That isn't fair. What game are you playing at? How will that help me be with Cyprien?"

Goldie took a deep breath and braced my shoulders in her warm hands. "This is no game. You will need to die in this life. But before you die, you will need to use the magic of Vida's elementals, she is willing to share the source of her essence with you and being you are already part soul shifter, by having her shared essence, you will be born again as our sister. I will be giving you the gift of my alchemy. When you are reborn, the gods will grant you immortality and you will be our fourth sister.

Doing this will give you the power to break Aza's spell and tie yourself to Cyprien in your next life. Because of the spell and the red thread, we have found a way for your soul to be reborn and retain all of your memories of this life. You will be an exact reincarnate, same face, hair, body, voice the only difference is you will be implanted in one of our followers on earth, far away from Aza. Your new family will raise you, and when you come of age the magic you placed on Cyprien will bring him back to you. You will be tied and meet again, and both of you will remember your love as if no time had passed and live happily ever after, connected for eternity."

It sounded so magical, and I wanted to believe it to be as simple and true as it sounded. "You make it sound so easy. I am not a witch, and I am not immortal. How will I be able to do this and still be me in the future? My mind cannot grasp any of this and where is earth? Is it far away? How will my spirit call Cyprien?"

"Vida has collected elements from seven dwarf stars and created a stone for each element. These stones are imbued with her magic, her life source. We are both determined to fix the errors of our and our sister's ways. Vida will teach you the spell to sever your current thread and create a new one with Cyprien. He will go into a deep sleep until you are reborn and will wake up when you are his age, and voila, you will have all your memories back once you see him and live happily ever after. Simple."

"So, all I have to do is use the thread that Aurora gets from the elf Alfrock then use the dwarf stones and spell Vida is getting from the soul shifter, and Cyprien and I will be together forever. Is that right?"

She nodded with a smile. "I love quick learners. Now the question is, do you want to live your happily ever after?"

"I do."

She breathed a sigh of relief. "Good. After you meet up with Cyprien to see if his way worked, you let me know. By that time, I should have the stones, the thread, and a plan. We will only have a short time to teach you everything you must learn to make this happen."

"Before I commit to this, I did mention to Cy that I overheard you and Aurora talking. I asked him if we could use magic, and he told me he wanted me with him but didn't want to use black magic. Please tell me this isn't dark magic?"

Goldie gave me a serious look. "What Aza did to you is dark magic. What Vida and I are trying to undo is not the purest of magic, but I wouldn't say it is dark. I like to call it healing magic. What Vida has is powerful elemental magic sourced from the universe. The universe is expansive and both good and evil, light and dark, and everything in between. It is what your intentions are when utilizing the magic. Love is pure. If you are using the magic for pure purposes, it isn't dark. But no matter if magic is dark or light when the source comes from the universe, a balance must always be maintained. That is why there must be a sacrifice to prove to the universe you are worthy. You, my dear, need to be willing to change not only your fate but his as well for your future. You must be bold and brave to weave the fate of your lives. And in doing so, you cannot tell Cyprien. It is the law of the fates never to allow the ones we are binding to each other to know. You must both find each other again in the future, but I promise you when you do, you will both remember everything. Your souls will remember. You will be immortal in that new life and have the gifts of the elements from birth. You will be special."

Panic rose in me. I would never grow old, and I would be making that same decision for Cyprien. Taking his choice to grow old away from him.

Goldie frowned. "You must hurry and make up your mind Delphine, what is your decision? Stay connected to a man who will never love you and end up killing you with his distorted love or sacrifice yourself for a chance at freedom to love the man you choose?"

I swallowed thickly on the verge of panic. I didn't

want to take his choice away, but it wasn't right that we'd been the victims of Aza's game.

"How much do you love this man?" asked Goldie. "Enough to be with him for an eternity? I know if it were me, I would risk it all for the man I loved. What risk are you willing to take?"

I thrashed in my bed. The pouch locked in my cupped hands. I tried to throw it from me, but I couldn't let go.

My decision was made the moment Cy limped into the glen.

There was no secret smile on his bruised face or split lips. I did love him, I loved him enough for eternity. "What happened?"

He grabbed my hand. "I asked Séverin to take a walk out back of the house with me. I didn't want our parents to overhear. I confessed to him that you and I had been meeting and had fallen in love. That you didn't love him, and I wanted to be the one to marry you for our family tomorrow instead of him.

"I tried, but he attacked me like a wild beast. I'd never seen him like that. I didn't recognize him. Even though as young boys we fought it was always just a scuffle. This—"

He turned to me the bruised eye swelling shut, his clear eye bloodshot and full of tears. "He was only throwing killing blows. If the groomsmen in the barn hadn't heard us and pulled Sév off I would have died.

"I didn't have it in me to fight back. I failed you."

He sat up and locked his arms around me and I kissed the brow over his bruised eye. Then above the cut on his cheekbone. I wanted to kiss away all his pain.

"I am so sorry I didn't listen to you. I didn't understand how much Sév had changed. Will you ever forgive me?"

I couldn't see him because of my tears, but I nodded anyway. The decision had been made. I couldn't let Séverin beat his brother into submission or allow Cyprien to give up on our love.

Goldie was right. I had to right this wrong. Later that afternoon, I found Goldie and Aurora in the parlor. My Aunt had just left after preparing the room for the wedding to take place. There were flowers all over the room and chairs were brought in and placed creating an aisle. Tomorrow was the big day and I had dallied too long. I was sad for my aunt to have to discover that not only did I run but that I died and left this life forever. The world would believe that it was either a double suicide between lovers or that Cy had killed me and ran off. I walked up beside my two friends. My cheeks were blotchy from crying, and they knew I had bad news. I had to be strong. "Tell me what to do."

"I am so grateful." Goldie hugged me to her. "We will fix this! Thank you."

I didn't know why Goldie was grateful other than maybe helping me heal the wound her sister had caused in my life,

Aurora came beside me and gave me a side hug, "I think you made the right decision. But oh, how I will miss you dearly."

I hugged her back with tears in my eyes. "I will miss you too; hopefully you will be my sister in the future."

I looked up at Goldie, "Do you think that is possible?"

Before Goldie could answer the howl of a wolf outside grabbed our attention. Goldie ran outside as Aurora and I ran to the window facing the back of the property. A huge wolf stood near the shadows at the edge of the woods.

"He has the stones!" Goldie called back over her shoulder.

I gasped. "Did you know they could turn into men?"

Aurora shook her head, mesmerized at the sight of a tall dark-haired man. She kept staring until with a blink of an eye he was back into wolf form and disappeared into the shadows.

Aurora held her hand to her chest as if to keep it in place.

Goldie returned to us fuming mad. She didn't explain and wouldn't answer any questions. Honestly, I don't know why seeing the wolf man surprised me, Nod was full of creatures hiding in plain sight, but they generally kept themselves hidden.

Humans and elves were the only two species in Nod who seemed to have good trade agreements and got along without pretending to be something else.

Goldie spent the rest of the night teaching me what needed to be done to detach myself from Séverin. We stayed up until dawn and I learned everything I could about the stones, the elements, and the spell Vida had told the wolf to give to Goldie. Aurora created a potion called sleep of the living dead and put it into the lip balm she had me use the night of the ball.

Today was my wedding. The carriages of guests started arriving and Aurora and Goldie helped me get ready. They wanted me to wear my wedding gown, but I couldn't bear to put it on. Instead, I had taken one of the serving girl's uniforms and put the simple dress and apron on. I thought I might have a better time of sneaking away.

Cyprien and his parents had arrived, and I had Aurora send him a note asking him to please meet me one last time in our spot. I had only two hours before the bell chimed for the wedding to take place.

Aurora stayed behind to cover for me, but she was to meet me at my final moments to complete the spell. Goldie confided in me that the wolves had taken her sister Vida prisoner because Aza had commanded them to kill her. She was still alive but mated to one of their own and in hiding. Goldie was worried what Aza would do next and went to try and soothe things over in hopes Aza wouldn't find out what I was doing.

She swore to me that Aurora would capture my soul and give it to her. She would make sure I would be reborn so my happily ever after could come true.

Cyprien was late and I was so scared that he wouldn't come. There was less than an hour before the service. I needed to finish this or run.

The snap of a branch brought me out of my thoughts. Cyprien had come. He was dressed in the wedding attire, and even though his face was bruised, my first thought was that someone hired a witch to create the illusion he was healed. He was as handsome as a prince. His amber eyes scanned me up and down. He saw my clothes and I could tell he was confused. He probably thought I was going to run. Misery and regret were written all over his face.

I inhaled and it came out as a snuffle. The weight of what I was about to do overwhelmed me for the first time since I'd made my decision. Cy hurried to me and pulled me into his arms. I wrapped my arms around his waist and inhaled his woodsy scent. "Phin," he breathed out, holding me in his embrace.

My cheek rested on his chest. His heartbeat was strong and quick as he tilted my chin up and kissed my poisoned lips.

When we broke apart, we were both breathless.

"I will always love you," he said, leaning his forehead against mine. But "I can't stay here and see you married to my brother. I will leave after the wedding."

"Without me?" I was momentarily stunned that, knowing his brother's temper, he wouldn't let me run with him. "Why can't I go with you?"

His once proud shoulders sagged. "I cannot dishonor my family. It will destroy them. They will lose the farm and their way of life. It is better this way. Once you are married, I truly believe whatever has come over my brother will be gone. Before I left two years ago, he was once a loving and compassionate person. I just think that all the pressure is on him from my father."

I backed away from him as tears fell from my eyes. "Please don't be angry with me," he said. "I know I seem weak by not taking you with me, but I won't destroy your life! You would be ruined; Nod is very small, and everyone will know. We would be treated like the lowest of creatures. I can't do that to you, living with my brother is better than starving with me."

I searched the conviction in his eyes. Nod was small, and even if we traveled the seas, the other nations would have heard about us. I was taking his choice, but hadn't he taken mine? By me becoming a sister of fate in the future and tying myself to him I knew we would be safe and protected. I would be magical and because I would become immortal, he would be bonded to me for eternity as well.

"I forgive you–always," I said as tears continued to roll down my cheeks.

I was doing this for both of us. I was changing our fate for the better. I placed my palm on his cheek and cried.

He wiped my tears away with his thumb. "Please don't cry. I don't deserve your forgiveness or compassion. I deserve your anger; you need to despise me."

"I could never despise you! I love you more than my life itself."

Cyprien's hand struck my shoulder as he stumbled and fell. He was on his back, and I was on top of him. His breathing slowed and his blinks became slower.

The poison was working.

His hand moved in the air a bit then grabbed the front of my apron. In a soft breathy voice, the words "I love you more" came out very slowly.

I kissed him one last time. "You are my chosen soulmate, my sayonee. I promise I will find you again."

The last thing I did was lay my head on his chest. His

heartbeat was faint but still beating. The potion had worked.

I wanted to tell him it would be all right and I knew what I was doing, but I couldn't. I quickly tied the red thread attached to my pinky to his and the rhythm of his heartbeat strummed through the thread connecting us. Soon our pulses equalized to a perfect rhythm.

The deep breath I'd been holding escaped. "I promise, I will come for you in my next life. We will forever be bound." I kissed him over his heart. "I will always love you."

Still on my knees beside him, I poured all my love for him into the thread joining us, slowly weaving reminders of how I fell in love with him, the feelings and sensations tingled throughout my limbs and followed the thread into Cyprien. I wanted to leave him with dreams of love and happiness so that when he woke up he would know how I truly felt.

Then the red strand did something I wasn't expecting. It turned bright gold, and I flew back from the jolt that ran through me. I could barely open my eyes as the thread was now as blinding as the sun.

Slowly the brightness faded and I could physically see not only the golden thread connecting me to Cyprien but the red thread connecting me to Séverin turning black. It was taut, and I could see it weaving its way through the wood to him. Never had I felt emotion coming from Séverin but now I could clearly sense his impatience and frustration.

How couldn't he feel the wrongness of our bond? Maybe if I had talked to him, he'd have wanted to help me. But it was too late now, I couldn't let anything stop me.

Séverin was probably standing at the altar wondering where Cyprien was and waiting for me to walk down the aisle. Maybe he figured out that we had one last secret rendezvous or maybe he was afraid I ran away with Cyprien. I couldn't take the chance of him coming for me early. I jumped up and focused on the rest of my spell work.

I needed to hurry.

No more second guessing, Hopefully I was doing everything right because Goldie never mentioned the thread would turn gold or the one connecting Séverin to me would turn so dark it nearly looked black.

No more thinking. Cyprien appeared as if he were sleeping peacefully.

He even wore his crooked half smile as if he were waiting for me to come near so he could play a joke on me. Then I realized he was healed, no more swollen black eyes, nor were his lips split. I kissed him one last time.

"Until we meet again."

I pulled the small tan leather pouch out of my pocket. Opening it up, I placed the hematite ring on my ring finger nearest my racing heart. Goldie told me this was the key to igniting my borrowed magic and what would help bind the magic to me in my next life. She called it the head dwarf star. There was a total of seven Vida had collected from the universe.

I then pulled out Malachite, the earth stone and Labradorite, the air stone. With both in my right hand, I did the spell that I had practiced overnight. I used the wind to create a bed of fallen leaves under the sacred willow tree. With a few words, I turned the leaves into a plush velvet sleeping pad. I used the wind once more and laid Cyprien onto the pad.

I took out the onyx and diamond combining the power of shadow and light to create a glass encasement to protect him. When that was complete, I took out the chunk of gold Aurora had given me. This spell would seal the coffin and keep Cyprien frozen in time. I placed it on top of the glass and once more used the malachite stone and created fire to melt the gold. Power rushed through me, a feeling I'd never felt before. I shivered, arms thrown wide as I held the air stone in my fist.

The gold melted, and the ancient Greek text appeared. It vanished just as quickly. Then the only thing remaining on the glass coffin was a beautiful golden filigreed design. I placed my hand on the top and spoke the words Goldie had me memorize. "You will awaken by my touch when I am reborn with the strength of the fates behind me. This I vow to you."

My heart felt like it was caving in, and I fell to my knees. The golden thread was broken. Both Cyprien and I wore the fragments as if they were now only rings of gold. Fear that I failed burned behind my eyes. The thread that was connecting me and Séverin was looser. Maybe the spell was starting to work. I couldn't give up.

I was running out of time. I had to finish this.

I gave Cyprien one last look and stepped away from the protection of the sacred willow. My hand brushed the sagging branches.

"Thank you for giving me peace. Keep my love safe until he and I can meet again."

The wind blew, and the branches of the willow swayed, sending soothing sounds my way. Deep in my heart, I knew she'd heard and acknowledged my thanks.

I rushed into the center of the glen. I hurriedly sprinkled the salt in a circle around me and placed all the stones back into the pouch, gripped them in my hands, and said the last spell I memorized. It was no language I ever heard. Vocalizing, the sounds came out of my mouth as if I were singing. The pouch grew warm in my hand as all the seven dwarves were activated—magic, earth, air, fire, water, light, and shadow.

The rutiles in the hematite ring began to glow. My time was up. Séverin was on his way. The thread tying me to him was growing in strength and that scared me. The fear of being caught and bound to Séverin outweighed my fear of dark magic.

I shouted the words and cast a spell creating a dagger made of water. Goldie had promised it would be painless, and she didn't lie. As I plunged it into my chest there was no pain only a heavy weight as if I were holding my breath underwater.

I looked up as Séverin rode into the clearing. As I rushed the last words, the water blade turned into stone. I collapsed to the ground. The pain was excruciating. My entire chest was crushed, and I felt myself contort in pain trying to gasp for breath and none would come.

Fear like no other overwhelmed me. Panic that I couldn't breathe and the pain... I prayed for death to take me faster.

The loud blast of trumpets was the last thing I heard.

Darkness

Silence

I was no longer living.

My soul left my body crumpled on the ground. The stone blade vanished. All that remained was a bloody hole in my chest and my hand still gripping the pouch of stones. How had I kept them in my hand in that much pain?

Séverin jumped off his horse and ran to my crumpled body. He knelt by my side and lifted my shoulders and brought me into an embrace. "What have you done?"

The black thread was still connected from him to my soul, not my body.

I felt so sad for him. He truly appeared like he loved me. Was I so unhappy that I was blind to him? If he loved me so much, why had he hurt me?

The stones fell out of my fisted hand. He picked up the blood-soaked pouch. I could see the energy move into his body just touching the bag. He turned to where I stood as if he momentarily saw me.

"Delphine?"

He came to stand before me. His hair stood on end as a golden light glowed around him. "What is this magic?"

Goldie didn't tell me that the stones could be used by Séverin. She didn't tell me he would still be tied to me and see my spirit. I tried to grab the stones from his hand, but my soul passed through the pouch and him. He walked back a step. I tried again. This time he stood and started to search the woods. What was he looking for? I tried to follow but my soul remained near my body.

Where was Aurora? She was supposed to be waiting here at my death. She was supposed to capture my soul for Goldie so that I could be reborn. She was supposed to leave right before I was expected to walk down the aisle.

This was all going so wrong.

If I failed what would happen to Cy? Would he die or stay frozen in sleep for eternity? Hopefully the sacred willow would take care of him and protect him. My ghostly hand still connected by a long black thread to Séverin and on my ring finger a golden thread... thankfully connected to Cyprien. Hopefully it was enough.

The wind howled, the sky darkened, and lightning struck the ground not far from us. Rain came crashing down. Séverin's horse started bucking and finally he came back into my view to reach his horse and soothe him. He treated his horse better than he'd treated me when I was alive.

He and the horse took refuge under the Doskurya tree, its large round plumes protecting them from the rain. Thunder boomed again and a soaking-wet Aurora finally arrived in dripping wet formal attire. She slid off the side saddle of her horse and ran to my prone body. She slid in the mud on her knees beside me and fell on top of my body and wailed. Her tears were loud, and I felt the grief pour out of her. I prayed to the gods that would allow us to be born again as sisters. She truly was the one person I loved beside Cyprien.

She sat back on her heals then gently closed my eyelids. "You did it!"

Relief filled me at her words. I did do it and now she will complete the final part. Goldie had instructed

Aurora what to do privately while I learned my spells. She pulled the hematite ring off my finger, put it in her pocket, and stood up. She spun around with arms spread wide; her face upturned into the rain.

Séverin's horse nickered and shrieked when the next strike of lightning hit nearby. Aurora stopped spinning and faced the direction of Séverin.

He walked up to Aurora leaving his horse behind and handed her the pouch. "It worked."

Wait! My spirit moved next to them. What was going on? This wasn't a part of the plan.

Aurora's wet scarlet hair was plastered around her pale face. She placed the pouch in the deep folded pocket of her cape and turned her back to Séverin. Faced my soulless body, as a wicked smile crept onto her lips.

It was a look that I'd never seen cross my sweet friend's face ever.

She laughed. "Poor dear, you really are a fool."

Chapter Seven

I woke up gasping for breath with my hands around my throat. I couldn't breathe. My throat and chest were dry, and I couldn't even make any spit in my mouth. Aurora came running into my room, flicking on the overhead light as she entered. I jumped away from her and nearly fell off my bed. My fear that was already at a ten jumped higher. I was scared she was going to...what? Kill me?

I tried to swallow, and I caught a shallow breath in. I tried taking a deeper breath and the horrible sound of gasping came out and panic struck again.

"Oh my god, you're turning blue. Breathe, Phin, dammit, breathe." Aurora pounded me so hard I nearly fell off my bed.

Never in a million years did I ever think I'd be grateful for spit. Aurora slumped down beside me. "Oh, thank God! What happened? I thought I'd have to call emergency."

"Bad dream." Taking slow, measured breaths, I rested

my head on her shoulder, no longer afraid. "Nightmare. I died, and my soul left my body."

She hugged me. "Was it that stupid dream from the drawings again?"

I pushed her away. "Why do you keep having that dream?" Aurora was still shaking.

Why in the world had I dreamt of Aurora betraying me? She would do anything for me.

"You scared me," she said, squeezing my hand.

"S-scared myself," I choked out.

"Do you want to talk about it?"

Did I want to tell her she betrayed me in my dream? No, I didn't but I did need to talk about the dream. "It's been happening ever since my birthday and it's just weird. I've never had recurring dreams like this before. The dream felt as if I lived it. I could see, taste, smell and remember each detail as if they were memories."

I took a deeper, still shaky breath. "Remember the drawing you saw earlier of me in the clearing, dead? This time it felt more real than the dream. I swear I felt like I'd died."

Aurora pulled herself all the way on my bed and sat with her legs crisscrossed. "I don't like that you keep having those dreams. Do you think your subconscious is trying to tell you something?"

"I have no clue, but Goldie said something to me earlier tonight, and strangely, it coincided with something in my dream."

"What in the world did Goldie tell you?"

I picked up the blood-stained leather pouch and almost dropped it again. Power exploded out of it, wrapping around my fist like a hand. It was exactly like the one in my dream.

"We found this," I told her.

I watched Aurora's expression closely. She appeared confused.

"Am I supposed to know what this is?"

"I guess not. It's just weird. In my dream, you were an alchemist and Goldie was one of the three fates of destiny." I shook my head. "Never mind it was just a weird dream. Anyway, before you got home, we found these in my memory box." I held the little pouch up, letting it dangle by the pull ties. "Goldie told me that I'm an elemental and that the stones chose me."

Aurora looked down at her hands, folding and unfolding around one another.

I placed my hand on hers to stop them. "What is going on, Aurora? What aren't you telling me?"

She didn't say anything, and I was starting to panic. My life just nose-dived into the I'm not mentally stable phase.

I couldn't handle the silence. "What! Tell me!"

She looked up at me. "You know I would never ever lie to you, right?"

"I would hope you wouldn't. We are family and best friends." Then my brain caught up with her words. "Wait, are you saying you lied to me?"

"Well, it's not really a lie. It's more like just withholding some information."

I stood up and started walking in circles in my room. I stopped moving, and with my hands on my hips, I looked down at her. "What aren't you telling me, Aurora?"

"Actually, Goldie kinda mentioned it last night, sort of when she asked Theo why he was hanging with an Alchemist. Do you remember that?"

I nodded. "Kinda hard to forget that weird moment."

"Well, she and I are members of a secret society that is called the Daughters of Fate. It's like a non-collegiate sorority for science geeks like me, and it is exclusive. You have to be invited in, and I was invited by Goldie during my first semester in college. I would have told you, but I was bound by secrecy, and I honestly didn't think anything of it. It's kinda like a small private group, and only a handful of women of all ages love the ancient art of alchemy. For the last three years I have been a practicing Alchemist learning from Goldie and a few others."

I sat back on the bed. That didn't sound at all like my dream version. It sounded kinda geeky and boring.

"I can see why your subconscious took off with the Alchemist bit, but what confuses me is what Goldie meant by you being an elemental." Aurora looked at the bag. "The only elemental period we ever talked about in the Daughters of Fate was the Rosicrucian movement. And the only reason we talked about that was because of Panacea. Some of the ladies were hoping to reinvent 'universal medicine.' But during this period in history, people claimed only to see elemental creatures."

"Creatures?"

Aurora turned to me all serious and grabbed my hand. "Well honey, I hate to be the bearer of bad news, but if you were born during that era and you are an elemental, then that would mean you aren't human and that you are either a nymph, sylph, pygmy, or salamander."

She chuckled as I swatted her on the leg. "Not funny. I was freaked out for a second."

"But seriously," a grin started on her lips that she tried to conceal. "I think I see it now."

"See what?" I asked.

"Maybe you're part pygmy." She giggled and I pushed her arm shoving her away.

"Not funny."

Aurora became serious again. "What were you doing with the magic in the dream?"

I felt my cheeks heat up.

Aurora grinned. "Ooh, is this about the mystery man?"

I nodded. "Yeah, I was fated and betrothed to Séverin, and I didn't want to be, so the only way to destroy the connection was to use the magic, die and have my soul reincarnated to break the tie. I was supposed to be brought back to life but –"

Her eyes opened wide. "But what?"

"I woke up not breathing. I never got past that part."

"All I can say is I'm glad it was just a dream and not real."

She pointed to the little pouch. "Are those the stones?"

I nodded.

Aurora picked up the pouch and looked at it from all

angles. "It looks really old, and the color is strange. It almost looks like dried blood."

I didn't respond because, strangely enough, that is what I thought too, and I saw my blood in the dream stain the pouch. Was it a coincidence, or is that something else I just subconsciously brought into the dream?

Aurora poured the stones out in her hand. "They are just crystals and gemstones." She put them back in the pouch one by one then held the smallest stones and turned to me. "These don't look magical at all; they look like something you'd buy in the bargain bin at the gem shop down the street." She placed the stone back in the bag with the others.

"Yep. What were you expecting?"

"I really don't know."

She held the ring up close to her eye. "The hematite is beautiful. The rutiles look like little streams of gold."

When Aurora was done looking at it, she handed it to me. It was exactly like the one in the dream, and on impulse, I put it on my left ring finger. Warmth radiated in me. I pulled the labradorite stone out of the pouch. The second I did, a breeze moved throughout my room. The curtains ruffled, but the windows were all closed.

"Woah! What the hell was that?" Aurora asked. She turned around, looking for where the draft came from.

My heart strummed heavily in my chest. At the same time I was intrigued when powerful energy coursed through my body. I didn't answer her, instead, I picked up the red carnelian. My hand became warm as the energy spread through my body again. The power made me feel ten feet tall. Within seconds all the candles in my room lit up with a small flame.

Aurora stood up. "No way! Oh, my gods! Was that you?"

She started pacing the room. "When I first joined the Daughters of Fate, I walked in on a conversation once when our oldest member, who is in her seventies, was asking Goldie if she ever thought that the elementals would ever show themselves again."

Aurora stopped pacing. Looked at the lit flames. "Wild! I didn't believe that there was such a thing, but I guess there is. You are wielding *magic*."

She pulled me up by my hands and started jumping up and down and spinning in circles chanting, "You are magical."

I couldn't help but laugh when I shared the exhilaration of the moment with Aurora.

Aurora stopped spinning. "But something feels off. When Goldie was talking to the lady, she said that her sister disbanded the Elemental section of the Daughters of Fate. Then she said something even stranger, a contradiction. She said her sister had been taken before the section was even created, and more than likely it was just a ploy to throw off the Fates. The old lady never questioned her, and I obviously couldn't because I was already eavesdropping."

She turned to me. "This is all so surreal."

I had no words. I rubbed my hands across my aching chest. I didn't know if it was from the pain of dying in my sleep or the ache of missing Cyprien, but either one could make my heart feel empty.

Aurora hopped back up again and quickly paced the small space in my room. "Why is Goldie involved in all of this? This is too bizarre, first that she invites me to a group that I didn't think much about and now she is involved in telling you you're an elemental. Who the hell is she? Why did she pick us? And what does all this mean?"

She was making me dizzy. I still wasn't feeling a hundred percent after nearly choking to death, so I grabbed her hand and made her sit beside me on the bed again. She turned to me. "This makes no sense at all. What does she know? Oh, my gods. I've been so narrow-minded. Geez, Phin, how are you taking all of this? How do you feel? Is magic painful?"

How was I taking this? I honestly felt almost numb except for the moments of pure power when the stones were in my hand.

"No, it isn't painful. Actually, I feel strong and alive when I'm holding the stones. They take away some of the cold sadness that I've been feeling for a long time. What I'd like to know is why am I taking this so well? I mean, shouldn't I be freaking out? I am manipulating the elements. That's huge, right?"

Aurora nodded. "It is. It is like massive, huge."

I fell back on my bed and stared at the ceiling. "Goldie said that I have been channeling the elements since I redesigned my room."

Aurora lay beside me. "Wild!" She turned her head to me. "Do you think she did something to make you dream things? Did she slip you anything to drink? Maybe she made some kind of potion to help you discover your magic. She is an alchemist and is good at it too!"

I lay quiet for a moment. "Actually, thinking about it, we didn't even eat or drink anything while here, and all she did was pluck the hanging pouch off Felix's paw after I pulled him out from digging in the box. After that was the news on TV, Goldie, and Theo's drama, and seeing Séverin crying."

Aurora squeezed my hand. She knew I still had unsettled feelings about Séverin.

She rolled over to look at me. "Anything else you remember? Anything that might help us figure out what is going on?"

I lay there for a while thinking, but the only thing that popped into my head made me giggle.

"What's so funny?"

I scooted over closer to her, rolled over to whisper in her ear, trying to create mystery. "Only that the stones are called the Seven Dwarves."

She laughed, shoving me to the side. "You're lying!"

I rolled back onto my back and crossed my fingers over my stomach feeling somewhat satisfied with that fun little nugget to break the strangeness of the night. "Nope, there was a little piece of paper inside with it written on it and a date."

"That is funny. I wonder why they call them the seven dwarves."

"No clue. But I kind of like it. I always did love Snow White as a kid."

"That you did. Remember when you made a coffin from our red wagon, a cardboard box, and cellophane paper? You laid in it for Halloween and made me pull you around to trick or treat."

I laughed. "Oh, my gods, that was the best Halloween ever."

Aurora rolled to her side. "Phin,"

I rolled to face her.

"I'm scared you might run into Séverin again," she said.

I blew out a breath. I was scared, too, "I'll be all right. That was five years ago and now I have magic, right? I'll just blast him with a flame of fire or blow him away if he comes anywhere near me. I just need to learn how to control it."

She gave me a half smile. "I'm still worried. I don't want you to run into him and think he's a changed man and fall for him again. You endured so much while dating him and lost way too much ever to forgive him. Promise me you won't talk to him if you run into him."

"I can't promise that I won't forgive him or talk to him. You saw him on TV. He looked broken. I am sure being in jail and getting clean opened his eyes. But I do promise I will try not to confront him alone. I am kinda scared of what he might remember from that day in court."

Aurora frowned. "I guess I have to accept that." Then she playfully punched my upper arm. I rubbed my bicep. "Ouch! That wasn't nice."

She rolled her eyes. "I didn't even hit you hard."

She put her left pinky out to me. "You better swear to me that you won't fall for him again. I can see all that compassion oozing out of your eyes. Need I remind you that he was and will probably always be trouble."

I linked my pinky to hers. "Promise, I learned my lesson. I won't date him again, but if I do see him, and I feel like there is unfinished business between us, I want to talk to him and make sure he understands what he did to me."

Aurora looked terrified. "Promise me you won't search him out!"

I tried to pry her fingers off my arm, but she wouldn't let go.

"Okay, already. If you let go, I promise I won't go looking for him."

But silently, I thought if we ran into one another, maybe I could overcome my fear of him with the help of the elementals and see if he had changed. Or figure out a way to cloak myself in magic and secretly follow him to see if he is a hazard to me before confronting him. The intensity of this new power running through my veins made me smirk. *He'll be sorry if he ever messes with me again.*

Aurora slid off the bed and jumped to her feet. "Why don't I think you're being honest?"

Because she probably could see the wheels in my head turning. What if his threat was real? What if he'd cried on camera because he was hoping I was watching the news and wanted my sympathy to try to lure me into a false sense of security.

Here I was moments ago, ready to forgive him because I felt bad for him. I really couldn't be naive about him this time. Just because I could light a candle with the stones or make the wind blow didn't give me power to fight or protect myself if he were still a danger. I needed to keep my distance.

With more conviction this time, I crossed my heart with my fingers. "I promise. I will never ever go looking for him alone."

She breathed out a sigh of relief. "That's better than nothing. Now, back to before you fell asleep. Did anything else happen? Did Goldie leave anything around the room to maybe make you have these weird dreams and be extra potentially forgiving to Séverin, because you had me seriously worried for a few minutes?"

I kicked her shin with my foot playfully, even though she was kinda right. I tried to remember. Had Goldie tried to drug me? Nothing came to my mind except Felix.

"Wait! Something did happen."

Aurora sat up. "What?"

"Felix climbed on top of me with the pouch clutched in his jaw. He dropped them over my heart, curled into a ball, and fell fast asleep right on top of them. I didn't want to move him and ended up falling asleep with the stones and Felix acting like a heating pad. It was so incredibly soothing that I forgot about the entire day and fell fast asleep."

"So maybe the stones were trying to communicate with you?

"Why would the stones try to communicate with me?"

Aurora had a strange look on her face, almost as if she might have felt the stones too. "Magic is magic, even though I love science, there are some things in the world that just can't be explained. Honestly, if I didn't see you do magic with the stones, I wouldn't believe it. I mean, I never thought my group was that big of a deal, but tonight has me second-guessing many things. What if there is more to being an alchemist? Never in a billion years would I have ever believed that stones can produce magic." Her answer erased my initial fear once again that she might be a part of the dream conspiracy.

She looked at me in awe. "But you are living proof."

I didn't feel any different. I still felt like me. The girl who prefers to stay hidden away licking her wounds. Why would stones choose me to be magical? What am I expected to do with this new gift? I'm not sure I wanted it. But I tried to think about what Aurora said. Were the stones trying to communicate with me? I was starting to worry that maybe they were trying to protect me from trusting the wrong people again. Maybe they were called the seven dwarves because, in the cartoon, they protected Snow White.

Were they trying to warn me to beware of Goldie and especially Aurora? No, that can't be. Aurora is my best friend and soul sister. We have been inseparable since birth, and she has stood by me through everything. She is the only one I love more than my life, which is what helped me keep on living. There is no way she would ever betray me.

Before my mind caught up with my mouth, I was already voicing part of my fears. "Do you think my dreams are coming true?"

Aurora had quieted down and looked to be lost in her thoughts, but when my question caught up to her,

her blue eyes darkened to a stormy grey. I was one of the only people she knew who could see so much from her eyes, maybe it was the artist in me, but I could tell my question terrified her. "What do you mean?"

"Well, do you think that I can make what happened in my dream happen in real life?"

"Girl, I have no idea." The worry continued and Aurora started talking faster. "All of this, everything that is happening." She looked toward the door to her room then took up and started talking with her hands making exaggerated movements. "I mean, everything that has happened in the last twenty-four hours is unprecedented."

She stopped walking, put her hands on her hips, took a deep breath, and placed her hand on my shoulder as I sat on my bed. She looked me in the eye. "I know I joked about making your dream guy come to life, but scientifically I can't believe what your subconscious mind created while you slept will become real in the sense of your dream. Dreams that are vivid generally are a way for you to piece issues that you are struggling with together. Practically everything in your dream was something that happened to you already or overheard in conversation, and your mind used its imagination to sort it all out."

She drew in a deep breath and shook her head, squeezing her eyes closed.

"I seriously don't want to think that the ending will ever come true."

I knew she was worried about me dying, but I really couldn't see that happening. Maybe I dreamed it because I truly was afraid Séverin was coming for me for revenge.

Aurora shivered and her eyes widened and glazed over for a moment the golden ring returning. That was the expression I'd noticed earlier when Theo was near. She cleared her throat then said, "But if any part of your dream would come to life, I certainly hope it's that hot guy from your drawings. The expression on your face kissing him is how I hope I look when I kiss Theo."

She pulled me into a hug. "Phin, you are my best friend, and I love you more than life. Please don't ever harm yourself, and out of everyone I know, you are the kindest soul on the planet and deserve to be loved. I hope you can find someone like the man in that drawing to bring pure happiness back into your life."

My cheeks heated up from her compliment. I didn't feel that kind a moment ago, especially when I was thinking she might possibly betray me. I tried to take the focus off me. "You don't have to worry about kissing Theo to get that look. You have it just looking at him."

She smiled, stood taller.

"I know we just met again, but I seriously think I am in love."

Aurora walked over to my desk and opened my iPad. She started looking at my drawing app and pointed to the file dream_5-5-23.

"Yep."

She opened the file and was flipping through the images. "Are these the same as last night's dream? You said the dreams were the same all week."

I walked up beside her as she scrolled. "Yeah, so far, they are the same."

"You drew Séverin and the hottie you were kissing

beside each other here. They kinda look alike side by side."

"Yeah, in my dream, they were brothers, and I was betrothed to Séverin but wanted to marry his brother Cyprien, who I called Cy."

"These drawings are the best you've ever drawn."

I looked down, not meeting her eyes, and just lifted my shoulders. "Thanks."

She flipped to the drawing of me stabbing myself. I pointed to it. "That is the part of my dream last night that felt so real and made me wake up gasping."

When Aurora looked at me again, she hesitated for a moment, then chose her words carefully. "I know I joked about the dream guy hopefully becoming real, but if the elemental magic is somehow responsible for these dreams...if they end up being some weird premonition caused by magic...I never want you to practice it again, especially if this is what it's leading up to."

She had tears in her eyes as she held the screen up facing me, and in an emotionally choked voice, she said. "This can never ever ever be real."

She put the iPad back down on my desk and slapped the cover over the image, trying to block it from her view. "Your dreams are just dreams," she stated with a deter-mined tone as if her words would make it true. "This whole thing is just a bizarre coincidence. We'll have to call Goldie in the morning. Being she is the one who knows about the elementals, I am certain she will be able to clear all this up."

Aurora fought a huge yawn that came upon her suddenly.

I picked up my phone on my nightstand. "Dang, it's three a.m. I'm so sorry I am keeping you awake. I know how you have to have a full nine hours to be functional."

Aurora yawned again, and this time it rubbed off on me.

"It's all right. I'll grab some coffee from Magic Brew before I head to school."

"I will set my alarm to wake you up, and I'll treat you to breakfast tomorrow morning. It's the least I can do."

Aurora gave me a hug. "You owe me nothing."

I was as stiff as a board for the first time all night with her. My old feelings of wanting to run and hide around her returned. It had been so long since I felt like that with my family. Was it because of my dream? Was it really trying to tell me something? She wasn't letting go, so I made myself try to relax and return the hug.

I tried to pull out of the hug with an apology, but she didn't seem to take my cue. "I'm so sorry I scared you awake, but thank you for coming in. It means a lot knowing you care."

Finally, Aurora pushed me out of her arms and looked at me as if I were delusional. "Of course I care, I love you!"

Felix meowed extremely loud at the door. He stretched his stubby front legs, then yawned. I crossed my arms around my chest, agitated by his abandonment during my nightmare. Maybe if he'd stayed with me, I wouldn't have had to wake up Aurora. He could have easily clawed me awake or something.

"Where were you, mister, when I needed your protection in my sleep?"

Aurora chimed in and turned to the cat. "Yeah, dude, where were you?"

Felix jumped up on the bed, completely ignored Aurora, and bumped his head into my hip. I immediately picked him up and cozied up to him. He licked my cheek, and I smiled. "All right, you're forgiven."

Aurora laughed. "I swear, you have to be the most forgiving person on earth. That took what? All of two seconds."

"Hey!" I objected playfully, "That isn't a bad thing."

"No, it isn't, but one day, I hope it doesn't get you in trouble."

It already did when I forgave Séverin a multitude of times and kept dating him. I momentarily curled in on myself, hugging Felix tight to my chest.

He squirmed in my arms, and I let him jump down. He meowed at Aurora then sniffed with his head in the air, turning his back on her as he gave her a nice view of his butt with his tail high in the air.

Aurora crossed her arms across her chest and pouted. "Traitor. Just because she forgave you fast doesn't mean my words aren't true."

I cleared my throat. "Awe, don't be mad at my boy." I nudged her shoulder with my finger and couldn't help but suppress a giggle. "You know... they say when a cat shows you their butt, they really like you."

Aurora huffed. Then her expression turned serious, and the topic changed completely. "Are you sure you're going to be okay?"

I nodded. "I'm sorry again."

"Stop it! I am fine. It's you that I'm concerned

about." Aurora yawned again. "Do you think you will be able to get some more sleep?"

I nodded for her sake. She needed to stop worrying and go back to bed. I kept her up too long, but honestly, I didn't think I could go back to sleep even if I wanted to. So many unusual things have happened in under twenty-four hours that my mind was in a whirl. I glanced at Felix and back at the bed, uncomfortable and not sure how to explain it.

Aurora hesitated. Felix meowed at us both and staked his claim on my pillow.

"Do you want me to sleep in here with you until morning?"

"No. You really need your rest. You have an early morning class, and I'm fine." I picked up the cat again. "I have Felix to protect me." I turned to him and rubbed my head against him. "Huh, boy."

He yowled at me and pushed me off the pillow.

"All right then." Aurora walked to the door. "Oh, don't forget to blow out the candles before you fall asleep."

"Will do, and thanks again for coming to my rescue."

"Always." She smiled, closing the door as she walked out of my room.

Chapter Eight

I couldn't sleep. I sat on my bed holding the carnelian and labradorite stone. I wasn't quite ready to figure out the others, but being I already made these two work, I played around with them the rest of the night. I tried to focus my thoughts on what seemed to come naturally to me. Over the last few hours, I have finally made the flame capable of rising and falling a good two to three inches and making a breeze either blow the candle out or make it flicker in a couple of neat patterns. Even after a few hours of playing around with the stones, I still struggled to believe that magic was real, and I was indeed a wielder of the elements. Each time I thought about it, I felt a little giddy. This is the first good thing that has happened to me in five years. Seriously, who wouldn't want to have magic at their disposal? I was a wielder of the elements. My mind said that to me in all caps and I surprised myself by giggling.

As dawm approached and the early morning light filtered into my bedroom, I imagined meeting Cyprien in real life. I didn't think I was ready to open my heart again, but deep inside, I couldn't help the sudden rush of happiness that filled me at the thought of seeing him, kissing him, feeling his hands in my hair and on my back bringing me closer, the taste of cinnamon that always lingered on his tongue, the smell of pine and spice and earth. My heart raced in anticipation as I flicked the flame on again. This time it glowed brighter and was a lot bigger. I wonder if it was affected by my emotions. I used the air stone to blow it out, and the wind was incredibly cold, making me shiver.

"Well, that was interesting." Note to self, emotions make the magic stronger.

I decided to try it out again after thinking about Séverin. The flames in every candle lit, and they all were so huge that I was scared they would catch my room on fire. I hurriedly picked up the air stone, and it was wild. The wind blew hard and cold and extinguished all the flames.

I steadied my racing pulse with a few deep breaths and decided to think of the love I felt in my dream for Cyprien. This time when I opened my eyes, the candles were all a soft glow flickering peacefully. What shocked me most was that I didn't even have the stone in my hand. It was still lying on the bed next to me. I tried to blow them out without the air stone, but it didn't work. I had to pick it up to blow them out.

"Well, that is interesting." I wondered if I practiced more what else I might be able to do without the stones in hand.

The alarm rang. I hurriedly turned it off and rolled

out of bed. I kept the ring on but put the stones in the pouch on my bedside table. Now that I didn't need the stones to make fire, I felt braver, more confident, but I wasn't ready to risk removing the ring. I'd been empty for five years and it gave me energy.

Aurora was sound asleep with her eye mask on and soft snores were coming from her lips. She was all curled up in a ball with all her collectible squishy dolls surrounding her. Her room was as opposite to her choice of clothing as mine was. Her entire room was Hello Kitty pink. She had a white four-poster cast iron bed with a hot pink canopy. She had a white desk with a pink furry desk chair, and her six bookshelves were covered in either her schoolbooks or the cute figurines she'd been collecting since she was a little kid.

I couldn't wait to see what Theo would say the first time he walked into this girly explosion.

I pulled her mask off her eyes, and she rolled over, putting her head under her pillow. The muffled sound of her voice was barely heard. "What the hell, Phin?"

I spanked her leg through the covers. "You have school."

"I can skip."

I started rocking her body back and forth. "Wake up"

Aurora growled at me and threw the pillow off the bed. She was a sight this morning. Her black, typically straight hair was standing every which way, and with no makeup on, you could see that she shaved half her eyebrows off again to draw them in the way she liked them.

I stared at them; I bit down on my lips to prevent myself from making fun of them.

"Ugh, stop staring," she said as she walked to the bathroom.

"I'm sorry." I looked in the direction of her bed. She must have slept horribly, her sheets were all over the place. I sat on the edge of the bed.

She returned quickly and sat at her desk, which was also her vanity, opened her three-way makeup mirror, and used a facial wipe to clean her skin. I watched her draw on her eyebrows. "What time is it anyway?"

"Six-forty-five or so. I left my phone in my room."

She got up and went to the bathroom again, and this time came back with a toothbrush in her mouth. With her mouth full of toothpaste, she started to shoo me out of her room. I think she was telling me to go get ready.

I did my morning routine and put on a new pair of leggings, my Converse, layered a t-shirt, and threw a flannel on top. Within minutes I was back in her room with my phone in my hand. "It's seven ten. You want breakfast, you better hurry."

She was still applying her eye makeup and not even dressed yet.

"I am not going to school looking half put together. Can you go down and buy us something? It will save some time."

"Sure." I hurried out of her room. Perfect, the sooner I left and fulfilled my promise to her of breakfast, the faster I could be back to practice my elements.

I left the apartment and was walking in the alley to get to the Magic Brew. Goosebumps rose on the back of my neck. It felt like I was being watched, and I turned around to see if maybe Bev was on her way in, but there was no one behind me.

Fear slammed into me. I crossed my arms around my waist, trying to keep my heart from pounding out of my chest and my stomach from rolling. All the bravery I'd felt in the middle of the night vanished in the light of day. I started to breathe heavier and frantically searched every face near me. The streets were crowded today. I looked in every direction, trying my best to see if I could see Séverin hiding behind the crowd. I squinted, trying hard to see through the shadows of the alley across the street where I thought I saw him yesterday but didn't see anything.

Before entering Magic Brew, I pressed my shaking hands to the window and stuck my face in between, trying to see if he might be lurking inside waiting for me. My breath fogged the window with a sigh of relief. It was practically empty, and he wasn't one of the customers. Bev was making coffee. I opened the door and rushed in.

"Morning," Bev greeted me without looking up from making someone's coffee.

I waited at the register for her to finish and come check me out. It didn't take her long.

"Two days in a row. Your Aunt Marie will be happy to hear you are getting out more."

I gave her a wavering smile. "Yeah, I'm trying."

Bev gave me a genuine smile. "That is so good, hunny! I'm so proud of you for finally moving on."

I never said I was moving on, but she could believe what she wanted. "I need to get me and Aurora breakfast."

"Do you want your usual?"

I thought about it and decided no, I really didn't want the same thing. "I think I will get something different today."

Bev's entire face lit up, and she stood up straighter. "Well, then, this is a cause for celebration. Your coffee is on me today, pick anything you want."

I swallowed hard. That was so sweet. "Bev, you don't have to do that."

"Shug, you've gotten the same thing for five years. It's my pleasure to expand ya taste buds. What can I make ya?"

"Um, I used to like Mocha Mambo a long time ago. Maybe I can try that?"

"Can I suggest something to ya?"

"Sure. I guess."

"I want ya to try the Mississippi Mud frap. I think you'll enjoy it."

I smiled at Bev's enthusiasm. "As long as it doesn't contain real mud, I'll try it."

She chuckled.

"Also, I need to get Aurora the Hair of the Dog espresso and two breakfast croissants."

"She got drunk last night?"

"No, we were just awake late talking, and I want to make sure she is fully functional for class. I feel bad for keeping her up."

Bev snorted, "Well that'll sure wake her up." She handed me back my debit card. "It'll be ready in a few."

The back of my neck prickled again. I walked to the front of the cafe and looked out the window. This time I did see someone. I saw two men, and I nearly passed out. I caught myself on the table and sat in the chair. Séverin had his arm wrapped around Cyprien's shoulder. They didn't even look inside the cafe and kept walking. I got up and ran outside; by the time I reached the sidewalk they were gone. My hand flew to my heart trying to slow the rhythm, and I squatted with my head on my knees, trying not to hyperventilate and fall onto the filthy sidewalk. I couldn't stop shaking.

Cyprien was real! My heart raced at the desire to chase him down and confirm what my dream was telling me, but at the same time the chilling sense of dread that followed Séverin around reminded me that wasn't a good idea.

"Hey, what are you doing?" Aurora said.

I shrieked and fell on my butt, knocking my head into her knees. Aurora jumped back from my reaction, and muttered a swear word. The street was suddenly silent, not even a local or tourist in sight. She held her hand out to me. "What the hell, Phin, you scared the shit out of me."

"Me?" I yelled, pointing to myself and gave her 'you scared the shit out of me look' right back at her.

"Sorry." She held out her hand to help me up. "Why are you out here squatting in the middle of the sidewalk?"

I couldn't seem to focus, trying to decide if what I saw was real or if I was becoming delusional. I felt sick and could feel myself turning in on itself and trying to pretend everything was ok and I wasn't going insane.

"Seriously though, you are so pale, I'd think you saw a ghost."

I shivered, and my teeth started chattering; the anxiety was getting to me again. I wanted to hide; I hurriedly scanned the area again, but it was to no avail. They, if they even existed, were gone; Aurora placed her hand on my shaking arm, and I turned to look at her concerned eyes boring into mine. Should I lie? But what good would that do me after telling her all about my dreams? I breathed out a shaky breath. "Almost. I think I just saw Séverin get in his car."

She hurriedly shoved me through the door of the cafe. "Why in god's name were you outside? Were you searching for him? I swear, Phin, you promised."

"I know... it just happened." She glared at me. My stomach knotted up and a vision of Aurora betraying me from my dream flashed. My trust in her waivered. Is this the same Aurora? I didn't want to tell her about Cy. I had to let her believe it was only my stupid obsession over Séverin. I shrugged. "I know it's just... I wasn't thinking."

I was worried that if I did, she would skip school. "I promise. I won't go searching for him. I will not act rashly in the future." I held up what I thought was the scouts sign. "Scouts honor."

We walked up to get the drinks and food. Aurora was wearing a color today. She had a black dress, stockings, and her docs on, but instead of a dark jacket, she chose her satin red bomber jacket. She also had bright red lips to match. "You look amazing."

"Thanks, Theo told me he thought I'd look stunning in red, so I figured I'd show him that I do."

I laughed. "It really is remarkable; it makes your skin look so creamy and vibrant at the same time. But most of all, it makes your golden eyes really pop."

Her grin kept getting wider and wider. "Then my plan will work. I am going to let my hair grow back to its natural red next but before that I will make him fall in love with me as I am. Or at least I can hook him with my looks first, then reel him in with my personality."

I made a fake gagging noise, and we both laughed.

We parted ways. Aurora was on her way to class, and I went back up to the apartment to feed Felix and to text Goldie and see what time she would be at work.

The weekend flew by. It was already Wednesday, and my tension was rising. The one friend I had besides Aurora was MIA. I texted Goldie the last few days more than I had in five years, and that same dread that attached itself to Séverin started to attach itself to Goldie. Where was she and why was she ignoring me?

I even went out of my comfort zone and went by myself to her new store Underground Sorcery and Co, and her one employee told me he hadn't seen her but she left a note with the key to open and close for a while. I bit my nail off on my walk home. Why did she disappear on me? I needed her. Even Aurora started to worry and messaged the ladies in the Daughters of Fate club but none of them had seen Goldie either. It was as if she vanished off the face of the earth.

I finally decided to ask Bev this morning if she'd seen her lately, and as she did with everything, she contacted Marie to instantly update her on all my woes. But Marie did have a small snippet of information. She said it was possible Goldie went to visit her family.

Goldie rarely talked about her sisters and honestly, I forgot she even had sisters. My memories on the topic were vague, but if I recalled her family was dysfunctional. Her older sister was a tyrant, but she had to check in periodically and her sister had no tech allowed in her home. Maybe that was what happened. It would make sense she was out of touch if that was the case.

But we only had two more days until the ball, and despite the fact that I didn't know more about this new magic, I was so confused about all the dreams and real life that I didn't want Goldie to miss the ball. Or have to go it alone.

I jumped off the sofa, Felix got startled and ran to the other room. "Sorry, bud!" I shouted. Poor little guy has been spooked lately and hiding under my bed more than he's been out. Theo had been coming over often to visit Aurora and his scent was everywhere. Felix didn't seem to like that too much and kept staying in my room.

I opened Aurora's door, and it flew open hitting the wall with a loud bang. She jumped off her desk chair when I threw the door open. Her pencil flew out of her hand and landed at my foot. "Sorry, but I just remembered I don't have a dress for the ball and it's in two days!"

Aurora gestured at the pencil, and I tossed it over. "Holy hell, I don't either. How did that slip my mind?"

I started making kissy noises. "I know how. You've been a bit preoccupied with Mr. Hottie."

She got a faraway look in her eyes. "Too true."

We laughed. It felt so good laughing with Aurora again. Over the last week I'd been so preoccupied with Séverin, shopping with my best friend lifted my spirits.

Aurora stood up, grabbed her purse, and looped her arm around mine. "Let's go thrifting. We have to find our dresses."

Without a thought, I hugged Aurora. She was stiff in my arms for a second, then she hugged me back. She didn't comment on my impulse, but I did see her eyes gloss up a bit. I was grateful that she just smiled and linked her arm into mine, leading us out of the apartment. For the first time in years, I wasn't going to think about anything stressful. I was going to enjoy the moment shopping for a dress with my best friend.

By the time we got to the third thrift shop, I'd had zero success. Aurora, on the other hand, found so many dresses that looked amazing on her. She was tall and lean, and she just tried on a red satin slip dress that hung on her body as if it were designed for her. It even had long sleeves which Aurora expressed she wanted because she didn't want to bring a jacket to the ball. The scarlet red matched the chunky streaks that she added into her hair over the weekend.

She turned around looking in the tall mirror outside the fitting room doors.

"You have to get it. Theo's tongue won't be able to roll back into his mouth after seeing you in that dress. I'm even having trouble keeping the drool in." I made a fake slurping noise and Aurora laughed.

"I typically don't like wearing color, but Theo loves me in red. Plus, I wanted to stand out from the crowd and not look like the typical vampire attendees."

"Well, you will. That dress looks like it was made for you. I also like the way the back is low and shows off your alchemy tattoo."

She turned to the lady hanging some clothes on the rack nearby. "Excuse me, this dress doesn't have a tag. Do you know how much it is?"

"Oh yeah, that one came in just this morning. I have more to put out but didn't get a chance. Let me check the price. I'll be right back."

"Wait," Aurora called out to the clerk.

"We don't mind waiting to see the other dresses. My friend is looking, too."

I could tell the girl was a bit annoyed at having to stop what she was currently doing, but she went to the back of the store and came back struggling with a huge box. I ran to help her carry it. Some of the gowns were hanging over the side and the box was crazily heavy.

"Thanks," she said when I relieved her of some of the weight.

We set the box down on the closest table. "Y'all are welcome to dig through the box. I currently don't have time to hang them all up right now, but my boss told me before she left that none of the dresses have ever been worn, and some of them had original tags priced in the thousands. So, today is your lucky day if you get one of those because everything in this box she is selling for thirty bucks a piece."

Aurora and I looked at each other with glee. "What a deal!" we both said simultaneously and laughed.

We started pulling the dresses out one by one, shaking the wrinkles out and holding them up. Aurora found another dress in black, and she went to try it on. So far nothing was catching my eye until the very last dress. It was a beautiful, corseted ball gown in royal blue velvet.

I walked into the dressing room next to Aurora's. "I found something I want to try on."

"Awesome, I don't think I like this one as much as the red one. Is it okay if I don't show it to you?"

"Yeah, that's fine. I thought you looked stunning in the red one anyway. You should get it."

"I think I will."

I walked out of the dressing room and stood in front of the mirror. I fell instantly in love with the gown, and it fit as if it were made exactly for my body. Aurora stepped out of her changing room, and I stood before her with a huge grin plastered on my face. "Oh my god!" I loved that her immediate response was her hand flying to cover her open-mouth shock.

My heart filled with joy; I spun around catching a glimpse of myself in the mirror envisioning my hair pulled up and Aurora in a similar gown helping me. This was the most beautiful I ever felt in my life. Aurora came up super close to me. Her eyes didn't look happy, they looked spooked and maybe a bit wild. I scooted back away from her, but she grabbed a handful of the full skirt and moved closer to me cornering me in the three-way mirror. In a hushed pained voice said, "This is the dress you were wearing in your drawing."

My head snapped up and my eyes caught her panicked ones. My heart dropped into my stomach. "What?"

She turned me around and I saw what she noticed. How had I not recognized it at first? Or should I say I did. I loved it just as much this time as I loved it in my dream. Only now I staggered back into Aurora. She caught me by the elbows and helped me into the changing room. She came in with me and closed the fitting room door. "This is so insane. I swear this is the real life version of the dress from the picture you drew of the dance when you are greeting Séverin and Cy. Remember, the drawing was in such perfect detail it could have been a photograph." She pulled up the skirt. "It even had the same embroidered vines down the skirt."

I couldn't breathe. "Remember it was the picture where you just found out they were brothers for the first time. Remember?"

I swiped her hand away and started fumbling with the buttons on the back. My hands shaking and my nausea rising, my legs gave way from under me.

"Phin!" Aurora caught me but I kept sliding to the floor and I fell into a heap. I swallowed the lump in my throat. My voice came out hoarse. "Of course, I remember."

A shaky breath escaped, and tears started to fall. As

my hands still shook, I reach for the button. Aurora didn't say anything but started helping me undress.

The insanity of the moment was too much, first I see Cyprien and Séverin and now this dress. What more will I bring into the present from my dream?

Instead of being excited to practice my magic when I got home, I was going to put the seven dwarves back in the bag and in the box in my closet. I never wanted to touch them again. In the dream, Cyprien called it dark magic. If what happened in the dream was real, he'd never want to be with me again. He would think I was a dark witch or something just as horrible.

Was I doomed to fall in love with him all over again? What was wrong with me? Why was I born to have broken love? What if whatever I was doing was starting the process all over again? Aurora might be on the road to wanting to betray me again because I kept chasing Séverin. NO! I wouldn't let that happen. I won't let anyone, or anything, do harm to the few people I have left in my life. I would not lose Aurora over a man. My life had been ruined by Séverin. I would not let another man ruin my life.

My hands fell into my lap shaking and couldn't stop. Aurora was done with the buttons, and I wanted nothing more than to be out of the dress and back in my own clothes. I looked up to her and saw the reflection of my fear in her eyes. My voice shaky and small, all I got out was "Help."

The dreams vs reality would stop now. I'd make them stop.

Aurora helped me up, and as I stood in my underwear all my energy drained. This time instead of falling to the floor I sat on the small stool, tears falling onto my chest. The dreams and feelings of fear of betrayal and dying overwhelmed me. In this moment both were real. I was so confused and scared, and at the same time, my heart had a rush of emotions that imprinted my love for Cy into my veins. I wanted to run to him even though I didn't know him yet. Had I finally snapped? I didn't want to tell Aurora any of this because I was not only afraid she'd worry about my sanity, but I'd see the truth in her eyes.

Aurora hugged my shoulder. "We'll figure this out. I promise. We will find Goldie and figure out what all of this means."

Tears still wet on my cheeks I asked, "What kind of answers would she have? I mean she isn't much older than us. Just because she knew what the stones were and belongs to your club there is no way she can know why my dreams are coming true."

Aurora nodded. "I know, but at least she is someone who knows something. Plus, she opened that occult store now so she may have supernatural contacts who have leads."

A laugh cry choked out of me, the way Aurora said supernatural so easy and believably broke me out of my spell. I sniffled and picked up my flannel. "I'm cold. I need to get dressed."

Aurora shivered. "It did get a lot colder in here."

My pulse took off like a bullet burning in my chest. I

took shallow ragged breaths trying to calm myself down. "This can't be real." I picked up the dress like it was poisonous and handed it to Aurora. She took it into her arms as I said, "I want to buy this dress and burn it. I don't want anyone else to have it. I don't want it to exist in this world."

Aurora bit her cheek piercing. I couldn't tell if she was contemplating if I was going insane or if she was assessing if I was serious. "Ok," she nodded, "we will buy the dress on my mom's credit card and burn it when we get home."

I exhaled with a sigh. Aurora opened the fitting room door, and with a new sense of purpose I threw my shoulders back and stepped out. Aurora quickly went into her fitting room to gather the gowns she'd tried on, then together we walked to the register.

"Phin, wait."

Aurora stopped a few feet from the check out and turned around. "You still need a dress."

She was going to buy the red dress but still had the black one in her arms. It was a simple long sleeve gown with black pearl buttons from the waist to the high neck. "I'll just wear the black one you didn't like."

"It will be too long on you though."

My shoulders slumped and I rolled my neck. I was tired and ready to go home. "I don't care. It's thirty bucks. I'll just cut it."

"Don't you want to at least try it on?"

How could she ask this after everything that happened? "No, I'm ready to go home." My voice cracked on the last word.

She nodded, "I will take care of all three dresses. Why don't you go get a breath of fresh air and I'll meet you outside."

I went outside and leaned against the wall of the shop. I pulled out my phone and called Goldie. The phone didn't even ring, it just went straight to voicemail. "It's getting colder," Aurora said as she walked out of the shop. She shook the bag and tried adding a playful lilt to her voice. "It will be fun to have a little bonfire in the courtyard."

"Yeah fun," I said with very little enthusiasm as I stepped away from the wall. We started to head home, and I couldn't seem to think of anything to say.

Aurora's phone rang.

"Is it Goldie?"

She shook her head and gave me a sympathetic look. "No, it's Theo."

Aurora was answering Theo with soft quick spoken yeses and nos. She glanced at me and said no again then looked up at the small bookstore that was run by a man who was ancient and hard of hearing. Aurora motioned that she was going in. I mouthed "I'll wait here." She nodded and walked into the book shop. I took the sign and walked several paces away from the shop.

They were either talking about me or something private. I'm sure she told him she was worried about me, but I wonder if she told him about my magic. I hoped not. I'd have to ask her later. I shivered as I clinched my phone in my hands, paying more attention to the phone than where I was going. I tripped over a loose brick on the sidewalk, my phone flew but I caught it in relief then face planted into the lamp post. "Ouch!" With eyes squinted shut, I rubbed out the pain.

When I looked up, I froze, and my fingers gripped the post trying to keep myself steady. I wasn't in the French Quarter anymore. I was on a dirt road, at a cross-roads and I was all alone.

Chapter Nine

My heart started racing and my chest ached. I crumpled to the ground, shaking, elbows resting on my knees. My fingers dug into my scalp trying to make sense of what just happened. First, I had to slow my breathing before I really did pass out. As I was pulling my hands away from my scalp, the hematite ring tangled in my hair, pulling a few strands out with it. I can't believe I forgot to put it away. Had I just somehow magically teleported myself somewhere?

Where was I? Was I dreaming again? A warm breeze caressed my skin. My flannel shirt started to feel too hot. In my dreams, even though they felt real, I don't remember noticing the weather so much. Was elemental magic that powerful that only the ring could teleport me somewhere?

The sound of someone in distress was coming from the left crossroad, I didn't want to be seen. I tried to make myself get up. My legs were like jelly, but I did it anyway. I hurried as fast as I could and tried to make myself as small as I could behind some hedges that were placed like a half wall surrounding a beautiful grove full of a large trees with giant fuchsia balls hanging from it. I'd never seen anything like it before in my life. They reminded me of something from a Dr. Seuss book I read as a child.

The climate was a bit warmer here than when I left New Orleans. I wanted to take my flannel off but was afraid that whoever was coming would hear me moving. Crouched down, my backside exposed to the grove but hidden from the road, I found a small gap in the hedge and peeked at the road. A small man was running and muttering. The little old man stopped running right in front of where I was hiding. Clutching a ton of red silk threads tangled around his gnarly knuckles, he shook his fist to the sky.

"How many more humans will I have to entangle my hands in before I'm allowed to live in peace?"

What the heck? The man hurriedly put his fist down as another voice from afar seemed to be calling him.

The other man arrived. "Ahoy there, Sir Alfrock. How are you this fine morn?"

He too was a tiny man. He was smaller and thinner than the one called Alfrock. This man was eccentric. He had on a pale blue suit, a hot pink vest, a psychedelic shirt with both colors and a tall top hat with peacock feathers. It surprised me that the fancy pants man addressed the frumpy dressed man with the title of Sir. Then I thought about it for a moment and thought it was kind of nice that they didn't seem to judge. Then again, I only have seen two men. Who was I to judge anyone? I had my own issues. If they met me, they would probably think I was some kind of freak. Obviously, something is up with humans here being Alfrock seems so distressed about them, and the other guy is asking. Maybe wherever I was frumpy was considered fancy.

I shook my head. What the heck am I thinking? Why was I getting all involved in these people as if I were watching reality TV. Two minutes ago, I was leaving a dress shop in New Orleans.

Alfrock was fidgeting as the fancy pants arrived. His wrinkled worn green cloak fell off his shoulder and hung at an odd angle. It looked like his breakfast stained his cream-colored pirate shirt which was half tucked in old fashioned button front britches with suspenders. The pants even had patched knees. The man backed up near my hiding place and hurriedly hid the hand behind his back. His gnarly old fingers were tangled with the red silk as if they were a sticky web. Finally, his hand found the pocket he was searching for in his cloak.

Then he said the most unusual greeting I'd ever heard. "Tickety-boo and you!"

The other little man answered just as oddly. "Frob-bly-mobly." He pulled an old watch fob from his vest pocket. "I'm in a bit of a hurry this morn."

Alfrock shifted. "Is that so?"

The top hat man seemed agitated. "The alarms went off again, interrupting my breakfast. You know how the Inflexible one is about time."

Alfrock nodded and started bouncing on the balls of his feet. "So, what particular alarm went off this time?" With his free hand he pulled out a handkerchief and wiped his forehead that was beading with sweat. "Are the wolves at it again?"

The other man sighed. "Thank goodness, no. They've been rather well behaved lately. I'm afraid this time a human has come into Nod. The Inflexible one hasn't been very happy with humans lately, especially the females. She has a new rule that I have less than an hour to find them and deliver them to her."

Were they talking about me? My poor heart had just calmed down, now it was strumming faster and harder than ever. My stomach quivered then flipped when I shifted, and the bushes made a sound.

The little man in the blue top hat turned in my direction trying to see through the hedge. I held my hand over my nose and mouth to make myself as quiet as possible. Thankfully, a small fluffy white bird hopped off a branch not far from me and flew away. Then tension in my shoulders released a small fraction because of luck.

Alfrock, the man hiding the silken thread, started rocking on the balls of his feet now and his hand in his pocket behind his back started shaking.

I wondered if the threads were hurting his fingers. From my view in the bushes, his fingers looked to be turning a strange colored purple. Maybe if the other guy leaves, I could help him remove them. I'm sure it would be hard to do it by himself. Then I thought better of it.

"'Tis a pity you've no time to chat. Gotta run

before–" He used his free hand and pointed his shaking finger to make a slice motion at his neck.

The top hat man huffed and started walking towards the way Alfrock had just come. And Alfrock ran off in the opposite direction from where the other man was going. I guess it's best. I didn't need to be stupid and help him when he could have turned me into the person called Inflexible. I don't think I want to meet anyone with that name.

I moved to the tree and sat on the ground resting my back on the tree. I needed to figure out how to get home. Aurora was probably worried like mad, especially if I vanished right in front of her eyes.

I pulled my phone out of my pocket, and it didn't work. There was zero reception wherever I sent myself. I wrapped my right hand around my left ring finger with the hematite ring. I closed my eyes and envisioned being back home in my room. I had a feeling when I smelled the fragrant blooms of the tree and felt the humidity of the air that I wasn't home but when I opened my eyes I was still hoping.

I thumped the back of my head on the tree. "Ouch." I rubbed the back of my head.

I heard a feminine laugh nearby and I jumped when I turned around and saw a tall lady who looked eerily similar to Goldie. They had the same tall willowy shape, the same long wavy hair, the only major difference was her hair was more copper.

"Delphine, I am so glad to finally meet you, but I wish it were under different circumstances."

The woman came towards me smiling in what

seemed an overly friendly manner then placed her hand on my shoulder. I jerked my shoulder and took a few steps back. "Don't touch me."

The corners of her smile dropped as she dropped her hand. "Please don't be afraid."

My instinct was to run away but my feet wouldn't move. It was like the dreams you have when your feet turn to lead. That's right I had to be dreaming. There are no such things as elves, "How do you know my name? Where are we?"

"My name is Vida."

I stared at her. Something seemed so familiar about her name. It wasn't a common name. Had I read it in a book? I knew I had heard it before, but I couldn't place where.

"You are in Elvindale." She must have read the lost look on my face and decided to clarify. "It is located on the main island of Nod below the Black Hills where my home is."

"Nod?" Nod sounded familiar. Mom used to read me books about the land of Nod when I was a kid, then I remembered Nod was where I lived in my dream. All of it was real. Panic started to rise, my stomach churned, my dreams were real, and that scared the bejesus out of me at the same time as feeling elated at the possibility of being with Cyprien again.

"The Realm of Dreams," said Vida.

Panic turned into hysteria; I was going mad. This was a dream, it wasn't real.

The wind whistled through the largest fuchsia plumed tree in the grove. I watched fascinated that the wind only blew on that tree. Vida's head snapped towards the tree. As she watched, she moved her hands and blew out a breath. It looked almost as if she were talking to it. Then she held out her hand to me. "Come, we must hurry. We shouldn't be here."

I didn't take her hand right away. Why would I trust this stranger even if she looked like Goldie. The wind blew past my ear and one petal landed on my cheek. When I pulled it off, I could have sworn I heard it whisper "run."

I shoved the petal in the pocket of my jeans, and I only had a second to pull my hand out when Vida grabbed hold of my wrist and started pulling me along through the grove. I grudgingly trudged behind her. I was tripping over my own feet. Her hand yanked my wrist and my shoulder jerked. "Ouch! Slow down."

The pain felt so real. "This is crazy. I must have fallen out of my bed or something because my shoulder is seriously hurting from you yanking my arm."

"My apologies, I forget humans are more fragile." She relinquished her tight grip but continued to urge me forward. "Come, come we really must hurry."

The wind was coming up from behind us rather strongly. "Is it about to storm? Are we trying to get away from a windstorm?"

She didn't answer and I ran faster to try to keep pace. Panting right beside her now I shouted. "Why are we running?"

"They cannot find me."

"Who?"

"The wolves."

Then that is when I heard them. It was one lone howl coming from the wind behind us. I eventually heard a few echoes of others from farther away.

"Why?" I started huffing harder as I tried to keep running beside her. I was so out of shape.

As we made it to the other side of the grove, the wind stopped, and the trees swayed their branches making the huge fuchsia balled plumes tinkled like bells. Vida whispered "Thank you, my friends. Give us a few minutes start."

I searched the grove to see who she was talking to and noticed the trees stilled.

I was so grateful we stopped, and I flopped to the ground trying to catch my breath. "What are you doing? This is not the time or place to rest. The Doskurya spirits will only be able to protect our scent for a few more minutes."

"I'm sorry I'm not used to running." I stood up and bent over, my hand gripping my waist placing pressure on a cramp that started seizing up the moment I sat down.

She turned back to the trees. "Please help us a little longer, friends."

One of the snowball shaped flowers blew some more petals in our direction. A few landed on me and several landed on Vida. "Thank you, my friends."

For all I knew she was crazy, but this was my dream. "Where are you taking me?"

"Home," she said.

Where was home? Hers or mine? Should I follow her? I decided that I needed to go with her.

She watched me as I took some slow deep breaths then asked. "I gave you my dwarves, why are you not using them?"

My hand was hidden, how had she noticed my ring? She made me nervous suddenly and instead of wanting to run from her or not talk to her, I did something completely out of character. I mimicked her actions. As I stood with my hand on my hip, looking her over as she did the same to me, something shifted inside of me. A warm breeze that felt like a hug drew me closer to her. She smiled when I took a few steps nearer. I teetered mid-step, stopping myself from being drawn in by her magic. Whatever she was siphoning out of me made me feel safe, and that surprised me. Very few people made me feel that way. Aurora came to mind instantly and Goldie followed a few thoughts later.

Vida really could be Goldie's twin. They were that similar. Again, I reminded myself that this was probably a dream, and my mind was playing tricks. I'd let the dream take me where it wanted. I'd follow Vida, maybe I will get answers if I do.

She turned around when the branches of the trees behind her started waving madly around as if the winds had picked up. But where I stood, there was no breeze nor wind. It was almost too quiet, and like in any suspense movie I'd ever watched, it foreshadowed something bad was about to happen. I followed her gaze and searched the area. When had we moved locations? We were deeper in the grove where the trees were dense, and a fog lifted around the edges of the grove, the trees almost obscured from my vision.

Vida turned to me, and her expression was one of surprise and what almost looked like joy? Her voice came out slow and steady, sending a calming wave instantly slowing my rapid heart into a normal rhythm. I closed my eyes and blew out a deep breath, I hadn't even realized how tense I'd been. When I opened my eyes, we were back in the small grove, no fog around us. How did Vida do that?

Before I could verbalize my thought, she spoke. "I think I may have harnessed too much of my power when placing it into the stones. I wonder if Goldie formulated it wrong..."

She knew Goldie? I was about to ask but she interrupted my thought with something that seemed to concern me more.

"Your powers are much stronger than anticipated."

What? She can't think I did that? A branch snapped and a low growl came from somewhere behind us. Vida heard it too and her words became hurried. "We must get to safety."

At the same time she said the words, we heard the howl of a lone wolf and the answering of many in the distance. This time she grabbed my hand. I ran with her.

The howl seemed to be getting closer. We headed into the foothills nearing the mountains. It was challenging running uphill in the dense woods, but soon my adrenalin kicked in. It was like a high I'd never felt before, my vision more focused as it guided me through the densely forested hills. I jumped over fallen branches with grace and a speed I didn't know I had.

Vida slowed her pace and released my hand. "We

need to climb from here but it should be easy. There is a path. Follow me, don't worry about falling. I have the wind at your back to keep you safe."

I wasn't even out of breath, I felt alive! We climbed. The trail started off as a ledge that we hugged moving sideways one side step at a time. I'd never been climbing before but thankfully the path was smooth even though it was narrow and the area for my hands to grip were secure. I thought I heard waves. So far, I tried not to look down but this time I did. We were moving fast. I couldn't believe we were already on the side of the mountain. Below me was a shear edge and if I made one misstep, I would fall into the huge, jagged spires of rocks jutting out from the shore of the ocean.

For the first time in my life, I was grateful I wasn't clumsy and had decent balance. But exhaustion caught up with me and after a few more steps I started breathing heavily. Whatever boost of adrenalin I felt early was gone. My body was close to giving out.

"How much further?" I puffed out.

"Not much. Just beyond that nook."

Thankfully she was right. The nook in the mountain was actually the small entrance to a cave. The only way to get in was by lifting myself up with my arms. It reminded me of having to get out of a pool without steps. My arms were shaky by this point.

Vida reached out her hand to me. "Give me your hand."

With one foot on a small toe hold on the mountain, I shifted my weight giving her my right hand. She pulled me up effortlessly as if I weighed nothing. Once inside, the sounds of the wolves seemed farther away. I sat against the wall, my entire body weak and shaking from using muscles that I doubt I have ever used before. I was so tired I could sleep.

Vida breathed out a sigh as she looked at me. "We can only rest here for a moment. You did well."

She pulled a leaf out of thin air. "Are you thirsty?"

I nodded, and she handed me the leaf cup full of liquid. It was sturdier than a paper cup, and the water was the best tasting water I'd ever had--so pure and clean. But most of all, it somehow replenished my energy. Pain and exhaustion ebbed away.

"What is this stuff?" I asked holding the cup out for her to refill.

It magically filled with the water again. "Ambrosia."

Before I could comment, she started talking and squatted in front of me, worry lines creased her brow. "Now that I have been with you for a while and was pulling energy from you to help you move along faster, I can see something went wrong in the past. Your soul shifted and is new, but I now can see your threads of life. They are all knotted up and one has gone black. This isn't good."

It was just like the dream. Séverin's thread went black. How did she know? Then the words soul shifted blared out. "I didn't shift my soul. I'm still me."

I scooted back away from her into the wall. Vida's expression went from concern to pity at reading what she must have seen as horror in my expression. She hurriedly tried to rectify her words. "You misunderstand. You had to give up your soul in the past and give it to the gods to hold until you could be reborn with power. You achieved that goal, however if I'm not mistaken you are still tied to the man you do not desire. Am I right?"

I nodded. She was right. "How do you know this? That is all from my dreams and my life on earth. How would you know this?"

"Because those dreams are not dreams, they are your past. When the time came, they reminded you of your purpose. Dreams are a way to help you learn and process your past. Did Goldie not explain this to you?"

I closed my eyes and tried to remember. The Goldie in my dreams did explain some things, but I didn't remember her talking about dreams. Goldie on earth tried to explain some things too but if she talked about my dreams, for some reason I had only locked in on the elemental magic part.

Vida closed her eyes and inhaled deeply, "Let me check something to be sure I am on the right track."

The energy around us became charged. The wind started swirling around us. She started moving her hands as if she were practicing tai chi. The leaves started dancing around us as she moved. Her Grecian gown flowed around her lithe body. As she did her slow movements, the atmosphere around us filled me with joy.

I hadn't felt this amazing in years, if ever. The earth was singing. I could hear the hum of energy bouncing on the walls of the cave like music. When she stopped moving all sounds ceased. She inhaled again and within seconds everything was back to normal.

She opened her eyes and looked at me; her expression changed to that of concern. Yet I was still smiling and floating on air. She gave me a sad sort of smile. "However wonderful that may have felt. The good news is your soul is pure, and the shift worked but I can sense something went wrong during the transfer. I have yet to place why you are so attuned to me yet not at the same time."

She glanced out of the cave opening. "Are you rested enough? I don't want to linger here much longer. I will feel safer if we are inside."

I nodded.

"So, what is wrong with me?"

We left the cave and started walking. She turned back to me, stopped, and placed her hand on my cheek. "Nothing is wrong with you dear child, but something is off with your destiny, and we need to figure it out."

"Do you think you can figure it out?"

Vida smiled at me kindly and patted my cheek. "I am positive we will. The night I gave Goldie the stones everything happened so fast. We were worried Aza was on to what we were doing and had to work fast to try to save you."

All I seemed capable of doing was either repeat her words or ask dumb questions. "Who is Aza?"

"Goldie, Aza, and I are triplets. We are the Moirae, the goddesses of fate."

"Oh." It took a second for that to process. "Wait! What? You are a goddess?"

She laughed a tinkling laugh. "That I am."

Vida grabbed my hands and held them in hers. The warmth buzzed up my arms. The sensation felt like home. I felt at peace. I wanted her to hold my hands forever.

"Aza can never have the elementals. She cannot ever become a weaver of life. Do you understand?"

She let go and the peace was gone. Tears filled my eyes. I didn't want to be sad anymore especially after feeling so good, but I nodded and responded in a choked voice. "Aza is bad."

She nodded at my child-like answer as if it were the perfect reply. Then hugged me.

"There is no need to be afraid. I promise we will fix this."

The peace was back, and I found myself hugging her tightly. She held me in her arms soothing my back with light pats as I cried. The release felt amazing and draining all at the same time.

I stepped out of the hug and wiped my eyes with my sleeve. I felt my cheeks heat up. "Sorry. I–"

"There is nothing to apologize for. This isn't your fault, it's Aza's."

I didn't know Aza yet but that is the second time Vida mentioned her name. She started pacing in between two of the trees. Every time she passed, they swayed with her. It was truly magical the way she had control over the elements as if they were friends.

She stopped in front of me again. "If anything, Aza is the one who was behind this. Whatever she did, or whoever helped her, somehow was one step ahead of Goldie and me. We made you immortal to be with your love, but I am still trying to figure out what exactly Aza did to strangle you with darkness."

My heart sank into my stomach, I did feel like darkness was always around me. I'd gotten so used to tuning it out and turning my feelings off I didn't even recognize how right she was.

It had been strangling me since I met Séverin.

This time Vida wasn't as perceptive, she didn't notice the shift in my mood and kept on talking. "Hopefully once we are in the safety of my home, I will be able to really assess your magic and figure it out. There is such a strong connection that I am sensing but I need guidance."

I stood there in silence. My mind started shouting for me to talk about this darkness, my immortality, or any number of questions I had, but all that came out was a strange croaking sound of jumbled nonsense. Her right eyebrow went up and gave me a look so very much like Goldie. I cleared my throat and tried again and the only damn word that I could get out was "What?"

Seriously, watching her the only difference between her and Goldie was that Vida's hair was more bronzy gold and her eyes were a bit more greenish blue. But her body language was identical. Even the way she tilted her head and raised her right eyebrow in question I would have thought she was Goldie playing a trick on me. Before I could compose one of my many real questions, I blurted out, "Do you know Goldie Spinner?" then I clarified to make sure we were talking about the same one. "On earth who lives in my time."

Vida laughed at me then graced me with the most beautiful smile. She came to me and hugged me tightly, saying, "You are such a funny girl."

A buzz of her energy passed through me filling me with her happiness. I found myself laughing in joy, my question momentarily forgotten. This woman was a balm to my soul.

"You've met Goldie again! I am so happy! How is she? I haven't seen her since–" She backed out of the hug. "I met my husband the night you sacrificed yourself all those years ago. That was nearly a hundred years ago in this realm."

She spoke about my death so matter of fact that it took me off guard. I whispered, "That's a long time."

"Wait!" I said louder than I meant. "A hundred years– that's impossible. Goldie is only a couple years older than me."

She released a big bell-like laugh.

"Delphine, there is much for you to learn."

The part of the cave where we had come in had torches along the walls, but she guided me to another hidden entrance. "We need to crawl through this tunnel for only a moment, then we will be in a larger area again to walk."

She led the way and as we crawled further into the tunnel we lost all light. I was blind. The only way I knew where I was going was because my hand would touch the sole of Vida's foot in front of me. I heard her feet drop to the ground, so I knew I was coming to the end of the tunnel. When I felt the lip of the exit, I scooted into a sitting position and dangled my feet over. "Is it a far drop?"

"No, just a foot."

I jumped harder than necessary, and my knees buckled for a second. She grabbed my hand. "It's darker in here but the path is smooth."

It wasn't darker. It was the same pitch black. I couldn't see anything. "Um. I must have awful sight because it is dark in here."

She chuckled as if I'd made a joke. But she grabbed my wrist and dragged me along behind her. I had never been in a cave before, and the further we went, the darker it became. I couldn't even see Vida's silhouette anymore. The only way I knew she was still with me was because my arm was extended and taut from hesitating with each of my steps while her hand held on to me. It felt like we had been walking for ages and every now and then I slid on the wet cave floor. Each time, my arm felt like it might be pulled out of the socket from her firm grip. I was glad she was strong and didn't let me go because being in utter darkness was very disorienting.

I shivered and I'm sure she felt it as my arm twitched. "How far into the cave would you say we are?"

"Around a mile or two."

We walked a few more minutes with no conversation.

"Here we are."

I wasn't expecting her to let go of my hand and felt myself fall forward. Thankfully, she was right beside me and I fell into her. She helped me right myself.

"Are you all right?"

"Yeah. Sorry, just very disoriented."

She let me go again and I could hear her picking up something and it scraped along what I assumed was the wall.

A cold hand grabbed my forearm and I screamed.

"It is just me. You are safe."

I took a deep breath. "I'm sorry. I thought you were on my other side."

"Have you not been able to see anything all this time?"

Well duh, we were in a cave with no light. But I didn't want to sound too rude. "Should I have?"

"I am so sorry." Why was she apologizing?

"What for?"

"I figured since you've exhibited such a strong control of the elemental magics that brought you here you'd also have the gift of night sight. I shouldn't have assumed, especially knowing something went wrong in the transfer."

Frustrated, I kicked my toe into the wall. I groaned from the instant pain then grumbled, "I still don't understand what all that means."

"I promise we will talk soon. I prefer speaking openly in the safety of my home. Wolves are good trackers, can be silent as a ghost, and have very good hearing and I'd rather not take my chances."

I wanted to ask more but I could sense she was telling the truth. Her voice broke through my thoughts." You may want to close your eyes. They may be sensitive when I open the door and turn on the lights."

I didn't want to close my eyes, but I had a feeling that any light would be like looking straight at the sun after being in pitch dark. Instead of closing them I placed my hand over my eyes using my fingers as a filter. Within seconds Vida started glowing. A golden light surrounded her as she held her hand up to the wall and started muttering some foreign words.

My hand fell away from my eyes, and I could feel my jaw drop as an ancient looking wooden door appeared.

When she pressed her hand against a large symbol made up of circles, triangles and lines, a door magically appeared inside the stone wall of the cave and swung open. She stepped through into a room that had flickering lights. "Come on this way."

I felt hesitant at first. What if this was a trap? Why was I blindly trusting this woman just because she seemed to know Goldie. Then I remembered her hug and the feeling of comfort I felt in her arms. Why would I feel like that if she were bad? I stood up straight with my shoulders back and stepped in.

The door slammed behind me, and a row of flame torches like the ones in old castles came to life along one wall. The other wall was like a huge built-in open cupboard or storage space like you'd see in a mudroom. As we walked further into the room, there were wooden racks with rods holding a myriad of different style clothing from all centuries.

"Where are we?" I asked.

"This is the secret passage into my mate's home. This is where he stores his possessions from the different centuries he visits. It is also how he saved me although I didn't know it at the time." She ran her fingers through a few pieces of clothing while we walked. I wanted to be nosy and ask her what she meant by first, centuries, and second her being saved, but at the same time, I didn't want to intrude because she seemed almost melancholy walking through this room.

I kept following her through the huge historical

closet-like space and we were about to enter another door but before we did, she stopped next to a door with four huge bolt locks on it. Vida's airy presence entering the cave became more stoic as we stood in front of the door. She made a gesture with her hand and the locks clicked open. She pushed the door wide enough for me to see in.

"This is for prisoners."

Chapter Ten

My heart pounded in my chest. I was so stupid. I should have known this was a trap. She was going to lock me up.

Vida walked in, sat on the small bed, bounced twice, and rubbed her hand on the wool blanket. "This is where I slept when I first came here."

I didn't want to go in the room. I didn't want to be seduced by her kindness and be trapped.

Next to the bed was a nightstand with a small oil lantern on top. Then through all my fear the craziest thought popped into my head that it was strange that the only lighting I've seen so far was old fashioned oil lanterns.

Vida stood up and gave the room another sweeping look and I hurriedly backed away further from the door and back into the big closet room.

She smiled at me then went to the other door. "That was before we knew one another. He believes that we are mates and after all these years is trying to figure out why we haven't been able to bond when he says he knows."

I was trying to make sense of everything she was telling me. So, she wasn't going to lock me in the room?

"What?" I asked, shaking my head trying to clear my confusion and ask a real question. "So, you aren't locking me in?"

She laughed. "Why would you ever think that?"

"Um, because I'm in a make-believe world that I somehow magically teleported to and met a woman who makes me feel..." I stuttered on the word "safe" as if it were a bad word, "and I just don't understand anything you are telling me. Like one day you're his prisoner and then you're not and now you're his mate? What does that even mean? A friend-mate or soulmate? Plus, how can this place even exist and how are you glowing again? Seriously, when you do that it's freaky."

She chuckled. "You are a funny little human. I like how you think." She grabbed my hand leading me into a hallway. "You are not my prisoner. You are my chosen family. I believe now I know why my eternal bond with my husband has been delayed."

She walked through the door of her supposed home and just stood watching me. I was now more confused. She was married?

I slowly followed her into the room. It was full of both antiques and modern-day furniture, and the décor of natural rock and wood wouldn't have been out of place in an architectural magazine. It felt like the homiest of homes. Even the crackling from the fireplace seemed to be saying welcome home. A well of emotions I couldn't even name enveloped me, and I was suddenly spent; my emotions had been more active today than in my entire life, and add it to the week I've had all I wanted to do was curl in a ball, hug my cat and cry. I started shaking and squatted, hugging myself.

"I think I'm having a mental breakdown." I cried.

Vida walked up to me and placed her hand on my shoulder, "Delphine?"

I could hear the concern in her voice and lifted my head, tears already falling. I shouted, frustrated and sad that I couldn't discern reality from dreams anymore, I pointed to the room around us. "This is impossible." The room was warm and cozy like a cabin in the woods. A plush brown leather couch, with a beautiful rug below, sat in front of a large stone wood-burning fireplace,, "This place can't be real? Nothing makes sense, this has to be a dream and if it isn't..."

My words trailed off along with the tear down my cheek. I ducked my head back down, my forehead resting on my knees.

Vida knelt in front of me, pulled my hands into hers, and said. "Look at me."

I didn't want to. If I did, I didn't think I would be able to stop my tears. She placed her hands on my shoulders, "Take a deep breath." She took a deep breath and I followed. She lifted my chin.

The concern that emanated from her eyes made my vision blur with tears. I sniffled trying to call them back inside of me. I tilted my head down but her grip on my chin was firm. "Look at me."

Instead of looking into her eyes I focused my watery

gaze on her perfectly shaped left eyebrow, "This is real. Nod exists in the Dream Realm."

My tears slowed and comfort filled me, relief swept through me remembering I was in the dream world. "Okay, I get it, its real in my dream, I am creative, this makes sense." I spoke out loud trying to make myself believe my own words. They were easier to believe than this being real.

Vida looked at me exasperated. "Delphine, listen to my words well. This is very real and not a dream. You are in another dimension. The Dream Realm is a plane that mortals cannot see unless they are descended from the gods. You are not mortal, but in the ancient years on earth, the gods and their children told stories to the earthlings. Those stories I am sure you are familiar with, they are where all fairytales and legends come from—it is the second realm of earth. There is one more above us and that is the heavens where I am from."

I breathed out a sigh. "This is too weird to be true."

Vida stood and pulled me up with her and dragged me to a bookshelf. She pulled down a huge tome of a book. She opened it up to a beautiful page written in ancient Greek with hand-drawn images. She flipped a few pages and as she did, I noticed a drawing of satyrs, Pegasus, and a griffin.

She got to a page that reminded me of a cover on a childrens' book my mother read to me as a child. "I recognize this." I pointed. She stopped the page.

Vida grinned wide, the golden glow around her brightened and I could swear I felt her elation that I recognized this picture. "This is the Coast of Slumber on the other side of Nod, it is where the Nyads live."

It was finally sinking in that maybe, possibly, this was real. Aurora's mom, Marie, used to make Aurora believe she was from Nod and expand on the stories from our childhood book. Mom used to joke that she wished one day we could go. Did Mom believe?

"My mom and her friend used to read us stories about Nod. But if its real, why are we always taught that it only happens in our sleep, like nod off and dream."

"Well technically, that is one term for it. All words come from something and the way the dream gods work is by using dreams as reminders of past existences. For some, like you, it was once your home before your soul was reborn. Nod is magical, it is the realm where all the children of the gods live now. Only a few mortals have come here and only in the last few hundred years. My sister decided she was bored and started playing with the love lives of earthlings and Nodians intertwining them through different centuries and realms. It is a horrible thing she has done. Goldie and I have been trying to repair the damage. Or I had until I got caught by her wolves. Now I'm trapped."

She closed the book now that I seemed to be listening "Would you like some more Ambrosia? You look a bit piqued."

I nodded and a cup appeared on the table in front of the couch. I sat down beside her, pulled my legs up under me and sipped on my drink. Vida had a glass of wine in her hand, and I think my mouth must have dropped open forgetting for a split second that she was a goddess and could materialize anything she wished. She chuckled and swirled her glass, "Bacchus had the best year." Then winked at me.

I shook my head, blinked my eyes a couple of times as she continued to snicker at me. I scanned the room and although it was homey and cozy there were no windows, no easy way out. Since meeting Vida, and knowing Goldie, both women seemed to need the sun and freedom and before I could stop my tongue from wagging, my curiosity of why she lived here leapt out of my mouth. "How did you get caught?"

"Demetrius caught my scent first and came after me. When he caught me, he ended up fighting to protect me. He took me prisoner until he could figure out why he believed he was mated to me. Because of being caught, it ended up good in the end because he was the man I was looking for to help Goldie. She had found another of our older sister's unfated matches. This time it was more complicated because the match was a bit more compli-cated. Aza must have figured out what we were doing and had her soul shifters hunt us down and kill us."

I gasped. "Your sister tried to kill y'all."

Vida gave me a sad smile. "She did."

I hoped it wasn't contagious. I still didn't know what my dreams were trying to tell me about Aurora. I wanted to believe she loved me, but that smile—maybe my dreams were telling me to be careful.

"That isn't important right now. What is important is that she didn't succeed. I am still alive and since meeting you I now know that Goldie is alive as well."

I bit my thumbnail. "I hope she is all right. I haven't

seen her since last Thursday. She was at my house and told me I was an elemental, and then she met my room-mate's boyfriend. They didn't seem to be on good terms, something about his family taking her sister and once she left, she's been missing since."

Then it dawned on me. Goldie said something about wolves and full moons and Theo, and that man look a lot alike. "Holy hotcakes. You are the sister who was taken!"

I jumped up and pulled out my phone wanting to text Goldie in hopes she'd answer this time. "Dang, I forgot my phone didn't work here." I flopped back down on the sofa.

"What do you mean Goldie is missing?"

"Well, I've been trying to reach her all week to hope-fully explain my magic to me, but she hasn't answered any of my calls."

This time Vida got up. "She wouldn't come back here, would she?" She mused then waved her hand towards a hallway or tunnel that led into another part of the cave. I could see what looked like snowflakes flying fast and disappearing into darkness. She started muttering faster and pacing. "No, she wouldn't, she knows that coming here will alert the soul shifters, she must be searching for—" She stopped talking.

Her pacing was making me nervous. The flames in the fireplace flared, Vida turned back to my direction; a glistening ball of water was circulated in her palm and her eyes vacant, she stared into the water ball. The irises of her eyes changed color; it almost looked as if there were moving galaxies swirling behind them; her voice monotone spoke to the water globe. "Is that the only solution?"

Vida stopped pacing, her eyes back to normal. The water evaporated, then she turned to me. "Who was the man she was angry with?"

"Theo Pantazis."

Vida sat back down and laughed but it wasn't a funny laugh, she was upset. "That is Demetrius's nephew. His brother likes to go back and forth to the human realm. He is power hungry for humanity and notoriety. Theo is his child and half human and was born in the human realm. None of the soul shifters ever believed they could procreate with women from other realms. But we found out later that the madness took over Theo's birth mother about seven years after he was born. Demetrius took him in as his own child and raised him. Theo just went back into the human realm a few days ago at his father's insistence to learn about his human half."

The entire time she was giving me a history lesson on Theo's ancestry my mind was practically stuck in a stutter. She said too many things that were creating a million questions, but the only thing I seemed capable of saying was, "Theo is dating my cousin."

Vida tapped her perfectly manicured finger to her lip, then spoke. "Well, isn't this interesting. Has he taken her into his possession?"

"What do you mean?"

"Has he tried to kidnap your cousin?"

"No. Why would he?"

"That typically is their way. We have two types of

wolves on Nod, animals that contain only the souls of the wolf and the soul shifters, the ones who have both souls of man and wolf."

"Soul shifter?"

"Yes, their souls were stolen from humans and wolves. Although they are Aza's creations, her children, and she designed them, there was a small flaw in her plan. She cannot control their destiny."

"Isn't she a fate?"

Vida rubbed her temple as if it pained her. "Yes, she is, but there are ancient rules, which you will learn over time, rules that are not meant to be broken but sometimes we gods find ways to blur the lines."

"What did she do?"

"She wanted all her children to be devoted and obedient. She wanted to be the alpha and the omega. To make this happen, she spliced the souls of wolves from another pantheon and a soul freely given from a descendant of the gods. For the most part it worked. She is their alpha, and they must abide by her wishes or die from madness and descend to Tartarus in never ending torture."

"That is horrible!" I said, shocked. "I mean killing them would be so much kinder than having to live an eternity in hell."

Vida's eyes were sad. "I didn't like hearing this about my sister and at first I denied it. But after meeting a few of the wolves who have broken free, I have learned some hard truths. One thing is Aza cannot cut their thread of life. She cannot kill them. They must die of natural causes or in battle. The life supposedly freely given must have been deceived because what Aza stole from the universe has a price... the price for that deception must be paid back two-fold."

"Then why is Demetrious afraid of her finding him and you if she can't cut the thread of your lives?"

"Ah, she may not be able to end our lives, but for the most part, she still has control over the other wolves' obedience. She is their master and creator after all, but the one thing she didn't take into consideration when creating her shifters was wolves of Nod, when they find their sayonee, her spell is broken, and they are free."

"What is a sayonee"

"Their other half, their soul mate."

"I'm confused. Then why don't they all go find their sayonee?" Before she could answer I rushed out the rest of my thoughts. "Wait. I thought you were the fate to choose who we love, and it got all screwed up and that's why I'm in this mess?"

Vida shifted her head down. "That is partially true, but even the fates have boundaries. We don't have rule over animals, only humans, Greek gods, and their progeny. Animal souls and their progeny are ruled by another pantheon. Even though Aza had taken it upon herself to manipulate the wolves souls and split them into men, they began to evolve on their own. Having more links and traits to the wolf and deity."

"Wait. So, they really are part human from earth?"

"Yes. Demetrius now believes Aza stole their souls, and he is worried that she is trying to create a new breed. There are new wolves, younger, different, and they are being integrated into her primary guard."

"I don't understand." I shivered at the thought that

she might be creating something evil. It was a bit too much to imagine, but things in this world didn't make sense like things did on Earth. The God's lives were even more convoluted than humans. Vida tried to explain. "When the wolves started finding their sayonee, it broke the spell, and Aza would send her wolf guard to attack the wife and child of the wolf. Once his new family was gone Aza would get control back of the wolf, but what she didn't expect was karmic debt."

"What is karmic debt?"

"By destroying what was intended for the wolves., they eventually went mad and into a frenzy, eventually taking their own lives. I've felt distraught over never once looking into this in the past. It was only after I met Demetrius and him keeping me hidden and learning and seeing the truth in his word and after meeting a few of the others in hiding, that I truly believed him. At that point, I felt the connection between us and didn't want to leave. I loved him and would never let him go mad because of me. And he will not let me leave for fear that Aza's new guard will find a way to end my life. He is my sayonee."

She looked at me with eyes practically pleading for understanding and for a moment, I forgot why we were discussing all of this. Then I was reminded that Theo and Aurora were dating. "Oh my god. I can't let that happen to Aurora. I can't let her become a prisoner or be killed. Is it possible that Theo will take her prisoner?"

She nodded. "It is possible, but Theo is different from the typical wolves. He has always been different. He prefers to be a man, but if he found his sayonee, there is nothing stopping his animal from taking over. Their wolf soul is possessive over their fated mate and self-preservation takes over their will, forcing them to do anything to avoid going mad. Even if Theo is stronger and more human than wolf and he can fight the urge to take her, he will still be fighting his innate animal nature and find that he will still act on his wolf instincts. He will always find a way to take her to his den to protect her until they bond. Why do you think Demetrius was so angry I left earlier?"

I struggled with my fear for Aurora. I thought Theo would keep her safe, but he was just as dangerous as Séverin. At first, I thought Theo would keep her from getting caught up in my drama with Séverin. Now I learn Theo might be just as dangerous to her. Then I heard what Vida implied and had hope that Theo might be strong enough not to hurt Aurora. Maybe keeping her hidden away would keep her safe, but I had to clarify.

"I thought you were his sayonee and married. How are y'all not bonded?"

Vida's shoulders slumped; her expression defeated. "No. We've tried but..." Her sad expression changed and brightened when she looked up at me. She tapped her lip and her eyes widened. "The thought crossed my mind earlier, but our conversation took a turn. I think I know why our bond didn't complete."

"Why?

"Because I thought I needed to give you a piece of my essence to be reborn, but I don't think I needed to. You came here without the stones. If you give me the stones back, I can absorb enough of what was lost to complete my bond as a goddess."

"No!" I shouted. I struggled to get my voice under control. "I still need them."

I'd just discovered my magic. I wasn't ready to give it up. Not yet, and maybe not ever.

I wasn't Gollum, crawling around and calling them my precious, but I could feel them calling to be used. They made me feel powerful and when I used them, I didn't worry about Severin.

"I still need them." I repeated, quieter now. "I just discovered my magic; I'm not ready to give it back, not yet."

If I didn't have magic, I'd be stuck in Nod forever, and I'd never see Aurora again.

Vida patted my knee and handed me my glass of ambrosia. I took a sip and Vida took a sip of her wine. "I will not take the stones now, only when you are ready. I will keep this between you and I until then."

I nodded. We both sat in a strange sort of comfortable silence.

Look at Vida and Goldie. They haven't seen each other in ages because of Vida's kidnapping. She couldn't leave because her bonding wasn't completed. My mind drifted to Séverin. I wonder if that is why Séverin was so possessive. Was he a wolf and going against his nature? Was that why he started drugs, because he was going mad? Nah, he wasn't a wolf, but I wonder if I would forgive him if he had been honest with me and told me he was from here and had been waiting centuries for me to be reborn to be with me? My heart accelerated a bit at the romantic thought. But I shook that thought right out of my head. Séverin was not romantic. He was sick. I looked back up at Vida, how could she love Demetrius after all he had done to her. And love him I had no doubt she did. I could tell by the way her voice and eyes softened when she spoke about him.

I circled my finger around the rim of my glass. "How are you okay with what he has done to keep you prisoner and still love him? How did you forgive that and learn to trust him?"

She vanished her empty wine glass. "My relationship with Demetrius is complicated. But love truly does conquer all."

She put her hand on my knee and her energy buzzed through me, then she moved her hand up to her heart. "You must learn to trust what is here."

My eyes burned with unshed tears. I could never trust Séverin even though my mind and emotions wanted me to. But my heart and mind know with certainty that I trusted Cyprien in my dream, and I knew if I ever saw him for real, I would instantly forgive him for not running away with me when we had the chance. A burning need filled me, if only he would have run away with me, I should have just knocked him out and headed for the boat. Then he would have been all mine.

My stomach churned at where my thoughts had turned. I was just as possessive as the wolves. I can see how easy it would be to escape society and not have to face the real world.

The feeling of true love and trust had been intense in my dreams, but the moment I saw Séverin with his arm around Cy had been too much. I felt like I was the one going mad. Maybe I was part soul shifter. Once more I found myself muttering "this isn't real."

I felt like a broken record, and I was annoyed with myself for my rollercoaster emotions. I had shut them off for so long that I learned to make peace with emptiness and not feeling. Butterflies beat their wings inside of my stomach. I had to stop my train of thought. How can I trust in love if I couldn't trust myself? I choked on my words. "I can't"

When the tears started to fall, Vida pulled me into her arms and started humming something that was soothing me as she gently patted my back. Grief that I'd held onto for the last five years flowed out of me and I sobbed deeply and brokenly in Vida's warm embrace. I missed old me; I missed my mom and dad, and I missed hugs and comfort and touch. But in Vida's arms, she felt like a piece of my past, present and future and I felt protected.

She slowly pulled out of the hug and created a light breeze that dried my tears. I blinked a few times, not expecting it.

"Do you feel the energy running between us?"

I swallowed and nodded. I did. Her energy calmed me.

She nodded. "That is what I thought. I can feel your energy just as you feel mine. The gods I entrusted to help me create the stones had another agenda. My magic in those stones became a part of you."

"I don't understand."

She seemed hyped up and started to walk around me

as if I were an anomaly she was trying to figure out. Then she did something with her hand and within seconds a golden mist was surrounding me. The mist shimmered so brightly my hands flew up to cover my eyes. Spots danced behind my closed lids. I heard her gasp.

"Fascinating." Vida whispered to the room. Then clapped her hands. "How did I not see it instantly. You have been chosen. You were brought here to complete our bond, yours and mine."

Um, did Vida just go crazy? I didn't want to mate with her. The mist heated up a bit more and she laughed jovially. The warmth and mist faded as did the spots dancing behind my eyes. I chanced a peak behind my fingers to make sure it wasn't bright. "What?"

Vida was looking at me strangely. Her mannerisms seemed to change from more erect and powerful to soft and almost nurturing in how she was staring. Oh, crap was she going to kiss me. I got up and hurried to stand on the other side of the room.

She sensed my fear, just as I sensed her concern over my fear.

"My apologies. Your power is so strong I wasn't expecting..." her voice trailed off and her eyes turned all white as a wind blew around her. She was standing still like a statue.

I rushed to her side and was shaking her. "Vida! What is it?" She was hard as stone and then within moments her body was soft and warm again and moving from how hard I was shaking her. Her arms wrapped around me and pulled me in close. She kissed the top of my head, and I felt warm tears land on my scalp.

I shimmied out of her arms confused and scared about what just happened to her.

But her eyes were shimmering with love, she wiped a tear and whispered, "My Blessing."

Enough was enough, I stood up straight, my shoulders back, and in a firm voice I demanded an explanation. "What the hell was that?"

Vida wiped her eyes, took a deep breath, grabbed my hand and led me back to the couch. "Come, we must sit. There is much to discuss."

I allowed her to guide me to the couch.

We sat facing one another. Then she pulled both of my hands in to hers. Her warmth and happiness radiated into my veins. The raw heat of her emotions made me jolt backwards. I didn't understand what was going on. How could her touch be comforting only moments ago and now her emotions were so overwhelming I didn't know how to hold on to so much euphoria.

I couldn't breathe. Her emotions too intense, I scooted further back on the couch trying to create space between us. My heart raced, and I struggled to understand my feelings of confusion, fear, and anxiety with everything that had happened to me in the last twenty-four hours and her immense joy and utter awe.

"Delphine, I understand that you are overwhelmed. I do apologize for not being able to control myself around you, but my child," as she said those words her voice broke as her smile grew "you have been gifted immorality not from Goldie and Me interfering in your life or Aza's plans, but you were chosen by the Primordial. I gathered the elements and enbibed them with my energy and the gods have allowed your soul to be my child. You are now my daughter, our meeting was not by chance, you were chosen to be my family in the most elemental way. I just couldn't see it."

My throat went dry. What was she going on about?

I shifted in my seat debating if I should jump up and run or not. I scanned the room, seeing no escape. If only I could teleport back home or wake up and be out of the Dream Realm, however it worked.

The scariest part of all of this was feeling the waves of truth coming from Vida. I stayed put and closed my eyes trying to discern my own feelings from her energy. I took a few deep breaths and the warmth of the magic inside of me bloomed. The intoxicating sensation swept through my veins, and I felt my head fall back in pleasure at the feeling of power.

I knew in that instant that everything Vida said was true. It was as if this truth had been buried deep within me my entire life and even though I loved my parents, I always felt a tiny bit disconnected from them and occasionally had wondered if I might have been adopted but loved them enough not to ask. I didn't want them to think I loved them any less. They raised me and I loved them and mourned them when they died. But now I knew why I felt that sensation. My earth mother's body was a surrogate to keep me safe for when it was time to meet my true mother. Vida.

My breathing was heavy, and my vision started to tunnel.

Vida came closer.

"Stay back." I rushed out in a breathy, uncontrolled

tone. I couldn't pass out. I had to get myself under control. I needed answers, and I couldn't do that freaking out, but it was a struggle as my head spun and a million and two thoughts sped by like a ticker tape in fast forward.

Vida stood up and walked away. With her farther away, my breathing slowly started coming back into control.

She held out a glass of water to me. "Here, drink this. It will help."

I took the glass and drained it in one gulp, then coughed because it was sweet when I had been expecting water, but my mind cleared almost instantly. The shock faded.

"What was that?" I asked, looking in the now empty copper mug.

"Pure Ambrosia, sourced straight from Olympus."

"What kind was the other ambrosia?"

"That was 99.9 percent watered down, this is pure and will be a necessary staple in your diet from now on."

"Why?"

"It is complicated. Once you find your place in our family and start hearing all the prayer requests and seeing everyone's futures, you'll go insane. Lethe helps us out.

"Lethe?"

"She is the Goddess of memories who helps wash away the past of those who die and choose to move on without remembering their past and enter the Elysian Fields."

I didn't know how many more times I'd be shocked that this was all real and not a dream.

I rubbed my temples, "Maybe I need to meet Lethe," I joked.

Vida chuckled.

I held the cup out to Vida. "Can I have a little more?"

Instead of Vida filling the cup, the cup disappeared and in its place was a small flask. Vida grinned at me. "You now have your very own never empty flask of Ambrosia."

I unhinged the top and took a deep sip. It didn't burn my throat as much this time, but I still coughed.

"You will get used to it in no time."

I was so relaxed and leaned back on the couch. "I feel so much better."

A loud sound of static crackled in the room and a piece of paper fluttered down into my lap. I picked it up and read *Welcome to the family*.

Holding up the note. "Will I ever meet the others?"

"Over time you will but we need to first take care of the bond you have with your unmatched fate." She lifted my left hand.

"What do you mean?"

She looked at me in question. "Now that the mystery of your existence is answered, I assumed the reason why you came here to begin with was to break the tie from the man in your past so you can find your true love? That is the entire reason you were willing to die in the past? Am I wrong?"

I shook my head. "No."

Strange how only seconds ago I felt so powerful and strong, and now I felt so human and powerless. The fear was overwhelming, having to deal with the reality that my past and present are both real and they are merging. I worry about Aurora— did she betray me in the past? And what about the present? Is she really the girl I grew up with or an illusion? And now that I know Cy is real, I will have to face his possible rejection because I went against his wishes and used magic.

My chest ached in pain at the thought of not being with him. I chose him and I still did but how could I keep him if the spell in the past failed and only made my relationship with Séverin more toxic. What have I done? How in the world did I screw up and ruin not only one life but two?

I opened my flask and took another sip trying to settle my thoughts again. Once more it worked.

"Delphine, be careful not to depend on the ambrosia too much. You don't want to create a pandora's box of lost emotions. It is what keeps us healthy and alive and can strengthen you when you are weak. But even as gods we have limits before consequences start to happen."

I screwed the cap on. I didn't want to become an addict.

"Okay. It does make me feel like a zombie. I guess that really isn't good, is it?" I looked up at her sheepishly, knowing that it would be really easy to keep drinking the ambrosia and forget my life.

"No, it isn't," she said softly.

I hesitated, "Why do you think I was chosen to be your child?"

"I can't be certain, but I can only assume that while I was collecting the elements for the stones across the universe, my intentions may have drifted to having a child of my own."

I struggled to believe. "Could it be that simple?"

She shrugged. "With the Primordial it can be simple or complicated, one never knows."

How does a human girl who never experienced anything phenomenal in her entire existence one day wake up and become a member of the Moirae gods' family?

I just sat their staring at her, believing every word she spoke, at the same time wanting like mad to believe this was some insanely intense dream.

Vida's eyes softened and she placed her hand on my knee and squeezed. "It must be so much for you to absorb. Delphine, you are still the woman you were before we met. That has not changed. You just found out that you have a different purpose than you did before."

I scoffed. "A different purpose? I don't think I ever knew my first purpose."

She smiled at me knowingly. "Well then that is something for you to discover and I know you will when the time is right. Her lips curved into a smile so large that I felt the happiness and love burst out of her and into me. She opened her arms wide, and this time she asked rather than just act. "May I have a hug, daughter."

Before I knew it, I was in her arms and wrapped in her loving embrace. A small ounce of guilt still lingered that her arms and comfort were so much more than my human mother's. And more comforting than anything I'd ever experienced.

When had I become such a crybaby? I let the tears fall

again unashamedly and enjoyed the safety of my mother's embrace.

I inhaled her sweet scent and wanted to crawl into her lap as if I were a toddler. I needed a mom. I had missed mine so much and since meeting Vida she had felt like home, like I had finally found my place. I felt safe and not only did I have a second chance at life, but I had a second chance at having a parent. This time I wouldn't let anyone take that away from me. Now, not only did I have to steal the scissors from Aza to cut my link to Séverin, but I had to protect my new mother from her sister.

Chapter Eleven

This time I pushed myself out of her embrace, wiping my eyes. "I am usually not such a basket case."

"This is something very overwhelming. Even I am trying to wrap my mind around it as well. I knew it was unusual for me to have felt your presence so strongly when you arrived."

Her smile once more was beaming. "Thank you, Delphine, for being you."

Before I could even respond to her a door slammed down one of the halls. A loud growl echoed into the living room.

"Wait here, I must speak to Demetrius before he meets you. There is much to be done and so little time."

She got up and went into the hall. I saw her light a lantern and I could have sworn I saw a large shadow of an animal follow her into another room.

Vida wasn't gone long. She took a deep breath as she smoothed her dress when she re-entered the room. She turned back towards the area she left and when she turned back to me, I could see worry creases on her brows. "Forgive Demetrius when you meet him. He is confused and in a state because our scent is similar."

Another door slammed and Vida raised her voice. "Demi, don't be rude, come on out and meet my daughter, Delphine Allard, from Earth."

She grabbed my hand, and I stood up beside her and slightly behind her. Her energy calmed my nerves and her voice whispered into my ear with a slight tickling breeze. "He is a bit apprehensive. Don't let him frighten you, he is really a gentle being." She was acting like he was a wild animal or something being all cautious.

I felt myself shiver as if her calming energy quit working. The shadow of a beast was creeping closer into the den. She whispered once more. "Do not be afraid; he can smell it."

"That's not helpful," I whispered. I could feel myself trembling. She grabbed my hand and forced her calming energy into me. I needed it because the confidence the nectar had given me vanished the moment I heard Demetrius' growl echo throughout the living room, shaking my bones with its vibrations.

His huge shadow was shifting from some kind of creature to something more human like. Then I remembered this beast was Theo's uncle, and my heart started racing in fear for Aurora. Shifters were freaking real!

I pinched my forearm hard trying to bring myself back into some sort of reality. "Ouch." I rubbed the sore spot.

"Why did you hurt yourself?" asked Vida.

"Because this is real and I'm scared, and wondering if I'm in a drug induced coma lying in a hospital bed somewhere in New Orleans. Maybe I fell and hit my head on the light post."

She shook her head with a silent chuckle. "You are not hallucinating."

When the shadow entered the den, I started muttering under my breath "Monsters aren't real." Then Demetrius appeared.

He was no monster; in fact he was completely opposite. He was an older version of Theo and all I could think of was dang, Aurora was lucky her man would stay attractive his entire life.

I could see all his muscles practically through his linen-like loose pants and shirt. He had a full black beard, his hair was cropped short to his head, and he had Theo's eyes. Like seriously, it was gross that I was googly-eyed over my what? Stepdad. Yuck! I shook that thought away. Vida walked over to him and linked her arms into his. He tilted his head down into her neck, inhaled then turned to me and pointed.

"Explain."

"Let us sit," said Vida.

He walked to the sofa staring at me the entire time. Vida sat beside me and Demetrius beside her. He grabbed Vida by the waist and pulled her onto his lap and he brought his nose to her neck and inhaled all the while giving me an evil glare. Just as I was about to sit next to them on the sofa he growled again, thankfully it didn't vibrate my bones. He then pointed to a hardback chair further away. "You sit there."

I jumped up and hurried to the hardback chair he was pointing to. My heart was racing again. This man was intimidating and scary as hell.

Demetrius growled as he rubbed his nose back and forth in Vida's neck. She brought her left arm up and gently rubbed his head. She was making shushing noises as if soothing a crying child. She spoke softly but I could still make out her words. "Babe, I'm still yours. Please, you are scaring her."

He grumbled and breathed out a harsh breath. "I don't like this. Aza finally quit hunting you. Now someone who smells like you walking free will make you a target again."

He turned his piercing blue eyes my way, and in that moment, I was scared he was going to try to kidnap me like he did Vida to keep her safe. I fidgeted with my flask wanting to take a sip but decided not to. Sipping in fear would only make me more dependent on the stuff. Instead, I prayed he didn't have any elemental powers like Vida because I think he would have burned me alive with that stare.

Vida shifted as if to get off his lap, but he wouldn't let her move. His arms tightened around her waist. "I'm not going anywhere, and Aza can't come to your home, it is protected. You know this."

"You weren't supposed to leave the house either, but you went looking for her." He pointed to me. "You took your safety out of my hands."

She crossed her arms around her chest. "I have lived docile in this home for over a hundred years without stepping foot outside. When I felt her enter Nod there was no way I was going to leave her to the wolves."

He growled. "My brethren would not have harmed someone who smelled like you. They know you are mine."

"But the majority still follow Aza, not you. If you remember correctly, you all followed Aza obediently until you met me. If you hadn't felt the mating pull, you would have killed me as well. So don't get all high and mighty because you have a few loyal followers who now believe my sister is a danger to them."

Demetrius growled again. "I do not like this. I don't like arguing. We need to send the child back to her realm."

Vida's expression turned sad, and she sighed. "Although I do wish she could stay longer now that we've met, I believe you are correct. There are things she must still do in that realm."

Demetrius gave Vida a long gaze. He almost looked as if he were talking to her silently. He puffed out his cheeks and blew out a breath. Vida placed her hand on his bearded cheek. "Can you call Theo to bring her back for us? She is powerful but doesn't understand fully how her magic works yet. I don't believe it is safe for her to go home on her own."

He didn't even respond, and within seconds, there was no man by the sofa, only a large black wolf with cerulean blue eyes who took off running out of one of the other halls leading out of the den.

"Oh my god, he really is a wolf." I held my hand to my heart and started rambling. "I know you told me about the soul shifters but seeing it in real life is startling. Especially being he was way bigger than the wolves at the zoo."

I looked at her dumbfounded as the stupidest words came out of my mouth. "My mother is married to a wolf man?"

She giggled at my statement. "And I love him more than anything. You will too once you get to know him. He will be a wonderful father figure or friend if that is what you wish. But now that you have met, I believe he needs a bit more loving tonight." She waggled her eyebrows.

Gross. "First rule of being a parent. No child wants to know about their parent's sex life."

I nearly gagged just saying the word.

Vida laughed. "Child, sex is natural. You don't need to be embarrassed."

My cheeks burned. I wasn't embarrassed by sex in general, but I had a good imagination, and I didn't want to think about my mother in the act. But now a strong image of Cyprien rushed to the forefront of my mind, so strong in fact that when I licked my lips, I could almost taste his.

Vida guided me to the kitchen. "I can sense you are reliving memories." Vida opened a cabinet and pulled out a dish that turned into a fully loaded charcuterie board. She brought it to the table, and I followed her there. We sat down and started eating. I didn't realize how hungry I was and ate four cubes of cheese before she spoke again.

"It appears Morpheus has been trying to help you remember and prepare you for your return to Nod."

"Morpheus?" I asked with a mouth full of Bree.

"He is the god of dreams who brings truth and helps you remember what is forgotten."

Vida was layering a thin slice of meat on her cracker and cheese, "Tell me about your current life."

She popped the cracker in her mouth without realizing a bucket of ice water filled my soul with that question. Shame filled me and Vida stopped chewing. "What has happened?"

I blew out a breath. "It..." I stuttered trying to find the right words. "It was a noneventful boring human life until I met my ex-boyfriend, Séverin, who in fact is the same man as the one I was betrothed to in my past. It was when I met him that my life altered. At first, I felt alive in his presence, then things changed." I was quiet and sat on my hands, then I whispered, "He killed my parents—"

A frown creased her brow and the corners of her lips turned down. Guilt at speaking to her about my earth parents blindsided me.

"They, uh..." I stuttered, "were in an accident that Séverin caused. because of that, he was sentenced to prison, and I've practically been living under a rock. I've turned into a recluse who is generally afraid of her own shadow and scared of everything and everyone except my best friend Aurora, who I hope one day you can meet. Then last week I turned twenty-one and all this dream versus reality started happening and now I'm here talking to my mom about having a past life that she knew about but wasn't my mom yet, and now have been reborn as a what–" I looked at her. What was my new species? Was I still human?

"You are a goddess" said Vida.

"Right. I'm a goddess." I didn't feel like a goddess. "That is the one thing out of all this that makes me think I am hopped up on some serious medication in a hospital right now."

Vida walked around the table to my side. Standing behind me, she placed her hands on my head and moved them down to my shoulders, stroking my head as if I were a small child.

The warmth of her love passed through me calming me once more.

I leaned back in my chair and closed my eyes. "Thank you."

Vida took my hand in hers and spoke softly, "I am so very sorry about your parents. I could feel the love and remorse you carried for them when you spoke about their death."

Grief I thought long buried crashed over me, and she pulled me into her embrace. Tears poured out of me like she'd somehow opened a faucet, and I gulped big ugly sobs as I snuffled into my flannel. "I hate this—I really don't want to feel this way anymore!"

Vida handed me a handkerchief. "I can see now how all of this must seem. It is a lot of information for a mortal, but just remember that you are also a goddess. You have power deep within your soul at your disposal. Once you organize all this information, the elemental powers you have inherited from me will come to you naturally. I have no doubt that with just a thought you will be able to utilize your gifts."

"Please don't be offended, but can you please explain to me how I got involved in all of this in the past. Why me?"

Vida led me back to the den and sat cross-legged on the sofa. I followed suit and sat the same way. She leaned forward, pulled the handkerchief away and replaced it with a new one.

"Goldie and I didn't notice Aza had changed until I discovered Goldie's sayonee. Aza had stolen his red thread and connected him to another person. When we confronted her, she became enraged and put a price on our heads."

I'd somehow managed to set the handkerchief on fire. I jumped up, flapping my hands like I could just fly away from everything. The handkerchief fell like a falling star and Vida grabbed my hands.

My skin was unharmed, but something opened inside me, like a big scream trying to get out. Why wasn't I burnt? How was I trapped in this never-ending dream, and where was I—really? I cupped my palms over my cheeks, my teeth chattering. Maybe if I pushed hard enough, I could lock the screams away and wake up. "How did I get involved?"

Vida gave me a concerned look and the blast of empathy I felt from her was intense.

"We set out to figure out who's souls were still alive for us to rectify Aza's changes. Goldie stumbled upon you when following a lead that a woman on Nod was consorting with Aza about making her and a soul shifter a forced mated pair. But before she could investigate it, she felt the pull of the sacred willow call to her. She discovered you and Cyprien and knew instantly it was you who was tied to the man who was destined for..." Vida stopped abruptly, closed her eyes for a moment, then started talking again, "for another woman. It was devastating for her to witness you meeting secretly with the man you were supposed to have but couldn't because you were tied to another. She came to me, and we knew we couldn't let your life play out that way.

My teeth stopped chattering. "No offense, but Aza sounds like a bitch." I hurriedly covered my mouth. "I'm so sorry."

Vida gave me a sad smile. "We have to call it like we see it sometimes."

"Poor Goldie, did she ever find her sayonee?"

"Yes and no. He doesn't see her because he is mated to someone else, and we still haven't figured out how to break the tie."

"Oh, that is so tragic. I guess y'all didn't learn anything from me because according to my dreams and still being attached to Séverin, it didn't work for me no matter how hard y'all tried."

She shifted in her seat and sighed. "Yes, sadly it didn't work out for you but so much else has happened since then. It seems that your failure was part of your fate. I am starting to think that my relatives are keeping me in the dark about something that may be important."

"What could it be? I mean, seriously, why me?"

"I am uncertain why they chose you but," she grabbed for my hand again, "I am so grateful to have you as my child. It has always been a secret desire to have my own child. There were many times I envied Aza taking charge of her own life by creating her own children."

I didn't quite know how to respond to that. Being immortal must get lonely. I can understand why they would want to find their sayonee to at least have someone to share everyday life with. I couldn't even comprehend living forever and ever.

Vida breathed out a strong breath. "Aza's powers were too great for you in the past but now you are descended from the Primordia's and me. I wonder if you are more powerful than Aza now. Someone in my family is keeping me blind in your future."

"Why would they?"

"That is something I can't answer, and I probably won't because if I leave again Aza will try to take me away from Demetrius and I will not allow that to happen. I will give you a message to give to Goldie. She is still somewhat free; she can ask our sister, Nemesis. She likes to hang out on earth, maybe she knows what is going on."

She lost her perfect posture and leaned back on the couch. "I am so used to seeing everyone's fate. It is frustrating not seeing yours as well as my own now that I am aware."

"Out of curiosity, did Goldie go to earth because that is where her sayonee is?"

Vida lifted her head up. "How did you figure that out?"

"Well, I've known Goldie for a while, and she disappears regularly. Now that I know she is a goddess, I figured maybe she was searching for him and once more stumbled upon me reborn. She obviously felt your presence in me, but didn't know what it was and that's why she always stayed my friend even though I was a pretty crappy friend the last five years. She was probably trying to figure out what went wrong in my past and maybe if she could figure it out, she could maybe get her love away from whoever he is with. How many times has her sayonee been born and fated to someone else? Is it always the same person?

Vida reached out and grabbed my hand. "You truly are observant. That is an amazing assessment."

I felt myself sit up straighter at her praise. I hadn't had anyone praise me in ages accept Aurora and maybe Bev when it came to my art.

"Her sayonee has a festering love for the same woman. I believe that she's only been reborn once. Goldie is still trying to figure out a way for them to break their red thread in this life cycle. She is hoping that this time it will work, and hoping things haven't gotten so screwed up that when they do end up together she can make him immortal, or she would have to find a way to become mortal. Everything is so convoluted. Aza has really altered the natural order of fate."

My stomach dropped. "Wait! If I'm immortal and found a way to be with Cyprien and he's mortal how would that even work?" Depression enveloped me as I acknowledged once more how unlucky I was with love. I should ignore my desire to be with someone and move on without love in my life.

"Technically, if they are a mortal from the Dream Realm where Nod is then yes, whichever being is immortal their fated mate will live as long as they do. If an immortal chose to die, then their mate will die with them. Your situation is different; I am not sure how it would work in your situation because you are created outside of the norm. Maybe your rebirth as my child is to reset the balance and you may be able to live eternally with Cyprien."

"I wish that Aza could have just left everything alone. This is all too complicated."

Vida looked down at her hands now crossed over her lap. "You must understand. We are selfish individuals. We really don't think like mortals do. At the time it made sense but as centuries pass, once again both Goldie and I are trying to rectify our mistakes, and this has turned into our biggest one yet."

Chapter Twelve

Demetrius arrived with Theo in tow. Theo looked at me in shock. "Phin, what are you doing here?"

Vida stood up and prevented me from speaking. "That is none of your concern and you must remember to keep this between only us three. You cannot even mention this to your father."

Theo scoffed. "I wouldn't tell him anything anyway. If you remember right, I was happy here." He then looked at me briefly. I could have sworn I saw remorse in his eyes, but I had no clue why he would feel like that.

Vida went to stand beside Demetrius. "We need you to take her home. Can you do that for us?"

He nodded. "Where and when?"

Vida turned to Demetrius. "I am sorry our talk took longer than I thought, and I forgot to tell her something vitally important. Will you excuse us for a moment?

He unwillingly let go of her hand and she told me to follow her down the cave hallway. We entered a huge cavern that was turned into a bedroom. The bed was four posters and huge and they had several rugs overlapping on the floor. The fireplace swirled to life as we entered the room.

"I need to show you the basics of your magic."

I don't know what I was expecting but that wasn't it. "I don't have the stones with me."

Vida moved a small table in between us and put a gold vase on it. "You shouldn't need the stones; this is very basic elemental work. You are my daughter you have my powers now."

In the namaste pose with her hands in prayer, she closed her eyes and took a breath. She did a pose that looked like a tai chi pose then moved her foot pointing her toe in a half circle in front of her. Then she stretched out her arms like an L and circulated her wrist.

The gold vase lifted off the table. She moved her wrist a little more and the gold melted. She stood straight again and using both arms started moving them as if she were a conductor in a band. The melted gold was moving and creating shapes like stones, and each had the name above, earth, fire, water, air, shadow, light, and magic.

"These are the seven dwarves. They are all formed from the minerals and gemstones found in dwarf stars. These are magical because they are the elements of the universe. I collected these when Goldie and I found you and wanted to help correct Aza's spell uniting you with someone else's sayonee. I made sure that they would find you when you were ready to understand your past and ignite the spirit of the fates to help you reunite with your true sayonee."

I had my arms crossed over my chest. All of this

seemed eerily familiar. I remembered very clearly in my dream making a golden filigree pattern around the coffin sealing Cyprien in a tomb to stay alive until I could be fated with him. I wondered if that was the same spell or something similar.

"You must be very careful with your thoughts and emotions when using the stones. They will be attuned to you and will react to your thoughts and emotions as if you commanded them. Eventually, you will understand your gift and you will be using them as easily as breathing."

The first one she brought forward was the fire stone. "For all intents and purposes this is the Carnelian and the fire stone. It is the easiest to work with of the elements. Fire is very close to our passions."

I shifted and cleared my throat. "I uh, I can do that one. Before I came here, I was making candles light and unlight with the wind."

She smiled. "This is wonderful news. Maybe the transfer was delayed for some reason. Have you tried any other elements?"

"No, I got scared when I saw the guy from my dream was real and he was with my ex-boyfriend."

"Wait, the man from your dream. You mean the one you tied yourself to with magic? Your true soulmate, the one who Goldie and I helped you spell? If he is on earth, who is your ex-boyfriend?"

"His brother," I whispered. My throat clenched tight, strangling the words.

"Oh my, and he found you again in this time?"

I nodded.

"That must be what went wrong."

She stopped talking and sat on the floor waving me over to join her. I sat in front of her. She grabbed my hand and again I surprised myself at not wanting to pull away. I didn't pull away. She took a steady breath and gave me a weak smile. "Being you are now my daughter; you may one day be gifted with the sight. Everything has changed, and even the Primordial are not disclosing everything to me. For the first time in my existence, I am blind to the fate of those around me."

"The sight? Like I might see the future?"

"That is one possibility, another is you and I may both be allotters and you will soon start seeing the fate of others."

I felt so uncomfortable hearing her say that it made me feel horrible that in my past I chose to become a fate because I was just as selfish as her and Goldie. How was I any better than them? I'd taken away Cyprien's choice, and something went wrong. Vida might get killed, and my dream, which was my past and not a premonition, may be happening again. Instead of me doing some sacrificial spell I might get killed by a crazy Fate.

I remembered Cyprien pleading with me not to do the spell. He didn't want me playing with dark magic, but I went behind his back and tricked him. How did that wonderful kind man ever love someone like me? I sucked.

Vida reached over and placed her hand on my knees. "Why the frown?"

I wasn't sure I wanted to tell her. "Do you think we can save the magic lesson for another day? Maybe Theo can take me home. I don't feel good." Vida twisted her arm and made a swirly motion, and everything was back to normal. "I understand and you are right; I am sure this is all overwhelming. Now that you know Theo and he is someone that Demetrius and I trust, we will have him bring you back for lessons to learn to control your magic."

She gave me a side hug. "Don't be worried; everything will work out the way it was supposed to from the start, and eventually, you will be strong enough to come and see me on your own."

As she led me out of the room, my mind went over her words. I felt the ring with my thumb spinning around my ring finger. I was desperate for information, but I wasn't sure I wanted the answers. I didn't want to be her replacement. I don't want this life we started in the past, but I also didn't want to be connected to Séverin. With who I am in this life, I didn't know if I even wanted Cyprien. What a horrible human being I'd become. I was ready to cave in on myself.

All I wanted to do was go home, crawl back in bed, cuddle Felix, and pretend none of this ever happened.

My life turned from a boring mess and not trusting myself with guys to my entire life being planned and manipulated. I wanted to cry at the thought that the person I trusted and loved most in the world was all a part of the plan. I had a hard time wrapping my head around Goldie being a goddess and Aurora and her family being my keepers.

Vida brought me to Theo's side. "Theo, Delphine is

ready to return but before you go I need to create a communication device for you both."

She plucked a few strands of my hair.

I yelped. "What was that for?"

She then turned to Theo, and he tilted his head down for her to pluck one of his hairs. She walked to her kitchen and took out a gold knife. I backed away when she came near me.

"I am not going to use this on you." She chuckled at my apprehension.

She placed it on the coffee table and melted the hair into the gold and then turned them into two gold necklaces. She placed the golden chain around my neck and said some words I didn't understand. The necklace became one solid cord that couldn't be removed. "This is for privacy. Theo has the ability to teleport to Nod."

She placed Theo's around his wrist and said the magic words again and his too became a solid cord. Vida looked up at Theo. "Whenever Delphine is ready to return she will contact you through this link. It will come as a whisper inside your mind."

She turned back to me. "I trust that you will not misuse this gift. When you are ready to return, you will need to hold the chain with your hand that your hematite ring is on and tell Theo what you need. He will hear you, and the bracelet will give him your location. He should be beside you within seconds."

Theo glared at Vida as she gave me a hug. "I would love it if you came back sooner rather than later. Maybe tomorrow evening."

"Maybe." I knew I wasn't ever coming back. I made

my choice. I wasn't ever going to allow myself to be a selfish fate and take people's choices away from them. I didn't have to finish a past I started.

Theo finally spoke up. "If I am bringing her back to the time she left, then she cannot come tomorrow because we already have plans to go to a social event that my father insisted I go to. Phin, Aurora, and Goldie will be in attendance."

"Oh, that is wonderful that you have met Goldie. Give her my love and tell her I think about her all the time."

He nodded but he gave her a hard stare. "I am sure she would much prefer if you told her yourself. After all, she wasn't sure if you were even still alive." He turned to his uncle. "Especially since you've been holding her captive nearly a hundred years."

Demetrius growled. "Insubordination. You know our rules. When you mate you can't have their scent around any others until bonded."

Theo clenched his jaw. "I understand very well, and I am determined never to let my animal destroy another person's life."

Vida shushed him. "Demetrius didn't ruin my life. I could have denied this claim and left."

Demetrius growled.

Theo rolled his eyes. "As if he would have let that happen."

Demetrius' voice was loud and firm. "Enough!"

Theo grabbed my hand and practically dragged me out of the room and back into the dark cave.

"Hey, do you mind?" I shook my wrist. "That hurts."

He let go. "Sorry. This is an old argument. I don't want my wolf to control me. It isn't right to hold anyone prisoner no matter if they are my mate or not."

I heard his jaw grind. He was trying to control his breathing. "I hate being forced to shift but the only way I can teleport is as my wolf."

"I'm sorry." I felt guilty that I somehow got Theo involved in my mess.

He held up his wrist. "Now that she bound us together, I am at your beck and call. Please try to be respectful."

"What do you mean at my beck and call?"

"This is a servant's chain. You are the master, and I am your hound."

I felt like I wanted to puke. "No... we have to remove them. I will not bind another soul to me."

I turned around and started pounding on the stone wall where the door once stood.

"It won't do you any good. Vida won't remove it. She wants you to have a way back."

"Then I won't come back. I do not have to be a part of this world. I don't want to take away any one's free will." I turned to Theo. "I promise I won't ever use the necklace, I will only call you on the phone.

Theo gave me a sad smile. "Thank you, but this has always been my fate. My species was created by Aza to always be servants to the fates."

I wanted to say something, but I didn't quite know what to say. Theo spoke first. "Come on, I don't want to stay here any longer than I have to. Let's get out of the dream realm and head back to the earth realm. Once I am in wolf form, I am still me, so you don't need to be afraid, just climb on my back. Oh, and try not to yank my fur. I can't promise I won't bite."

He grinned at me and gave me a side look. Then made a little shooing sweep with his hand for me to back up. I did as he requested. I started swaying from side to side and my breathing got faster. How will I know if I pulled his fur to hard? How will I explain Theo biting me to Aurora?

Theo rolled his eyes. "It was a joke. I don't bite."

I stomped toward him. "Not funny! This whole thing is insane to me."

"How did you get here? No human has ever come here."

"I guess I'm not human. Can we just go?" I snapped, agitated at this whole day. Everything was becoming overwhelming. How many lives have I ruined already as a newbie immortal being. Theo didn't' deserve my frustration. It was all on me and my past judgment. Defeated, I turned to him. "Sorry, I'm just ready to go home."

"Where do I return you?"

It felt like ages ago that Aurora and I were at the dress shop.

"You had just called Aurora and I walked ahead of her to give y'all some privacy."

"I tripped over a paver and caught myself on the streetlamp." I looked up and tried to remember what stores were around. I squinched my nose and closed my eyes trying to envision the exact location. "I was in front of Artist Alley. Do you know where that is?"

"Thankfully I do, and let's just pray no one is in the alley to see a giant wolf with a girl on its back."

I snorted. "I can see it now. First a glass coffin like something out of Snow White, now wolves in the Quarter. What's next, vampires?"

Theo laughed but I gasped when I realized the man in the coffin was Cyprien. How had I been so blind?

That's why Séverin was crying. How had he broken the spell? I was supposed to be the only one able to wake him up.

Theo waved a hand in front of my face. "Phin? What is it?"

"Uh..." I stuttered out a few times, totally blank. "I was thinking about the coffin. What happened to it?"

Theo moved away from me. "According to the news, they found the family. They took the coffin to their family property to bury him properly. His relative said that they buried him down in St John Parish, and when it flooded, his brother's casket was missing."

"That is so sad." My voice caught. "Did they say why the body was preserved after so long?"

"Because the coffin was sealed incredibly well," said Theo. He gave me a strange look. "I'm going to shift. I want to get this over and out of there before Aurora sees it."

"Wait!" I shouted.

His eyes darkened. "What?"

"Does Aurora know about Nod?" Theo shifted, his muscles bunched and tensed. "She has no clue and I'd like to keep it that way. She is the first person to ever like me, and I don't want that to change."

"Um, excuse me for saying, but she doesn't know you for you, if she did she'd know that you aren't even human."

He looked sad and just turned into his wolf. He laid down so I could climb on his back. "I'm sorry that was harsh. I guess you deserve to have someone only see you as a person but if you really like her you need to tell her the truth."

I heard his voice in my head. "Will you?"

"Of course not!"

Abruptly we were in the alley. Theo waited for me to dismount before starting away. I called after him. "I'll keep your secret if you keep mine!" He nodded and took off in the opposite direction.

A few seconds later Aurora came out of the bookstore.

"Sorry about that." She linked her arm in mine. "Let's go burn that dress."

Chapter Thirteen

Aurora was still thankfully ignorant of my travels to some alternate world that I never knew existed. I swear, thinking of it made me think I was trapped in a horrible misrepresentation of a fairytale land. It was even named Nod. I was personally struggling to believe it because I thought I'd literally nodded off. Or maybe I'd fallen, hit my head and woke up right before Aurora found me waiting for her.

Later in the afternoon Theo came over to pick up Aurora. She'd been getting ready for hours. It was like she'd never had a date before. "Aurora is still getting dressed." I held the door for him. "Do you want something to drink?"

He shook his head, and I sat down on the other side of the sofa, wiping my hands up and down my thighs as I rocked back and forth.

"This is all real, right? I didn't hallucinate it?"

His head whipped in my direction so fast his canine's bared. He shushed me, his ear still human in appearance twitched like a dog when alerted. He scanned the area. Aurora was in her room, then he looked back to me. I felt the anxiety rolling off him.

His voice was hushed yet gruff. "It is very real. Remember to keep your promise."

I stood and took a few steps back, worried he might lose it. "But I have so many questions!"

"Now isn't the time. I can take you back after the ball."

I gave him a grudging nod, anxiety knotted up in my stomach like a big ball of dread.

When Aurora entered the room, he relaxed just enough to give her a fake smile and they left, with Aurora swinging his hand and doing her Snoopy dance beside him.

By the day of the ball, I thought I was going crazy. No matter how many times Theo had told me it was real I was sure I'd finally snapped.

Aurora was my lifeline. She'd bullied me into getting ready and sat me in a chair with Felix while she started her makeup routine early.

Watching her was soothing. It took at least an hour for her to perfect her brows. She drew them on, wiped them off, and asked my opinion before starting it all over again.

Felix nuzzled my hand, purring.

"What do you think?" Aurora raised her brows. I shook my head, and she wiped them off again.

The knock on the door made me jump so hard Felix fell off my lap and yowled.

We had another three hours before Theo was to pick us up, but I was too stressed to answer the door. Thankfully, Aurora opened it as I escaped to my room.

Goldie opened my bedroom door. "Knock, knock!"

She was smiling, but her eyes had guilt written all over them. Anger and frustration rose inside me, and the flames of all the candles in my room lit up even though I didn't have a firestone in my hand.

I panicked at the height of the flames but Goldie grinned wider. The acknowledgement in that smile made me even more frustrated. Before I knew it, I decked her. She staggered back eyes wide. I slapped my hand over my mouth shocked at my violent behavior. I'd never hit anyone in my life. Was this what Séverin felt? Was that why he'd hit me in the past? I never wanted to be that person.

I pulled Goldie to her feet, tears burning the back of my eyes. "I'm so sorry!" I had to talk to Goldie, but this was the worst timing. I'd just punched her. Was she going to turn me into a toad?

Could she turn me into a toad? Aurora had been looking forward to the ball. I didn't want to let her down. Tonight was a night we dreamed of as teens, but now all I could think about was getting information from Goldie. I peeked into Aurora's room; she was sitting in front of her vanity still working on her brows. Her eyes caught my reflection behind her in the mirror, and she smiled at me. I asked out of courtesy but had my fingers crossed behind my back. "Hey, do you want to get dressed together in my room when you're done with your makeup?"

She turned her music down and grinned. I could feel the excitement bubbling up inside her. Since coming back from Nod, I've been slowly feeling energy coming out of everything elemental. I never realized our body had so many elements in them because I could now sense the energy from emotions. Emotions must manipulate the elements in our body.

"Absolutely," said Aurora.

I gave her a wry smile.

I'd been so consumed with reading her energy, I'd forgotten asking her.

"Would you bring my dress to your room?" she asked, gathering up her makeup.

"Sure." I walked over to her wardrobe and pulled out her dress. I was heading back out of the room when our eyes caught in her mirror. She had only one brow completed and the other looked so funny only being a half of a brow because she shaved off the ends to achieve the look she wanted. Tonight was a classic 1940s high arch. She even dyed her hair scarlet red last night after coming home from her date. She wanted to surprise Theo with it. Even though it wasn't her natural red it looked amazing. It softened her appearance more than the black.

"I'll probably be another thirty to forty minutes finishing up my look."

"Sounds good," I said.

The second I was back in my room, Goldie stood up from where she was lying on my bed. I hung the dress in my closet and turned to her. "Close the door. We need to talk."

A breeze slammed the door shut. "I am so mad at you right now."

Goldie rubbed her jaw. "I can tell. Nice right hook."

I rolled my eyes and flopped down on the edge of my bed. My energy was pouring out of me like she'd opened the faucet.

"Why would you tell me I'm an elemental then abandon me for a week? Seriously, I almost died and then went to a faraway fairyland, saw elves and wolves, and met your sister, Vida."

Goldie rushed me, shaking my shoulders so hard my teeth chattered.

"Vida? Where did you find her? How is she?"

"Vida is fine." I shook her hands off and stepped back, trying to make my five-two stature more powerful. I had some unsettled concerns about the way Aurora and Séverin had acted at my death. And I had no clue if Goldie was a part of it or not. But I didn't quite trust her.

"What am I?" I asked, picking the most important question.

"You are you."

The candles burst into flame. Goldie grinned, which only aggravated me more.

"You aren't taking me seriously." The candles blew out like the flatness of my words had smothered them.

She had the gall to clap.

This time the candles flared tall enough to reach the

ceiling. "Stop it! You know what I mean." The windows blew open. "What is going on? Vida told me I was supposed to remember but why don't I remember? Why didn't you look for me? Why did I have to be reborn as your niece? Why am I immortal? A fate? All I wanted was to love the man I chose. WHY ME?"

This time the candles roared, and the magic came—tearing into me like knives. Not the warm, happy feeling I'd experienced before. This was a raging inferno of power lifting me off my feet and throwing me into the wall. My hands clawed at the plasterboard. It was earth and it was *mine*. I could feel it sloughing away beneath my grip like it'd been pulverized.

Goldie rushed to my side and hit me with a broom handle.

I collapsed to my knees and angry tears started to fall. I haven't felt this mad in years.

"Breathe!" snapped Goldie.

"I don't like feeling all these emotions again," I said, pulling the broom to me. It was non-conductive and sat in my grip like a brick.

Anger fled, the fires went out, and the window closed. My room was back to normal. Goldie breathed out. "This is so complicated."

I shoved away from her. "My magic is out of control."

Goldie flew back. Guess she wasn't made out of wood.

I wiped my eyes. "Is this Aurora the same as the past Aurora? We all look the same and our situations are similar."

"Yes and no. I was trying to help her too, but something I couldn't control happened, and now she has yet to remember her past as well."

I nodded. At least this Aurora had my best interest at heart and didn't remember her past betrayal, whatever it might have been. "Tell me exactly why you found me in Nod and started this whole thing?"

Goldie got back on her feet. "Nod is the land that my family created when humans stopped believing. It is another realm that is connected to earth but not of earth. It is cosmic and only the Primordial and some of their descendants can pop in and out. You were unfortunately chosen by Aza in her games. I'm sorry to say it's as simple as that. My other sister and I were trying to fix Aza's meddling with fate."

Before I could ask any other questions Aurora opened the door. "How do you feel?"

My blank look prompted a quick hug. "Nervous?" she asked.

I'd been so consumed by my past I'd forgotten we were going to the ball, and I hadn't been around people in ages. Crazily enough, being in a crowd didn't frighten me anymore. I was ready to get this ball over with so I could break the thread tying me to Séverin.

Aurora knocked my shoulder with hers. "It will be all right. Right, Goldie? We'll stay by your side all night if you want."

A rush of affection choked me. "I'll be fine," I said when I could finally talk again. "I want you and Theo to eat, drink, peruse and have fun. I have Goldie as my date, and we'll be fine. Right, Goldie?" I gave Goldie a look to make sure she knew I wasn't done talking with her.

She walked to the wardrobe and pulled out the gowns. "Absolutely! We will all have a ball." She laughed at her own pun and laid the gowns out on the bed.

"Now let's get dressed. It's almost time for your date to pick us up.

Aurora gave her a blinding smile, dancing around and swaying side to side. My life totally sucked but seeing her so happy made me smile. "We're going to the Vampire Ball," she said.

I squeezed into my gown and buttoned the cold black pearls. I only hoped they weren't real vampires. The fates were bad enough.

Chapter Fourteen

It was a breezy night, the river was calm, and the moon was high and close to being a full moon. I glanced over to Theo and wondered if he was affected by the moon like the legends declared.

I wanted to ask but didn't want to break my promise to him.

I watched all the people in line move up the ramp onto the boat, giving their tickets to the person collecting them. They were all in gothic or medieval-styled clothes, representing the vampires of the past. Mostly, their colors were black and dark red. Goldie, Aurora, and I stood out because we didn't look like the typical vampires. Aurora looked more like a 40s glamor girl. Goldie wore a flowing floral dress and looked like a flower power from the sixties. My dress was a simple dress that looked more like Wednesday Adams than a vampire. I didn't even remember picking it out. All I remembered was the joy of burning the gown from my dream after my visit to Nod and learning it was real. I had really hoped it would help erase some of my angst over the raw deal I got in not one but two lives.

Finally, we got to the ticket person. Theo handed over our tickets and we walked in. The steamboat was gorgeous. Aurora was bubbly and practically bouncing around Theo. He was smiling, looking down at her in a love-sick way. Goldie looked to be taking in the décor, which I had to admit was beautiful. The walls were a rich, deep red historical accurate wallpaper with dark wood wainscoting and chandeliers hung from the ceiling, casting the perfect ambient lighting.

I was glazing over from the beauty of it all, desperately searching for Cyprien; my heart rate skipped a beat at possibly meeting him again. And just as suddenly, my heart fell into my stomach, knowing that if he would miraculously be here, then Séverin would too. Although I had my magic and boasted to Aurora that I could take care of myself being in a room full of people, because of its unpredictability, the possibility I'd set the whole place on fire didn't sit well.

We all sat down at a round table and within about thirty minutes every one was on board and the musicians made a trumpet-like sound that brought our attention to the stage. The host of the evening was standing there with the mic and gave a speech.

"First, tonight wouldn't be possible without Antoni Vesalius of The Vesalius group swooping in at the last minute and allowing us use of the magnificent Natchez Queen Steamboat." I was a bit confused because I thought Aurora told me that Theo's dad gave them the tickets.

Theo noticed my confusion. "That's the name my father goes by." His expression was grim, and he muttered under his breath, "I despise that man."

I wonder what his dad did to make him dislike him so much. Clearly, there was zero love in that family, and that was sad. I glanced at Aurora smiling and hoped she wouldn't freak out terribly when he finally told her his secret. He needed someone like her in his life.

I redirected my attention back to the host "...and a seven-course dinner followed by dancing. This is the first year with this setup, and if all goes well, the Vampire crew would love to continue working with Mr. Vesalius, who couldn't be here this evening, but I hope we all have a fun night. We will be taking off shortly. We are waiting to make sure there are no late arrivals."

Aurora leaned over Theo to talk to me. "This is so exciting."

I nodded in agreement. The boat had pulled away from the dock and Séverin and Cyprien were nowhere in sight. Aurora and Goldie struck up conversations with the others around us, and even though I remained quiet through most of the dinner, I started to relax and enjoy the atmosphere. Sitting back in my chair, people-watching, I held my hand to my stuffed stomach. I hadn't eaten so much in ages.

Just the memory of the blackened creole chicken and the white chocolate praline pecan bread pudding made my mouth water all over again. It was to die for.

Jazz musicians played softly in the background. Through the corner of my eye, I noticed Theo stiffen as he literally sniffed the air. Seriously, his entire body language in that moment was so dog like, I turned to Aurora. Thankfully she was still engaged in conversation with the girl across from us and hadn't noticed.

Leaning further back in my chair, I caught Theo's eye. "Is everything all right?"

His head barely shook. He got up quickly, and Aurora turned to him. Without any explanation, he practically dragged her from the table. Aurora gave us all a wavering smile. "It's all right." She hurried to keep up with Theo, trying not to look like she was being dragged away.

Whatever it was made Theo uncomfortable. I had a feeling he was very much like his uncle and found his mate in Aurora. If my suspicions were correct, he was struggling to keep his wolf hidden and protect her at all costs. It relieved me knowing Aurora would be protected. Theo would keep her safe from my drama, and I could figure out and come to grips with my new eternal future and how to eventually tell Aurora about everything. I felt a bit guilty keeping it from her because since we were kids, we told each other everything. Now that I knew our pasts were also interconnected and messed up from the god games, I needed to wait until I knew her past motives. She had to get her memories back before I could confront her.

A shiver ran down my spine and my magic flared to life. A strong gust of wind blew the doors open and everyone seemed to be searching for the cause. Goldie's eyes widened. Whatever made Theo leave with Aurora was from Nod.

I wanted to run too; my insides were jittering. I bit

my lip, trying to contain my shivering. Could Séverin teleport? Or was it someone else? I scooted in the chair next to Goldie. "Did you feel that? I think something dangerous is here?"

She scanned the room and the color drained from her face. I turned to see where she was looking, and my heart sank into the pit of my stomach. Séverin was here. He was in a dark suit that eerily resembled the one he'd worn for our wedding day in my past life. Before I knew what I was doing I had stood up. Goldie grabbed my wrist, thankfully preventing me from rushing into danger. But my sudden movement drew his attention to me. For the first time since knowing him in this life, my eyes were opened to the magic inside and not only was our black thread visible but the dark energy emanating from him reminded me of death.

My knees went weak when his hate-filled gaze connected with mine. My heart started pounding heavily in my chest and I struggled to take a breath. He wanted to kill me. I shook Goldie's hand off. I had to get away before I became a fool and ran to him. "Gotta go."

Trying to run in a crowded ball room was challenging, but magically a path between the dancers cleared straight to the bathroom and I locked myself into the only available stall. I wanted to hide there for the rest of the night. My heart felt like it wanted to explode. I am sure people could hear my breathing. I was too loud. I had to calm down. I tried to take slow, deep breaths, but thought of Séverin finding me kept popping into my head. He wouldn't come in the ladies room, would he? How did he even get an invitation?

A hard knock hit my stall. I jumped and my heart flew into my throat. I spread my hands to each wall of the stall to keep from falling. Shaking, I didn't say anything, then I heard Goldie's voice. "You okay in there?"

The last time I'd seen him I'd been sixteen. He'd thrown me against the stairs and nearly killed me, then he'd stolen our car and killed my parents in his drunken rage. He warned me he was coming. He was sick from Aza's poison and my manipulations. Even immortals could be killed and having a long life meant nothing. "No," I said, my voice thin, barely a whisper. "I'm not. Séverin is here. He's going to kill me."

"No," said Goldie. "I won't let him. I will protect you and don't forget you can protect yourself, too. Don't forget who your family is; we are with you."

I understood I wasn't weak anymore. I'd been born again with more power than I had back then. The only problem I had was that neither my past self nor my current self was trained, and I was afraid I'd hurt innocent bystanders by accident or catch the boat on fire and unintentionally kill everyone. Even though I loved the idea of my magic, the weight of what I could do with only a thought frightened me.

The lights in the bathroom flickered and the others in the bathroom all started making comments. Goldie snapped her fingers, and the lights came back on. "Come out, Phin, I promise it will be all right."

Vida trusted Goldie and Goldie was a goddess, and she definitely had more power than Séverin. I exhaled heavily and climbed off the toilet.

The lock opened itself and the door swung open. I squeezed my eyes shut. "I still don't want to face him."

"You won't have to. Now that we know he is here I can make sure we are always diverting him. If he comes near you, I will find a way to lead him away."

I looked up at her. "You promise?"

She held out her pinky to me and I linked mine to hers. "I swear you will not die again. I will protect you, sister."

I felt somewhat relieved by that. I had to remind myself that Goldie has been here since the beginning of humankind. She was a Moirae, and somehow, somehow, she and Vida made me one too. Now it was up to me to learn to protect myself and find a way to cut the thread connecting me to Séverin.

The second we walked out of the bathroom, Goldie tapped her nose on the side and blew a slow breath in the direction opposite us. Séverin turned around and I saw an image that looked like me running away. I turned to her, my mouth opened in awe. "What was that?"

"An illusion. It won't last long. I will follow him and keep it going. Find Aurora and warn her."

I took off in the opposite direction and went in search of Aurora. I looked everywhere inside and tried to avoid Goldie and Séverin. I texted Goldie to let me know if she saw Aurora and she responded with a simple k.

I went onto the main deck weaving in and out of people, not caring if they brushed up against me. I was too focused on running to worry about physical contact until a large hand clamped over my mouth and I was pulled backwards. I reared back to kick at him, and he turned me in his arms.

"Shh, it's Cyprien."

My heart raced. My hands splayed on his chest. "Cyprien."

I'd wondered how I'd feel meeting him again, but I wasn't ready for emotions I didn't know I had. I choked and gasped, drowning under a tidal wave of grief and love. Relief filled me. I'd done it! *We'd* done it! We were together again, and I was never going to let him go.

He picked me up as I wept, walking to the front of the boat. He sat down behind a large covered electrical box with me still in his arms. We were hidden from view, the music was muted from this far away, but we could hear the lapping of the water in the large paddle wheel.

My hand caressed his cheek. "You're real!""

He shifted me on his lap, winked, then kissed me, reminding me how real he was. My fingers feathered into his hair and our lips furiously tried to take in every lost moment. It was as if no time had passed. The intense chemistry that had been in my dream was a shadow of what I felt in this moment. Our lips broke apart and we both breathed heavily. He rested his forehead on mine. "This world is strange but since waking up, I have felt your love inside my heart, and I knew I'd been given a second chance."

This time I felt Cyprien's tears "I am so sorry I didn't fight harder for you in the past. I don't know all of what you've done, but I beg of you to let me fight for you this time."

I was crying too, and he buried his face into my neck and hair that had fallen out of its updo. He started nuzzling my neck. "I've dreamt of you for centuries. Your love had me wrapped in a cocoon and the scent of you right now is driving me mad." He inhaled deeply making goosebumps trail down my spine. "You smell of all my favorite things, fresh rain, pine, and the tang of the sea."

He kissed me again and my heart raced in happiness. This is what I had been missing. I knew deep inside Séverin wasn't right for me, but I never fully understood why I always made excuses for him. I never once felt the passion in Séverin's kiss like I did when in Cyprien's arms. But I couldn't let the passion stand in my way of finding out what Cyprien remembered.

I placed my palms on his cheeks and gently felt the slight stubble that was growing in. I pulled away and gazed into his deep green eyes. He brought me in closer. "What did you do to me?" Kissing my jaw he said, "I cannot get you out of my head." I leaned my head and his lips started trailing down my neck. I closed my eyes relishing in them. He whispered, "It is driving me mad, and I have been searching for you since I woke up."

"You have? What about your brother?" I didn't want to say his name and ruin the moment. I leaned my neck the other way and he started kissing that side.

He spoke in between kisses. "I couldn't care less about him. All I want is you. You were right, we should have run away all those years ago."

"Cyprien"

I pushed him back, his hands tightened around my

hips keeping me planted in his lap. He leaned his forehead on mine and inhaled deeply.

"Look at me. I need to know what you remember before you woke up."

He looked up. His pupils were dilated so large that I could barely see the green. My finger burned and the golden ring appeared. His desire was potent, but I couldn't let it distract us again. His eyes went to my full, well-kissed lips, and I tilted his chin lifting his face up so our eyes met again and asked, "Cy, please, I need to know what you remember."

He closed his eyes and sighed. "I remember you, holding you, feeling you, and loving you." He leaned in for another kiss.

I brought my hands up to his face, holding his cheeks with my palms to stop him from kissing me again. His eyes were glazed and staring at my lips. He licked his lips as craving stirred in my gut. I loved the feeling of him and us, but I was a different me. I needed to explain.

"Cy, I need you to focus. Please."

His eyes flickered up to mine. The need in them burned my insides, and I leaned in to kiss him. His hand had somehow unbuttoned the front of my dress and when his hand touched my décolleté and was moving further down a strong wind wrapped around us cooling me down. My hair swirled around my face.

Cyprien blinked, and the lust cleared from his sight. He leaned back and rested his head on the wall that was hiding us. "I am so sorry. I don't know what came over me."

I was still on his lap and I rebuttoned the top of my dress. "It's all right. I missed you too."

I did. I meant it. Now that I was with him it was as if I never left him. My past was as clear as my present.

He gave me a confused look. "Phin, what happened? Why are we here?"

I curled into him, and his hand gently rubbed my back.

"I did something either really brave or really stupid and I am worried that you won't forgive me."

"It is I who needs forgiving. I needed to fight for you, and I didn't. I want to now. Although my brother is happy to see me alive, I can see he is still obsessed with you."

"Did he tell you what happened then?"

"Only his side. Neither of us can understand why the gods made him immortal or banished to earth. He told me he had been roaming this area for hundreds of years. Then, a few years ago, he stumbled upon you in a museum. He followed you around and purposely ran into you to talk, but you had no clue who he was. He was angry and confused, and no matter that he hated you and thought you were dead, he still wanted you."

"We need to hide," I said. "I don't want your brother to find us."

Cyprien pulled me close. "Don't worry about him. If he comes this time, I will protect you. I won't make that mistake again."

The corner of my mouth lifted. If only he knew that once I could control my magic better I'd be the one to protect him.

I took a deep breath and explained everything I'd learned and discovered over the last few days. He stiffened when I told him I'd gone against his wishes, used magic, and failed to break the tie with Séverin. I laced my left hand into Cyprien's, and our threads touched, shining brightly.

He hissed and shook his hand in mine. I could tell he saw our broken golden thread. He pulled his out of mine and looked at it, then lifted my hand to look at mine and kissed it. A tingle of love shot through my finger straight to my heart. In awe he whispered, "I never saw this until you touched it."

The golden thread was glowing as if our togetherness charged it. I then showed him the long black thread that was still connected to Séverin. He asked, "How will we break this? We need to do this not only for you but for Sév also. He needs to be with his real mate."

"I don't know how to break it," I said. "I failed the first time and made it worse by turning the red thread black. I think that is why he is so full of hate towards me."

"Maybe I can talk to him and tell him what you were trying to do in the past and maybe together we can figure out how to cut the thread. Did you tell Sév any of this?"

I shook my head. I took his freewill away just like I'd taken Cyprien's. Shame filled me as I realized how horrible and selfish I'd been. Cyprien slid a finger under my chin. "What's done is done. It is the past; it's what we do with this knowledge that is important."

He was right. Maybe there was still a way to make this right. I hugged him hard. "Thank you."

He retuned my hug and added a kiss to the top of my head. "Do you think you can get the wolf to take us all back to Nod? Maybe Goldie and Vida can help us all figure this out."

Fear slithered through my stomach. "I don't know," I said carefully.

"What if he beats you up like last time? You may not stay here on earth."

He wrapped my hand in his. "Then we will speak to the fates and find out what we can do to break the tie. There has to be a way."

I laid my head on his shoulder. For the first time in years, my heart felt full. His arms felt like home, and he lifted my face to his. "Please don't cry. This time we will do this together."

I turned to look at him. He wiped the tears from my cheeks with his thumb. Before I could stop myself, I said, "I love you."

"Always" he replied and kissed me.

A throat cleared beside us. A man in a captain's suit was standing. "The ball is over; we ask that you gather your belongings and disembark."

We both got up and my legs were stiff. I didn't realize we had hidden the entire night. The time flew by. As we stood, it was the first time I noticed what Cyprien was wearing. He was in the same suit he had on when I had kissed him with the potion.

He was holding my hand in his and I stopped, and his arm extended back as I pulled at him. He turned around. "Everything okay?"

I nodded. "Thank you for trusting me again."

"What do you mean?" He looked confused.

"I told you everything I did, I even poisoned you with a kiss, yet the first thing you did when you found me was kiss me. Thank you."

He tucked a stray hair behind my ear. "While I slept all I felt was your unending love. I knew that whatever you did was because you truly loved me. There is no way you could ever have given me those feelings if you had ill intentions. Phin, I may not have said it earlier but I will love you and only you always. I don't need a thread of fate to tell me what my heart knows."

He kissed me again and once more the captain cleared his throat. "Move along."

Cy and I separated. My cheeks ached from smiling. I don't remember ever being this happy in my past or present.

As we exited the boat neither Goldie nor Séverin were there. Actually, no one was there. The captain walked beside us, and I asked. "Where is everyone?"

"They left over an hour ago. I was doing one last look around before locking the steamboat and ramp."

"Thank you for finding us," I said.

The captain nodded and walked away.

"Do you know how to get back home?" I asked Cyprien.

"I'm afraid not. Sév's been driving me around in what he calls a car. I must say this world has grabbed my attention. So far this is my grandest adventure ever. The things in this realm are truly remarkable and the advancements should be brought back to Nod."

I agreed. "You can come home with me. I live with

my cousin. She might be shocked I'm bringing a guy home, but I don't think she'll mind."

We walked hand and hand back to my apartment and as we were walking up the stairs, I started to get a flutter at the thought of sleeping next to Cyprien.

Chapter Fifteen

My apartment was dark, and I had Cyprien wait in the living area while I went to check on Aurora. The lights were out but her bed was still made. She and Theo must have decided to extend their night. When I went back into the den, Cyprien was pacing around the room.

"Are you tired?" I asked.

"Are you?" His eyes twinkled.

The squirmy flutters in my stomach grew stronger. "Sort of," I said. "Do you want to see my room?"

He nodded.

I led the way and when he walked in, he inhaled deeply. I could see him taking in my space. He walked to my nightstand and picked up the portrait.

"Those were my parents on earth. They raised me in this life."

He placed the photo back down and Felix jumped up on my bed and meowed. Cyprien turned to him and placed his hand near the cat's nose. Felix bumped his head into Cy's hand in invitation to rub him.

"He likes you."

Cyprien smiled and picked up the cat and started petting him. He was purring so loud. I walked to my closet and pulled out some night clothes for myself. "I'll be right back; I want to get out of this dress."

"All right. I'll be here," he said with a grin as he sat on my bed with Felix still in his arms.

I felt my cheeks burn and my heart race. He was on my bed. My bed! The temptations that flew through my mind needed to be shut down. I couldn't move that fast. I had to slow my hormones down.

After changing, I went into Aurora's closet to search for some oversized pajama pants. She was taller than me but hopefully they would be decent enough for Cy to sleep in. I found an old pair of her brother's grey sweats she stole years ago shoved in the bottom of her closet. Justin wasn't as tall as Cyprien but at least they were men's pants, hopefully they would fit him.

"I found an old pair of sweatpants from Aurora's older brother. They will be more comfortable for you to sleep in. I can show you to the bathroom."

He placed Felix on the bed who curled up in a ball and went back to sleep.

I pulled out a spare toothbrush and gave it to him. "Take your time. If you want to shower the towels are in the cabinet under the sink."

Cyprien shook the toothbrush at me. "Thank you. I'll be out soon."

I heard the shower come on and in less than five minutes he was back in my room wearing only the joggers. His skin was bronzed all over, and he was ripped with lean muscles from his years of sailing. His pants rode low and left little to my imagination. I forced my eyes back to his face, and good lord, his grin made me want to melt. It had to be the sexiest smile I'd ever seen in my life.

He walked toward me like a predator, and I backed up, knocking my knees into my bed, I fell backward. He leaned on top of me, and I was trapped in his arms, one of his knees on the bed, the other straddling me but still on the floor. He leaned in to kiss me, and instead of ripping his pants off like I was imagining, I panicked and shoved him off. His elbow folded in, he fell to the side, and I hurriedly jumped under the covers, bringing them to my chin. He sat up on the edge of the bed and laughed. "Where will I be sleeping?"

I took a deep breath.

"I can sleep on the floor; your rug is much nicer than some of the boats I've sailed on."

I scowled at the floor. I didn't even have an extra blanket to offer him. I didn't think this through.

"Or I can sleep in the living area on the sofa."

I shook my head. "I don't want to freak Aurora out when she gets home."

His eyes landed on the empty space beside me. If he slept with me, I didn't think I'd be able to stop myself from moving this relationship to the next level; and from all the heavy kissing we'd already done I doubt Cy would say no if I jumped him. I glanced down his body and notice that I was right, he was more than ready also ... I closed my eyes, a heavy breath exhaled out of my nose and all I could see behind my closed eyes was him in my bed.

I gave in, scooted closer to the wall, and flung the covers open, in invitation. "You can sleep with me."

He didn't hesitate. Before I could blink, he was lying on his back, the covers folded up to his hips. He moved one hand up behind his head and the other rested on his stomach. Suddenly shy, I didn't know what to say or do. I'd never had sex or initiated it before, but my body was humming with need. I rolled to my side, and he shifted an inch closer. Before long I was lying my head on his shoulder, with my arm wrapped around his body. His hand was rubbing slow circles on my back and the heat of his skin was penetrating through my nightshirt. All the candles in my room flickered on.

Cyprien chuckled. "I need to get used to that new talent of yours."

He shifted to his side, and we were facing one another. He wrapped his thick thigh around my hip and shifted me closer. I could feel all of him, his hand that was resting on my hip was now under my shirt rising slowly. He kissed my eyelids, then my nose, but before he got to my lips I whispered, "Thank you for not being mad at me."

Our eyes focused on each other's. He pulled back, then unfolded himself from me and laid back on his back. My heart sank. I ruined the moment. Did I do it on purpose because I was scared?

Before I could dwell Cyprien spoke. "I have to be honest."

I stiffened beside him. He was going to leave me now, my heart hammered in my chest afraid of what he might say.

"Although I love you and I know you love me..."

What does that mean - there is a condition?

"I'm disappointed that you didn't discuss this with me before you sacrificed yourself. But in all honesty, I am more upset I didn't fight for you. I should have run away with you and built a life together away from my family. The thread between you and Sév may not have turned black and changed him and you wouldn't have had to die and be reborn. It's a lot to consider now, especially because I am not immortal but Sév is. How long do we have? I will grow old, but you won't, how is that our happily ever after? What is the purpose of fate if it will always be a game to them? This is a horrible spell that keeps on punishing."

The candles blew out and the wind turned icy. I shivered in Cyprien's arms. He pulled the blanket up over us and rubbed my back with his hand.

"I worry about our future. If you can't break the thread with Sév, he will live forever, hunting you down, trying to kill you to end this? And that life would be torture for us all."

I remained silent, watching him in the thin light from the street. I wouldn't lose him again. I had to make this right.

The following morning. I slowly woke up to a hand

inside my pants holding on to my butt. My cheeks burned, remembering that after a brief nap, the rest of the night was of fire. I giggled because my butt cheek felt just as warm. We had fallen asleep attached after we both had our release and obviously hadn't moved an inch since. I slowly tried to slide down his body hoping not to wake him up, but moving that slow was a mistake. I felt his arousal and he gripped me tight, his voice rough and sexy, "Please don't move."

His eyes fluttered open. Rolling me over, I could feel every inch of him. On top of me, he braced himself up on his elbows and kissed me. I was timid to kiss him with morning breath, but the sensation of the kiss took over and all I could do was bring him in closer. When he started making slow circular motions with his hips, I moaned in pleasure.

As his head was moving lower down to my breast he groaned, "You are beautiful," and within moments we were both lost in our passion.

I woke to the sound of my phone ringing. "You've got to be kidding me," I groaned out in frustration. No one ever called and the first time in years that I slept well I forgot to turn off the ringer.

Cyprien rolled over and picked my phone up off my nightstand. He laid back down with his forearm covering his eyes. Smiling, I couldn't help but admire his smooth chest. I sat up and opened my phone to see what was so important.

The missed calls were from an unknown number and some texts. I listened to the messages, the first two had hung up but the third was Theo.

Theo: Aurora lost her phone at the dance. She is staying at my place for a few days. This is my number if you need anything. Aurora will text you her new number when she gets a phone. No need to worry.

Phin: Thanks for letting me know. Tell her I'm all good and not to worry about me either.

Theo: She's sleeping. I will make sure to tell her.

Theo: If possible, please don't use the necklace to call me, I'd rather not be yanked away with Aurora present.

I sat staring at the phone and brushed the necklace with my fingers. It was so lightweight that I forgot I had it on unless I noticed it glinting in the mirror.

Phin: Now that I have your number I promise once more that I will never use the necklace on you.

I went to the last unread message.

Goldie: I noticed that you and Cyprien found each other again. I didn't want to break up your reunion, so I led Séverin away with the illusion of following Cyprien into the city. I hope you both got to talk and get reacquainted.

I texted her back.

Phin: Thanks! We did. HE SLEPT OVER! We need to get together and figure out how to break the thread between Séverin and me. Can you take us to Nod so we can go talk to Vida?

Goldie: I can't see Vida. Aza has made it that I can't go in wolf territory. Have the mutt take you.

Phin: If you have any ideas on severing that thread, please keep me posted.

Goldie: I will

Cyprien had been watching me text and I could tell the phone was a marvel to him. "It's called a cell phone; you can communicate with people through it. It is pretty much instantaneous, but some people are slow to respond."

"Is it like telepathy?"

"No, it's more like... honestly, I really don't know how to explain it. I just know that it's called technology here and I type something in and attach it to their phone number and poof like magic they get the message."

"Ah, so it's like sorcery."

"I don't think it's the same thing as magic in Nod."

"Black magic is the same no matter where you are." He shifted uncomfortably.

"Wait. There are people who can talk to each other in their minds in Nod?"

"It's a rare trait but some of the gods have gifted their children with it."

"I wish I had it then I could always find you in the future."

He smiled, "I think you might be thinking of mind trackers."

I smiled back. I still had a lot to learn about my other life. "Goldie doesn't have any new ideas on how to break the connection between me and Sév and she can't see her sister because of the wolves. I need to ask Theo if he can take us back."

I clapped my hands. "Plus, I'm really excited to learn more about my magic."

Cyprien shifted both hands behind his head and his stomach muscles shifted. A thread of drool tried to creep out of my mouth.

He changed the topic. "I think it interesting how both you and Aurora were both reborn and she is mated to a wolf. I know you keep saying Aza is the fate who is playing games with our lives, but how can we trust the others? How can we be sure to trust others?"

"Goldie is a friend. I can't see her betraying us. She works too hard to keep us safe."

His hand reached for her. "Promise me that you won't use their twisted magic. The gods have their own agendas. I don't want them to corrupt you."

I got my pillow and slammed him over the head before he could react. "That isn't nice! I am not going to play games with the lives of others. That isn't who I am."

Crossing my arms across my chest, I glared at him but all he did was lift one brow.

"Okay, so I did screw around with your life and Sév's, but I swear I learned my lesson. I don't want to be that person."

"Power can be helpful or selfish, and the majority of those with power are selfish."

My jaw tensed. As if I would use my magic selfishly. I glared at him.

Now my past and present had finally merged, and I felt the magic inside me shift. The earth and air elements were a part of my nature. It felt freeing and I never wanted to give that feeling up. I resented that he would even think I'd use power selfishly. I would gain control and prove him wrong.

The wind fluttered the sheers over my window and dumped Cyprien off the bed.

He grinned, so handsome my heart hurt. "Great power." he said, rubbing his hip. "I could use a pillow."

I threw the pillow at him again. This time he laughed. "I'm sorry, I shouldn't have spoken my concerns aloud. I really don't believe you would do anything bad."

My indignation faded. "You have that right! I'm a good person."

He winked at me. "Technically you're a goddess."

"I will admit that overnight something rather big shifted inside of me."

He wagged his brows up and down, I blushed furiously and kicked my foot under the covers at him leaning on the bed. "Stop."

He held my foot and started rubbing the sole. It felt so good. A warm hum of energy spread throughout me, and before I could say more, the dried lavender I had in a vase for decorations rehydrated and filled my bedroom with fragrance.

Cy smiled. "Something shifted last night..." He encouraged me to continue.

"Yes. It was after we— um," I stumbled for the right word. "Our union."

He bit his lip.

I glared at him. "Don't make fun of me. I can feel all the elements running through my veins. I know it sounds strange, but it was as if I needed to meet you again to become whole. And even though I hate to agree with you, I do feel a connection to both good and evil and my power to feel the elements is getting stronger. I just wish I knew what to do with it. Will I wake up one day and feel like it's my destiny to make choices for others? I don't like this."

Cyprien stood up, tugged my hand, and led me to kneel on my knees; he laced our fingers together. "Let's not worry about it anymore. I shouldn't have made you second guess yourself. I know you will grow into your role, and I will find my place beside you because that is what we are choosing."

He leaned over to give me a kiss and I wrapped my arms around him. "Thank you."

He flicked my nose with his finger. "Let's get some clothes on. I worked up an appetite and need sustenance."

My stomach growled as if on cue. He winked at me and laughed.

"After breakfast maybe you can use your cell phone to reach the wolf. If he can take us to Vida we will see if she has any solutions."

"We can do that," I said, feeling a warm glow inside me that wasn't from the heat.

I climbed out of bed, and he pulled me into his arms and gazed into my eyes. His playfulness vanished and his brows scrunched in the middle. "Phin, I vow to you, from this day forward as long as I live, to always be here for you, but right this second, I am ready for our next adventure together."

I smiled up at him when I noticed the playful twinkle in his eye return. "I've heard so much about beignets but never had one. Can we have those for breakfast?"

I laughed when his stomach growled so loudly I could have sworn it echoed. followed by a low meow from Felix. "Sure! I'll feed Felix first, then let's get dressed. Maybe you can just wear the pants and shirt. I have an oversized sweater you can borrow if you're cold."

Neither of us took long to change. We walked in front of Magic Brew Cafe and Bev waved at us through the window. She looked shocked and dumfounded when she noticed I was holding the hand of a man and smiling on top of it. I could see her pull her phone out of her pocket, her mouth already moving.

I pointed to the cafe. "I used to work there when I was in high school. My earth mom and Marie, Aurora's mom, own it and the rest of this building."

I could have easily given him breakfast at the cafe, but I had zero desire to explain my behavior or introduce Cyprien to Bev. Instead, I led him further away from my home and continued telling him about places around us as we walked and I told him stories of my life here before I remembered my past and him. He was quiet most of the way, but he never let go of my hand. Having him with me was so incredibly reassuring.

We walked up to the counter at Cafe du Mondé. "This place makes beignets. They are like a sugary treat. You will love it. I promise."

I ordered two orders of beignets and some of their famous chicory coffee for each of us. I hadn't had chicory in ages. It didn't take long for us to get our food and find a table. We sat down and looked at all the powdered sugar. "How do I eat this?" His eyebrows scrunched in a quizzical expression.

I smiled and picked it up letting the sugar spill all over the place. I know that it was everywhere and as I licked my fingers he stopped and watched me. "Just enjoy it," I said.

"Oh, believe me I am."

I gently kicked his shin with my shoe and smiled at him. "I meant the beignet."

He took a bite of his and I couldn't believe that he was able to keep himself practically powder free. I was about to take a bite of mine but stopped with the beignet halfway to my lips.

Séverin stood right behind Cyprien. He was wearing the same clothes as last night. He was pale and had dark circles under his eyes. He kept walking as if he were a zombie, not looking at anything or anyone.

Cyprien turned around to see what caught my attention. "Don't worry. I promise I won't let him hurt you." He shouted his brother's name. "Séverin!"

He turned in our direction and when his eyes met mine, they turned dark as ash. He wanted to destroy me. I felt his barely controlled rage through the black cord and started shaking. Even though I had magic and could protect myself, how could I use it on earth and in front of humans? It would be caught on some persons cell phone and spread all over the internet in seconds.

Cyprien noticed also and stood up blocking me from Séverin's view.

Séverin jumped over the barrier into the outdoor café

and punched Cyprien in the jaw before he could protect himself. Cy didn't fall; he stood strong and only made me stumble a bit back into the chair behind us.

Sév's teeth clenched, he rolled his neck and with eyes blazing into his brothers, he yelled, "How dare you betray me and start seeing her again after what she has put me through. You are my flesh and blood."

Cyprien put his hands on Séverin's shoulders "Stop! Just listen."

Séverin's face reddened and he punched Cy in the jaw. Cy stubbled back but didn't fall.

"I deserved that." he said.

Cameras were all out and not a soul tried to stop them. Power roared inside me, demanding I step in.

Sév glared, and stepped like he was going to punch him again only this time Cy was ready. He punched back. Sév grunted and with a triple punch he enunciated each word. "I don't need explanations."

Panicking, I reached out holding Cyprien's forearm. "Please. Stop. Both of you."

Cy stopped, but Sév ignored me and hit him once more. I fell back onto my butt and cried out landing hard on my tailbone, and Cy was lying on the ground, not knocked out but not getting up either. Powdered sugar exploded off the nearest table, sending beignets flying as the doors and windows blew open. People were shouting, trying to get out of the sudden gusts of wind.

Sév gritted his teeth, glaring back and forth between Cy and me. His eyes burned into mine and sneered. Fear ran down my spine when he growled out, "I need her dead."

The people around us were all watching the scene and I could see some already starting to video. I held on to Cyprien, the heavy weight of my ring like ice."

"Brother, sit and let me explain."

Séverin gave me a wicked glare over Cyprien's shoulder.

"Alone." Cyprien caught his arm and started walking away with him.

Plates and glasses flew off the tables and knocked Cyprien to his knees.

"No!" Everyone turned to me as my voice carried.

Cyprien looked up at me, his face pained. "Dark magic..."

"No," I said quietly, holding my hand out. I couldn't let him go alone. I needed him. All the heat had left me the second he moved away, and I couldn't allow it. I hated needing anyone, but I did. I needed Cy's warmth.

Cyprien got back on his feet. The look he gave me was disappointed, but I hadn't been using dark magic—or had I? My hands knotted in my hair, holding my runaway thoughts in place.

Yes, I'd been foolish, but my elemental magic wasn't dark.

Cyprien started away with his brother in the lead.

My insides froze at the thought of never seeing him again. "Stop," I screamed louder than before. In that moment, everyone around me froze. Cyprien was the only one not frozen and I held his hand. Séverin was partially frozen and his eyes, still black, stared at me with even more hate then earlier. "We all go together; this is important. You have to give me a chance to explain what

I recently learned. We were both toys in a game played by fate and we must stop them."

He blinked. His pupils started to constrict, and the color started to return. I had his attention and I believe he would be willing to give me a chance to explain.

I placed my hand on his ice shoulder and blew out a breath I didn't know I had been holding. Everyone around me started to unfreeze. They all shivered simultaneously, but no one seemed to have heard my conversation with Séverin. They completely ignored us. Had I somehow inadvertently wiped their memories?

I pulled Cyprien after me and Séverin followed. We walked to Jackson Square and sat on the ground by one of the large palms away from most of the pedestrians roaming the area.

It took us nearly an hour and a half to explain what was going on to Séverin and I could sense his anger brewing. "I want to meet this fate who gave you the ultimatum. I recognized Aurora again when we met years ago, but I knew she was not the same just as you weren't. Even though I knew you had no memories, I was still drawn to you. I knew that what I felt wasn't mine. I knew it was— a sickness. Call this Goldie and let me hear what she has to say."

I did as he asked and called Goldie. She picked up on the first ring and I put her on speaker. When I didn't say anything right away she asked, "Phin, are you okay?"

Something changed in the black thread connecting me and Séverin.

"Séverin wants to..." he reached over to the phone in

my hand and instead of talking he ended the call and threw my phone back to me hitting me in the chest.

"What the heck, Sév?" I scooted closer to Cyprien who laid his palm on my knee—then I straightened my shoulders, annoyed.

I opened my phone again to call Goldie to apologize for the hanging up. The word out of Sév was strained. "Please." I looked at him then Cy who nodded, my hand fell to my lap. "Then what should we do?"

He raked his hands through his hair, looking lost and confused. "I don't understand but something strange is happening and I can't trust that woman. We must talk with the other one. Call the wolf."

This time I called Theo. He didn't answer.

"Call again!"

I did and still no answer.

"Are you sure I can't try Goldie again?" I asked, not knowing what else to do.

Séverin got up, hands clenching and unclenching. He blew out a long breath and turned to me. "I believe you. I believe my brother. But I still believe that the woman Goldie is not innocent in our ill-fated string. The moment I heard her voice I felt something. Like an old memory or something that has been removed. She has something to do with this ill fate of ours and I don't want to be anywhere near her."

Before I could say anything, my phone rang, it was Theo.

"I am sorry I couldn't answer your call. What do you need?"

"I need you to take me, Cyprien and Séverin to Vida. We have questions that only she can answer."

He growled at me over the phone. "This is not a good time. Try to use your magic first and portal yourself like you did last time. If you can't figure it out call me after the full moon."

He hung up and when I tried calling him back it went straight to voicemail.

Chapter Sixteen

Séverin swore and turned to me. "Show me this magic source."

Cyprien stood and held his hand out to me to help me up. He didn't let my hand go even though Séverin was giving us the evil eye. I led the way back to my apartment. When I opened the door Felix was waiting for us. He hissed at Séverin and ran into my room.

"Aurora, I'm back with company." She didn't respond.

Maybe that was why Theo was abrupt on the phone because we were keeping each other's secrets. But now it sucks that he is the only way to get in touch with her until she gets a new phone. I'll need to call him again and ask to talk to her.

I turned to the guys. "Y'all can have a seat, I'm going to see if she is in the shower."

I headed to Aurora's room. She wasn't there or in her bathroom. I pulled my phone out of my back pocket and called Theo again. Once more there was no answer.

Rather than keep calling I left a message. "Hey Theo, this is Phin, can you please tell Aurora that I have company if she heads this way but if I'm not home tell her she doesn't have to worry. I'm all right."

Knowing her she will probably still freak out whether I'm home or gone. Seeing Sév and Cyprien will make her think I've lost my mind. We really should leave before she gets home. As I made my way back into the living area, I was contemplating reasons for me needing to disappear.

The best and the only one that seemed realistic was that I decided to lead Aurora to believe I would attend the animation meeting in California at the last minute. I had to pack a backpack and leave before she came home if I used that excuse because she knew my fears of leaving town too well. If I told her in person, she would instantly read the lie in my eyes.

I'd be better off just leaving her a note and asking Goldie to cover for me.

I had never taken the ring off, but I picked the pouch of stones off my nightstand and headed back to the living area. I stood before Séverin and handed him the pouch. He turned pale and looked sick the second it touched his palm.

"Do you recognize the pouch?"

He started to tremble. I wondered if the memories from a hundred years ago started to replay in his mind. I hoped he'd volunteer what happened after I died?

He dropped the pouch suddenly as if the stones in it were burning his palm. "I don't like this."

"Do you remember them?"

He nodded once.

I couldn't wait for him to volunteer the information. I had to ask. "After I died, I saw you hand them over to Aurora. Why?"

He crumpled to the floor in a fetal position clenching his hands around his head. He was rocking as if in severe pain. Cyprien hurriedly got up off the couch and was at his brother's side. He placed his hand on Séverin's shoulder but Sév rotated his shoulder, shoving him off and groaned out. "Don't touch me."

Cyprien looked up at me helplessly. I stood frozen just watching as he sobbed and rocked back and forth. I heard a whispered voice as if the air spoke to me. "Remove the pouch from the room." I picked up the pouch off the floor and ran to my room shoving it under my pillow.

When I returned, he was now sitting up with support from Cyprien and taking deep breaths. His head was resting on his knees and his fingers were still rubbing his scalp.

He let his hands fall and hang loosely over his knees. His eyes were red ringed, and his lips were practically white. "The pain..." He swallowed.

I ran to the kitchen and got a bottle of water. I unscrewed the top and held it out to him. He took a sip and exhaled a deep breath. Color started to return to his complexion.

Cyprien asked, "What happened?"

Séverin held his hand out to his brother. "Help me up." Cy stood and took his hand helping him up. Sév finally spoke. "Someone took my memory. All that's there is pain when I try to remember."

His eyes squinted as if just trying to think of it again and he started trembling. His brows pinched together, and he started turning pale.

"Stop thinking about it. It's okay. I don't need to know." I didn't like seeing him hurt. It hurt me knowing I caused this, my heart ached. I still loved him. And I know he felt my love and pity coming from our black thread when he looked me in my eyes.

He squinted his eyes, frustrated and angry because I could feel that he hated making me hurt. His voice even changed and became softer almost but still ticked. "You may not need to know but I do. Someone stole my memories and punished me by making me immortal and exiling me to earth. I will kill whoever destroyed my life."

Strangely enough I didn't want to disagree with him. He had a right to be pissed. We all did. I tucked my head down. I felt so incredibly horrible because I'd made it worse. Guilt—If I hadn't wanted to break the thread in the past, at least Sév would have died after living a normal life.

The room started heating up. Cyprien grabbed my hand and led me outside. It was much cooler today than it had been all week. I shivered at the temperature change. He brought me into his arms and held my head to his shoulder. "It isn't your fault." His words came out tumbled and rushed.

I pushed away from him. "How did you know that was what I was thinking?"

"Your elemental magic started heating the room, I brought you out to prevent a fire."

My mouth dropped open in shock. Worried, I turned to my apartment. Could that happen?

Sév stood in the open doorway watching us.

"Close the door," I said. "I don't want my cat to escape."

Before he could turn around to close it, the wind slammed it shut from the inside.

They both turned to me. Confused, not knowing how I did that, I started stuttering "I–I–" I heard Cyprien chuckle under his breath and turned to him. He was trying not to laugh at me. I felt my cheeks heat up embarrassed for some reason.

"It seems that your magic doesn't need the stones anymore. It uses your emotions. Good job!" He brushed a kiss on my nose. I lifted my shoulders up and down. A bubble of happiness entered my chest that Cyprien was giving my magic a compliment.

I looked down at my hand. The hematite ring was on the same finger with my golden thread ring. I wonder if the combination of the two were the source of all the magic. After he said that it made sense. I'd been emotional when I went to Nod the first time. I wanted to find answers and I ended up practically in Vida's front yard. Maybe that was the key to helping us get back.

"Maybe that is what I need to get us to Nod. Maybe we can backtrack and go to the spot where I was when I went there the first time."

Séverin answered first. "It's worth a shot. Let's go" and he started heading down the stairs.

Cyprien stopped him. "Wait. Maybe we should bring some supplies. What if we end up on the other side of the island than where we need to be. We will need some things for trade and food and water if we have to walk."

I didn't even think of that. I guess last time I'd been lucky. "Oh!" I said rather loud. "I just remembered. They have alarms now for when humans enter through magic. We will have to be careful."

Cyprien smiled. "You don't have to worry about that babe, none of us are human."

My heart fluttered when he called me babe. That was the first time he ever used an endearment.

Sév made a gagging noise and walked past us into the apartment. "Let's get the damn supplies. I want to end this shit."

Cy grabbed my hand and kissed the inside of my palm. I turned to him, "I'm glad you were an explorer; hopefully you will know if I have anything worth trading for things in Nod."

After filling a backpack with things that might be useful, I sent Goldie and Theo a text telling them I was going away for a few days for work and to take care of Felix for me. I picked him up and hugged him. "Buddy, we will be home soon. I put out a huge bowl of kibble and a lot of water just in case Aurora doesn't come home today." I kissed the top of his head and locked the door.

We went back to the street next to Artist Alley. "Should we hold hands or something to make sure y'all come with me?"

"Might be a good idea," Cyprien said as he grabbed my hand.

I held my hand grudgingly out to Séverin. He took it. My nerves were bouncing inside my chest at holding both of their hands. Cyprien's felt so right. Sév's felt warm but the black thread was so tight it felt like it would cut my finger off. It wanted to suffocate me.

Nothing happened. We didn't disappear, we didn't land in Nod. I closed my eyes trying to think of Vida and needing her again, but nothing worked. I still heard the traffic of the city and the pedestrians walking by. I groaned and dropped both of their hands. "If I can't figure it out, we will have to wait until tomorrow or the next day for Theo. The full moon should be over then."

Frustrated after trying a few more times, I said, "I am going to call Goldie again."

"NO!" Séverin snarled.

I completely ignored him. Cyprien pulled me back into his arms as if to protect me from his brother who glared at me the entire time I dialed her number. Once more She didn't answer. "This is ridiculous."

Frustrated, I stomped my foot hard, the concrete breaking beneath my foot as the earth trembled slightly.

"Did you just do that?" Cyprien asked.

"I think so."

"It really does seem like your magic only works with high emotions."

Séverin's scowl transitioned into a wicked grin. His eyes remained focus on me as he stalked a few steps closer. Cyprien noticed as well because he wrapped his arms around me, bringing me closer into his chest. Sév didn't seem to care and sandwiched me between the two of them. My heart started pounding hard. I hadn't been this close to Sév in years and strangely enough, I didn't feel as scared as I should have. It really was remarkable that I never noticed how similar the two were in appearance. How had I not noticed in the past? Seriously, they even had the exact same eyes and eye color. Only Séverin's eyes always seemed so much colder and Cy's were more playful and had happy squint lines. When I heard Cyprien's teeth grind, guilt flooded my soul.

"What the hell are you doing man?" Cyprien seethed through his teeth.

Sév lifted his arms as if he were going to hold me. The strum of my heart picked up a beat, but he bypassed my shoulders and went to his brothers. I was so confused, yet my body was awakening with all sorts of feelings having both men so close. A breath I was holding shuddered out. Sév winked at Cy and then he did something so completely unexpected. He kissed me and I stupidly closed my eyes and let him. It wasn't just a peck on the lips, it was a full mouth experience and I fully responded, tilting my chin up to receive more.

Cyprien's arms pushed into my stomach bringing me back to reality and I realized that he was trying to detach my lips from his brothers. In shock, I stopped kissing and pulled my head back. I felt my cheeks heat up and the knowledge that I was an active participant created a heavy wave of guilt followed by a tightening of my gut with remorse. The wind picked up and the temperature dropped.

Séverin took a step back and Cy's hands released their grip. My heart sank at what I had done. And my reflexes finally kicked in too late but without another moment's thought, I slapped Sév across the cheek, his head flew in the direction of the swing from the impact. As he caught his balance and gave me a look of not anger but satisfaction, I couldn't help but notice the vivid red imprint on his skin. Why was he gloating as if he liked it? I didn't want to think of that, instead I allowed my betrayal to Cyprien fill me.

"What the hell!" My voice carried and echoed. I was both embarrassed and surprised by the power in my voice. I was fighting within myself. I had kissed him back in the heat of the moment and despised myself for responding, despite not enjoying it at all.

Turning around, wanting to apologize to Cyprien for my behavior, instead my mouth gaped open in awe as I took in our surroundings – we were in Nod.

Cyprien stood there, his arms crossed over his chest, shooting his brother a menacing glare. In stark contrast, Séverin was unfazed, chuckling nonchalantly at the success of his plan. "It worked. Now let's cut this thread. I'm sick of being a dick," he remarked with a smirk, referring to the scheme he had executed.

Cyprien, with a sense of protectiveness, immediately took hold of my hand and ensured I was positioned at a safe distance from Séverin. It was clear that even in the midst of their tense situation, Cy cared about my well-being and safety and that helped me calm down. The temperatures returned to the more tepid heat from our arrival.

He turned his attention to me, his expression softening. "Do you remember how to find Vida?" he asked, shifting the focus back to our objective.

I scanned the area taking in where we entered Nod.

This was a different location than the first time I had come. We stood in a heavily forested area near a river.

"Honestly, I'm not sure. Do either of you recognize the area?"

Cyprien picked up a dry leaf and crumbled it in his hand. He threw it into the air and the wind blew it to his left. He turned to Séverin. "It appears the wind is blowing to the north." He pointed to the other side of the river and to my left. "If I remember correctly, to head home we would just need to follow the river."

"Were there mountains near your home?" I asked.

Cyprien answered, "No, the mountains are in the south; we all lived in the farmlands."

I nodded, my full memories of the past were coming back slowly, but I do recall being very isolated and naive to what was out in the world. "Vida lives in the lower caves. The place I landed last time was a fork in a dirt road and a grove of strange trees that had huge fuchsia blooms. She found me there and it took us a few hours to walk to her house."

Séverin turned to Cyprien, "I wonder if that is the Doskurya grove near Elvindale?"

"I did see two small men when I was hiding."

Cyprien said. "Then the mountains she lives in are in the Black Hills. That's definitely wolf territory."

He pulled the backpack over his shoulder and pulled out the flashlight. "It will be getting dark soon. We may have to find a place to sleep for the night and start early in the morning."

"Do you know where to go?"

He pointed across the river to a pastoral view. It was

farmland of what looked like lavender. Behind the fields were some hills and a forested area further back. "Over those hills and through the woods."

He started to lead the way to a small bridge not that far away. "To Vida's house we go," Cyprien said in an exhalation.

I couldn't help but chuckle.

"What is so funny?"

"It is just what you said reminded me of a nursery rhyme we used to sing. It just seemed so out of context here."

I sang a few words and both men chuckled.

After miles and miles of walking, my feet were starting to kill me. I was about to whine and beg for another break when I finally saw the Doskurya grove. We were almost there, and the sun was starting to set. I really didn't want to have to pitch a tent. I was ready to find Vida but from this perspective the Black Hills really seemed black. I didn't know if I could do the climb without sun light.

"Shit." Séverin's exclamation copied what I was just thinking. "Looks like we'll have to camp here. It's too dark for the mountains and I'd rather not alert the Elves to our presence."

"I wish we didn't have to stop for the night," I said. Then to my utter delight the path to Vida's lit up with a fairy light trail and I giddily laughed. "Wow. Looks like she might be expecting us. She turned the lights on to guide our way."

Cyprien and Séverin both looked at me as if I'd gone mad. Cyprien was by my side and the back of his hand went up to my forehead. Then he held my head between his hands and looked into my eyes. "When was the last time you had some water?"

"Not even ten minutes ago. What is up with you? I'm not sick."

"There are no lights. You couldn't possibly see her home from here?"

What was he saying? Of course I could see lights. The path was so bright that it appeared to be daylight guiding us. I could clearly see the path lit up for miles, conforming to every twist and turn on the way to the cave. Then it dawned on me, "Are you telling me that neither of you see all the lights showing us the path?"

Cyprien and Séverin both gave each other a look as if they were talking to one another about me.

"Stop! I'm not crazy."

"We never said you were," Cyprien stated. "We just don't see the lights. Maybe it is a part of your magic or your connection to Vida that is helping guide you."

"Y'all don't see the lights at all?" I asked, my voice coming out a bit whiny thinking that maybe we won't be able to go tonight as I hoped.

They both shook their head.

I plopped down on the ground sitting with my legs crossed. "Well, this sucks big time. The lights are so bright to me that we could easily make the trek tonight but now I guess we are stuck sleeping here." I leaned back and looked at the darkening sky and the two moons starting to rise. I closed my eyes wishing that I was powerful enough for the guys to see it.

"What the hell? Cy, do you see that?"

"I do!"

I opened my eyes. Nothing was there, just the guys staring off towards the mountain.

"What is it? Is someone coming?"

Cyprien held his hand out to me as if he wanted me up. I grabbed it standing. His smile was huge. "Looks like you may have done a little more magic because now we see the lights and you are right, they are as bright as daylight."

"Seriously?"

He nodded. "How do you think you did it?"

"I just wished it. I really didn't want to stop again for the night."

Séverin had started walking the path. "Maybe you should have just wished us there. That would have been easier."

Cyprien whacked him on the back of his head with his hand.

"Hey," he rubbed his head "I'm not trying to be an ass on purpose. Let's get this quest over with. I am ready to have this bond severed."

We started the long trek. After we climbed a few of the rougher parts of the mountain, I started to wonder if I was going in the wrong direction. I ignored my fears and thankfully after only another half hour I finally spotted the cave.

This time I was grateful for Cyprien's foresight in packing flashlights. We walked about a mile in and that's when I found the hidden spot where the door was supposed to appear. I pounded on the rock wall because I didn't know the password she used to make it visible. "Vida please, it's Phin– Delphine. We need your help."

Moments later the door opened, and Vida and Demetrius were in their night clothes and hurriedly pulled us in.

Demetrius growled. "You brought more strangers into my home." As Vida said simultaneously, "It's dangerous to be out after midnight."

"Hi" I waved. "Um, we have questions, and I wasn't sure this would work but here we are." An uncontrolled nervous laugh escaped my lips at the deep scowl I kept getting from Demetrius.

Demetrius stormed back into the den and Vida turned to the three of us. "Don't worry about him. He is more afraid that Aza will figure out where I am than having strangers in his home." She turned to the men beside me and held out her hand.

"Séverin, so nice to finally meet you and you as well, Cyprien. I've seen what your destinies were supposed to be before my elder sister changed them and from the bottom of my heart, I am sorry that you have had to endure such hard lives."

"Come, let us go inside and discuss what is on your minds."

We followed Vida inside and she led us to the long dining room table. We all sat down and Demetrius, who had been pacing the living area, came to the table and slammed his hand down. "I don't like this. Between this girl and my nephew, Aza will be hunting us down."

I was curious about what was going on with Theo and wanted to ask but Vida interrupted. "Demetrius, the fabrics of their lives are all changing. Aza distorted their timeline and we tried to fix it once before, but it didn't turn out like we wanted. We must correct this. We must stop Aza from doing this again. I don't want to live in hiding for the rest of my life either."

He growled then sat down. "What must we do to stop it?"

Everyone looked to me. "Why are y'all looking at me. I have no clue what to do, that is why we came here. Goldie said she couldn't help us and we needed to find you."

"Séverin and I want to cut the thread connecting us." I leaned over the table to look at Séverin who was sitting beside Cy. "Right?"

"Absofuckinglutely!"

Demetrius muttered under his breath and rolled his eyes. "Foul earthly language." Then he said loud and clear. "Why don't you just go and cut the damn thread yourselves."

We all looked at him. Vida spoke first. "I will not end their lives."

He turned to her. "Not with those scissors; with the one she keeps down in Erebus that she used to create us." We all turned to him.

Vida looked surprised.

"How could you not know she had another pair? Didn't you wonder how she was able to cut the original tie between him?" He pointed to Séverin, and Vida put her hand over his mouth.

"You must not tell him of his future. It is against the

Moirae rules. He must discover her on his own since their link has been broken."

Demetrius nodded and removed her hand from his mouth. "Moirae rules went out the window whenever Aza went behind your back and started making her own rules. The boy should know."

Séverin snapped. "No." He slowly met eyes with each of us. "None of you will fuck with my life again."

Sév was right. It was time for all of them to stop. If Goldie and Vida hadn't tried to fix the past by looking for me, I would probably have lived my life with Séverin or run away. Because of their interference, giving me more choices, and manipulating me, I chose the sacrifice. Look at what that choice did to Séverin and Cyprien. Who knows how many other paths changed because of my one choice. For all I know, that was the reason why Aurora in the past betrayed me. Maybe my choice turned her evil or something. I wish that Sév's memories wouldn't have been erased. I would sure like to know what had really happened after my death.

I glanced at everyone at the table. My choice had affected all these people. Vida wouldn't have gone to the wolves if Goldie didn't ask her for the soul shifting spell. She wouldn't be hiding away from her sister, Aza, Demetrius wouldn't be so angry and stressed because he was afraid of Vida disappearing, and poor Séverin had been exiled and had to live hundreds of years never aging, always in hiding, waiting for me to be reborn.

"All of us, including my Cy, have been affected. I may have made this choice for love, but I never really thought about the consequences. I never thought about what being turned into a goddess or having power would entail. All I had wanted in the past was to love the man of my own choosing. One that made me feel happy and whole."

My breath started to increase and the panic inside of my chest tightened.

Cyprien reached under the table to squeeze my knee. My eyes flew to his, our connection filling me with warmth.

"It'll be okay," he whispered.

I placed my hand on top of his and he flipped it over, lacing his fingers to mine. He was worth every tear, every mistake. He had always been what I was fighting for.

"I promise in this moment, if I continue to have the powers of fate, I will never take away someone else's choice. I will talk to them and try to let them understand all the consequences first."

I stood facing each of them. "I messed up. In trying to get my way, I have affected each of your lives in a negative way, and I ask each of you to forgive me. Moving into the future, I want to be honest and open, and I want each of you to know that I never meant to hurt any of you."

Cyprien grabbed my hand. "We all make mistakes; what is important is what we do with the information we learned from them."

Vida nodded. "I can promise you I have had my fair share of mistakes and failures, we all do and Cyprien is right, it's the changes we are willing to make to grow."

I sniffled. Cy rubbed his thumb over my palm

sending me comfort. "All of my past choices have been bad."

Demetrius answered this time. He looked at Vida and pulled her into his lap. "Sometimes bad things have to happen for us to see beauty."

My eyes burned. "I appreciate you all, you are my family, but I promise that as a new member of this family things will be changing. I will be an advocate for free will and I will make it my sole purpose to be a fate of choice."

Séverin laughed. "Damn you all for making me feel like shit."

Cy stood, confronting him. "Back down, Sév."

"No!" Séverin pointed his finger at Cyprien, dead serious. "You stop. All this touchy-feely shit is making me want to puke. Screw your feelings, her feelings and their feelings. I'm ready to kick Aza's ass to Tartarus, and you can join me or get fucked."

Cyprien looked lost for a second then clapped his brothers back a couple time. Demetrius snorted. Vida looked like she was agreeing to disagree, and I busted out laughing because for some reason I needed to hear that too. Séverin gave me a half smile and I think I felt his forgiveness coming from his black thread.

I looked up at him with watery eyes and nodded that I got the message.

Chapter Seventeen

Séverin was the first to speak. He turned to Demetrius. "Where do we find these special scissors?"

Demetrius stood up and went to one of the bookshelves near the large stone fireplace. He picked up a large book of Shakespeare and laid it on the table.

I kinda laughed, surprised that he had a human book. "You like Shakespeare?"

"He's a good friend. He and his wife live on the other side of the caverns."

"That's impossible, he died in the 17th century."

"That is what he wanted everyone to believe. He was ready to move back home. He faked his death on earth, returned to Nod, and went in search of a way to help his human wife, Anne, to live a longer life. That was how we got involved with alchemy."

My mouth dropped open. "There is no way Shakespeare is a werewolf!"

Demetrius gave me a rare partial smile. "More like a soul shifter wolf."

"So cool. He is my literary hero. Will you introduce me one day?"

"Once Aza is out of the picture and we are safe again I am sure he would love to know that his writings are still cherished in the modern world."

"Seriously, if y'all can time jump, why hasn't he ever gone back?"

"That is not my story to tell."

He opened the book to the last page, tapped it three times with his forefinger. The book turned into a large map.

"He and I developed this map before our exile when we realized Aza had been the one killing our sayonees and letting our brothers go mad. We think she is trying to create a new breed, one that won't ever stray from her. I knew one day we'd need it."

Demetrius glanced at us all. "It appears I was correct in my thinking." He blew on the map and the image grew and hovered above the table. The map became a three-dimensional hologram. Each layer was a different dimension or realm.

"Delphine, I am entrusting this knowledge to you as my future daughter. You must steal Aza's scissors and bring them back to us. We must destroy them so that she can never abuse her powers again."

Séverin butted in. "But before we return them, we will cut our damn thread."

Demetrius gave him another half-smile. "Yes, you have earned that privilege."

Vida spoke softly. "I wish you would have told me of these scissors when we first met. Maybe we would have been able to prevent all of this misfortune."

I looked up at Vida. Did she already regret that I was her daughter? But before my thought could evolve further, she spoke again, wrapped her arm around my shoulder, and squeezed it briefly. "Well, one exception. I am so grateful to have you in my life."

I smiled back at her as I felt her happiness fill me up. For a brief second the room glowed as the lights all brightened. Cyprien kissed my cheek and I blushed furiously. "I need to work on my emotions having more control over my elements than my mind."

Everyone chuckled. Vida spoke again softly. "That will come with time. You are still part human after all, and the elemental magic was dormant until the dwarves ignited them. Then they became full power when we met, and our mother-daughter bond was completed. You will be more powerful as they develop and in time it will be second nature."

"That will be good. It's a bit embarrassing that the room can read my emotions better than I can."

Everyone laughed again, then Séverin said, "Let's get back to business. I am ready to get this ball rolling." He then turned to Cyprien and me. "No offense."

Cyprien chucked Sév on the shoulder. "None taken. I'm ready to have Phin all to myself."

"Yeah, yeah." I blushed. "So, where are these scissors?"

Demetrius pointed to one of the areas on the map and

the words in the upper right-hand corner came into focus. Realm of Dreams. A large body of water surrounded several different land masses. He used his index finger and thumb as if using a phone to enlarge the image to bring the area closer. The largest land mass came into focus. The name Nod was scrawled on it. As he continued zooming in there were beautiful, detailed images of large farmlands and several large homes along the river reminding me of where I lived in the past. Cy leaned over my shoulder, and I felt the exhale of his breath near my neck when he spotted his home at the same time as I did.

I hurriedly shifted my eyes to another part of the map and followed the river up to the mountains where it began at a large lake created by a flowing waterfall on the map. Off to the right was another river and a forested area that Cy and Sév followed to find the caves. I noticed the grove of the strange trees, that I now remembered were Doskurya trees.

I pointed to it. "That is where I appeared the first time I came, and Vida found me." I noticed little specks moving on the map. "What are those little things moving?"

Demetrius zoomed in. "The citizens of Nod." The map was practically a living image of this world. The awe I felt at the magic in this once book turned map amazed me.

"We are here." It took me a moment for his words to click as he pointed to the top portion of the map. I couldn't see our dots in the caves where we currently stood.

"Why are there only two little people here when I know that there are five of us?"

"Because Aza created her soul hunters to be untraceable, and you will never see any descendants from the Primordial gods on any map, enchanted or otherwise. That is why you are only seeing these men."

"But I'm part human. Why am I not on the map?"

"You are different. Your goddess blood must outweigh your humanity."

I burned with more questions about the map, about the way their genealogy worked, but before I could wrap my mind around a specific question I was too late.

Demetrius moved his finger down the map following the network of cave trails. "You will need to travel to Erebus."

The way he said Erebus made my blood chill. As I followed his finger, it led down to one of the lower levels of the map. The label Realm of Erebus materialized.

I swallowed hard when the word Hades Gates to the Underworld appeared past a maze of tunnels below Erebus.

"We have to go to hell?" I choked out as my knees went weak. I was grateful that Cy was beside me. His hand lifted to my waist so fast helping me stay upright.

I lifted my head up to look at everyone. "I don't want to go to hell."

Cy brought me into his chest wrapping his arms around me. I watched as the map's tunnels of Erebus started to change and blur together. It looked like a puzzle maze that had no actual entrance or exit. How would we ever find our way if the map couldn't even show us?"

"Is this the only way to get the scissors?"

"You will not be going to the underworld. You will be traveling parallel to it. Aza has made a haven for herself closer to Tartarus."

That didn't sound so bad but when the room was eerily silent, I glanced at Cyprien, and his face had gone pale. "What am I missing?" I whispered, regretting that I wasn't as knowledgeable in my mythology.

Cy cleared his throat. "Tartarus is the abyss, the deepest parts of the world where all the wicked receive divine punishment. It is a torturous prison for all our kind." I looked around the room and everyone was solemn.

Vida tutted and gave Demetrius a hard stare. "That is impossible, we are triplets and created with equal parts light and dark. It helps us remain impartial in discerning the fates of each person and god. There is no way she has chosen to live there. It would damage her soul."

Demetrius grabbed Vida's hand. "You are blinded, love. Her soul was damaged the day she called upon Chaos, Thanatos, and stole vials of Lycaon blood to split her soul magic to create us."

Vida pulled her hand out of his. "That is impossible. We Moirae cannot be dark or light."

"Well, you are a balance of the two, but I can assure you Aza is not what you believe."

"I know she has made some mistakes, but it was only because she feared our separation. We were never meant to find love—or so we believed."

"Vida, I never wanted you to worry because I wanted you to never question staying with me, but Aza's mind and powers are no longer the sister you knew. She is changed. She has morphed into her own chaos."

Vida turned to look at us all. Horror struck, her hand flew to her mouth. "She wouldn't!"

"She did."

Tears started to fall from Vida's eyes. Demetrius pulled her into his arms and turned to us. "Aza has used the powers of Chaos to prevent anyone from finding her. That is why the map is constantly changing. But she has her guard. They are loyal and have access to the key to the maze. I hate admitting now that I was once one of those shifters."

He turned to Vida. "When I met you, my universe shifted. I knew Aza was wrong, but my brethren don't understand. I know one or two who are still open to speaking to me. I will confer with one of them to see if they will help me."

Vida shook her head. "No, you can't risk it. They will tell Aza."

"I will come up with something. Don't worry."

She nodded.

I was sad for Vida that her sister had gone bad, but at the same time she needed to face the reality that things were not like she wished. I was grateful to Demetrius's warning so that we knew how horrible Aza really was if we ended up meeting her in hell. I tried to think of something to change the topic and get us back on track.

"Why is there zero movements down there?" I pointed to the map of Erebus.

"Because those who enter are either dead, shifter, or immortal. You will need to cloak these two men with your magic. We don't have a golden fleece for them, but from what I understand, your powers, once unleashed, will be powerful."

That stopped my mind in my tracks. My cheeks grew warm from his praise while my stomach churned because I still had zero control over said power. "Um, how am I supposed to do that when I have no clue how to use my magic? So far, it's only been affected by my emotions."

Vida took a deep breath. "I will help you learn before you embark." She turned to Demetrius. "Help them gather some gear for the cavern trails and get them all some dark clothing and proper shoes for their journey." He nodded.

"You two come with me."

Cyprien and Séverin, who had been quietly observing, both looked to me as if asking for my approval. I hesitated for only a moment then nodded in one quick motion. As they turned away, I hurriedly grabbed Cy's hand holding him back.

I didn't know what I wanted to say, but I wasn't sure I was ready to part ways with him. I had just gotten him back and for the first time since my human parents died, I felt whole again.

"Phin?" he asked softly linking his fingers into mine.

"I'll miss you," I whispered.

"We will be back. I promise."

Sév groaned and patted Cy on the shoulder. "We are just packing supplies, Delphine, he isn't leaving to go on a tour of the world. Geesh."

Cy smiled a toothy grin and for a brief moment my heart fluttered in double bouts of joy. It was the first-time seeing Cy so happy in person and Sév actually sounding like he's teasing us. That one act reinforced that I needed to learn the spell to protect them in Erebus, so we could get the scissors and break the thread of fate. I would make sure I could do that for all of us.

I turned to Vida. "I'm ready, teach me what I need to know."

"We will go over some of the basics of elemental magic. And being you are able to call upon air and fire, the easiest we will start with that."

Vida started the lesson. "Stardust is the element of the gods and is similar to both air and fire. It lives within each of us because we are all our own universe."

"Wait. What?"

She smiled. "Delphine, you are made of all the elements of the universe. Your eyes are your own. They are a replication of your universe, the one that created you. It is how we are all designed. Bits and pieces from myself and you and the Primordial."

So overwhelming.

"We can discuss our genetics at another time. Now, you must learn to call upon your stars to create a fine mist to cover the boys as if they were a part of you, hiding them when you are traveling through the Erebus."

I didn't have enough moisture in my mouth to speak so I nodded hoping she would get started. What I was about to embark on started tremors in me as uncontrolled shivers started to wrack my body.

Vida grabbed my hands, warming them up in her

own. "It will be all right, you may not understand much about what you are capable of yet, but I promise this will become as easy as breathing. It is in your blood now. You are now my family."

I nodded again as my teeth started chattering, and I tried to speak. "Let's do this."

She tapped under my chin with her finger. "That's the spirit. I will guide you."

I nodded.

"First, take a deep breath. Allow the air to enter into your lungs. Feel the weight of it filling you up inside, then release it. As you release it, feel the power of the universe inside of you. It is flowing in your veins. Call upon its power, let it build inside of you, visualize the stars giving you their protection. Hold your hands out and allow it to flow out of you into the palms of your hands and create a cloak of protection."

After a half hour of concentrating and slow deep breathing, I was no longer anxious. I had turned frustrated and threw my hands in the air. "This isn't working. I am useless." But not as useless as I thought. The fireplace flared up and sparks shot out of it like holiday sparklers lighting up the room.

"Hmm." Was all Vida said.

I rolled my eyes. "How will I protect us if all I can do is make magic when I'm emotional?"

"Did you bring the stones with you?"

"No, Séverin was having a bad reaction to them, so I left them at home."

Vida closed her eyes and within seconds the stones were in the palm of her hand.

"Here, use them as a conduit for control. If I remember correctly, you had pretty much mastered the art of fire and air while holding the stones when I first met you."

I felt a bit of relief hearing her say that. She was right. That first night I discovered I was elemental from Goldie, controlling the fire and wind was easy. I was just afraid of the power.

I tied the pouch to the belt loop of my jeans and started over.

Sweat dripped down my spine as I stayed hyper focused on calling on the stardust to me. It had taken me an hour just to finally have it appear. Now that I had it, Vida and I were practicing creating something that looked like a blanket. I would wrap it around an object and make it disappear. It didn't hide people like it did objects, but it would hide Cyprien and Séverin's auras from the maps and keep the guardians of Hades blind to them.

Then she said "Good, you are back."

I stopped what I was doing, and all the bright lights of the stardust rushed back into my palms as I turned around to see Cyprien and Séverin had returned.

"I need you boys to stand right here." Vida pointed to the spot right in front of me. "Now Delphine, I want you to call the stardust to you again." Vida opened the map and zoomed in on our location.

I glanced at the image and could see the two of them on the map. I took a deep breath and called the stardust to me. It only took half a thought now. Vida was right. It was easy once I got used to it. Within moments I had a cloak around both Cyprien and Séverin and both disappeared from the map.

Cy hooted in happiness but Séverin didn't look so good. He appeared as if he were about to puke. In fact, he took off running to the sink and did just that. Vida went to him and laid a cold cloth on his neck. "What is it?"

"The stones. She has them again. I can't be in the same room with them; it completely drains me. Makes me ill."

Vida snapped her fingers, and the stones were removed from my belt loop. Séverin whispered his thanks as his color slowly started to return.

Fear replaced my happiness over my success. "How will I do this without the control of the stones? I've failed before we even started." I flopped onto the sofa and held my head in my hands. Cy came to sit beside me. "You are not a failure. Phin, look at me."

I lifted my head to him.

"You have the power inside of you. Believe in yourself. I believe in you." Then he kissed me. It was a sweet soft kiss and my heart swelled. I needed to do this. I had to so that I could be with him.

Séverin's sighed and rolled his eyes at us. But his word betrayed his annoyance. "You can do anything Delphine, you just need to believe in yourself and if you don't, I'll just force it out of you again."

I stood up. "I'll pass thanks. Okay Vida let's try this again without the stones."

She smiled. "That's the spirit. We all believe in you. The power is a part of you. You have felt it already. You know what to look for now. All you have to do is remove your barriers of disbelief."

I closed my eyes and took a deep breath. I started the entire process again. I was lost in my visualizations until I heard a howl.

Demetrius was shaking me out of it. "Where the hell is Vida? What are you doing?"

The second he broke my concentration his hands were off me, and Vida was in his arms soothing him. "Demi, we never left. That is just her magic. She is truly stronger than any of us ever imagined."

Demetrius turned to me with a look of awe and residual anger from his initial fear. "It appears you are more than ready for this trip. I will guide you to the entrance then you will be on your own."

I grabbed Cy's hand and looked at Séverin and nodded.

Séverin spoke first. "Let's get this show on the road." He threw us each a bag with supplies and a change of clothes. "Get ready."

Chapter Eighteen

We said our farewells to Vida and Demetrius and headed into the caverns that would take us to Erebus and our descent into the underworld. Never in a million years did I ever think this would be my life. I was willingly going to hell!

I cast the blanket over Cy and Sév. Vida was right it was just like breathing. I had to remind myself that I didn't need to try so hard. When I did, they tended to completely disappear from my sight. Especially in the darkness of the caves. Each of us had a light on a helmet and we were all tied together by a rope line. That was the only way I knew they were still with me at times. The first mile or so wasn't so bad, the cavern was smooth and more like an enclosed hallway. There was enough room for both Cyprien and Séverin's height, but once we got into the actual realm of Erebus the ceiling dropped lower and it grew eerily quiet. Huge stalactites and stalagmites crowded in around us, and tumbled rocks cast scary shadows on what little was left of the floor.

My heart was pounding so hard, it was a wonder I didn't cause a landslide. Was it my imagination, or were the rocks pressing in closer? I scraped my shoulders on the slick stone and could only imagine what Cy was going through. The first time I squeezed through an increasingly narrow opening, I shouted out with the guys rushing to me, thinking I was in trouble, but it was only the caverns creating monsters out of stone. I slapped a hand over my mouth, silencing my fear as we passed the back gates of Hades.

The hellhound on the other side of the gate stopped and sniffed the air. A scream struggled in my throat. Cy grabbed my wrist when he heard my breathing hike and added his hand to mine. Together, we hurried past the gate. We were now in the large chamber that would take us to Aza.

The first challenge was to find her symbol on one of the hundreds of small tunnels. Some were so high we would have to do some serious mountain climbing—something I had never done in my life. I pulled out the paper map I'd sketched. I had drawn the symbol: a double-ringed circle with a hyphen in the center of the circle and a pair of scissors that almost resembled a butterfly of sorts. Aza's symbol would guide us through the maze to Tartarus.

"Let's each take a different entrance to look for the symbol."

Séverin muttered. "This is going to take forever."

Cyprien agreed. "The sooner we start the sooner we can get out of here. The silence is freaking me out."

The guys took some of the higher tunnels, Cyprien

being the more experienced adventurer had done climbs before. By the time he reached the top level, Séverin and I had already searched the bottom two rows. Now I had to start climbing.

Cy called down to me when he saw I was starting to climb below him. "I already searched the tunnels in my path on my way up. Start from the other side."

I nodded. I went to the middle as Sév went to the opposite end. By the time I got to the third level I was panting. My fingers hurt and sweat was clinging to my skin under my bra making me want to remove it. I tried adjusting the band and lost my footing for a second and was hanging on a small lip by my rope. I heard Cy gasp. "Phin!"

"I'm good. I just slipped."

"I'm coming down. There was nothing on my side."

Cy made his way down to my level. "Sév, do you see anything yet?"

"Nothing. It has to be in the middle somewhere."

I scowled at Séverin. "How in the world are you already done when I barely made it to the third level?"

"You were climbing slower than a snail, that's why."

"It's not my fault I'm more artistic than athletic."

Sév laughed. "How is that not your fault. You are the one who chose not to be athletic."

Frustrated, I gave him the stink eye that he probably couldn't see in the dark with my head light shining in his eyes. "Forget it. Let's just find this stupid symbol."

Cy helped me the rest of the way. It took so much longer for him because he was helping me, but I was grateful. The climb was easier with his help. We were now all congregated at the last tunnel and there was no symbol.

Sév cursed at the same time as I said, "What the hell?"

Cyprien was scanning all of the tunnels. It was then he looked up above us, and there it was in the center of the ceiling—the symbol.

"How the fuck are we supposed to get there?" Séverin said.

Both guys turned to me as if I'd have the solution. then Cy said, "You know this is supposed to be a magical entrance. Do you think you could use your elemental air maybe like a lift and get us up there?"

I blew out a deep breath. "Honestly no."

"Come on, Phin, don't sound so defeated," Cy encouraged her. "Vida said you just need to believe in yourself."

Sév butted in, "Yeah, and with that attitude we will never get this damn cord severed. Are you trying to tell Cy you don't want to be with him and would rather be with me?"

I glared at him. "Stop being such an ass. That is not what I'm saying." I practically growled in aggravation at his stupid implications. Of course, I wanted to be with Cy. Sév was a grade A asshole. Before I knew it, I was at the top of the ceiling and the guys were hanging from the ropes below me. The moment I realized I was at the entrance, I had a mini panic and we all free fell a few feet.

All of us screamed something different and then I made myself focus on saving us and getting back up there. Obviously, I could do it. We stopped free falling and I felt a tug and heard a loud groan from the guys.

Cy shouted up at me, "Babe, I appreciate what you're doing, I really do, but could you maybe hurry it along a bit?"

I looked down at Cy and panic started to form again. The entire bottom of the cavern had disappeared and Cyprien was almost about to be stabbed through the gut by a spear shaped stalagmite. Séverin was just dangling and looked like he might have passed out. At least this panic didn't make us fall more. Now that they were both in trouble, I really put more effort into it. I held my palms open. I was already floating and holding the two guys by our ropes. I could do this.

Before I knew it, I was at the entrance to the tunnel on the ceiling of the cave. Once I was inside gravity changed and I fell to the ground. My feet connected to the floor and the ropes were still dangling out the entrance. I started trying to pull the rope, but it was burning my hands. How was it not hurting my waist? I didn't understand but I didn't have time to think. I laid down on the floor of the cavern entrance and pointed my palms to the guys. I used every ounce of concentration I had and tried to make the air lift them to me. The first one to come up was Cy. He grabbed my extended hand so I could help pull him in.

I was lying on my back panting. He kissed my forehead. "I'll pull Sév in. You rest."

I nodded as I listened to him strain to pull the dead weight of his brother up.

Once he had Sév on the ground he did a complete assessment of his body.

"Is he okay?"

"He hit his head, but his pupils look fine. I think it just knocked him out when we fell fast." Cy then ripped the bottom of his shirt and made a wraparound Sév's head to stop the bleeding. "I think we may need to stay here for a while. We all could use the break."

"I don't feel safe here," I whispered.

"Neither do I. I think we all came into this a bit ignorant of just how long walking and finding our way to the first entrance would be."

"I know. For some reason I was thinking it would be just a short little hike."

Cy opened his camp bag and took out a small can. "Do you think you could start a fire in this for me?"

"Sure, that is something I know I can do." I didn't even have to point at the can, I just imagined the fire inside it and within seconds we had a very small fire lighting up our surroundings. "What else can I do?" I asked.

"Take out Sév's blanket and cover him, and maybe put something under his head. I am going to try to heat us all some soup for dinner. Hopefully he will wake up soon."

I did as I was told and covered Sév. When I got to his head, I placed a pair of spare pants under his head for a pillow. As I was lifting his head he groaned, and before I knew it he had his arms around me, pulling me down and he was kissing my neck.

"Séverin!" I screeched. "Stop it!" I shoved myself off of him.

He opened his eyes and groaned as he slowly sat up. "Why does my head hurt so bad?"

"Because you just kissed my girlfriend, and she paid you back for your obscenities." Cy laughed.

"I did not!" Then he looked at me and I was glad it was dark inside because I know my cheeks were burning.

"You did, but that isn't why your head hurts. We had a bit of a hard time getting into this cavern and you hit your head."

"Damn. I think I'd rather a beating than a lame excuse of me being knocked out from falling."

We all chuckled at that.

"That smells good. Is it almost ready? I'm starving."

Cy stirred the small pot over the flame. "Yeah, shouldn't be too much longer. Phin, would you get the bowls and spoons out of my bag please."

"Sure." I started digging through his bag and as I pulled out one of the bowls a small velvet pouch fell out. When I picked it up the ties were loose, and a beautiful, filigreed ring with an oval raw opal that shimmered like the galaxy fell out. I put it back in the pouch and back into his backpack. Was that for me? Was Cy going to propose once Sév and I were no longer attached by the thread of fate?

He still wanted me, literally with no strings attached. My heart soared knowing that I didn't need fate for someone to choose me and I would definitely choose him. I didn't need anyone to tell me that. I wanted to be with Cy in the past and in the present. I couldn't hide my smile when I looked at him. He smiled back at me, and we just stared at one another all sappy like.

Séverin sighed. "I can't watch this anymore. Can you

please stop staring at one another all googly eyed and serve the soup."

"Of course, we can."

When Cyprien gave me my bowl he kissed me on the head. "Thank you for saving us back there. I forgot to tell you that right away."

"It was no problem; I'd do it again and again if I had to."

He kissed me full on the lips this time in thanks, and Séverin started muttering. "I'll get my own damn soup."

Cyprien laughed and moved away. "You, brother, especially need to thank Phin. She saved your life after all."

"Thanks" he said quick as lightning, then started eating his soup against the wall hidden in the shadows away from the fire.

Cy sat beside me, and we all ate in silence. When we were done, I tried to fill my bowl with water to rinse it. Amazingly the water from the caves flew into the bowl and swirled around inside it. "Well, that was cool," I said aloud.

"Here, try again with mine." Cyprien handed me his bowl.

Once more I called for water, and it did it again. Giddily I laughed. "That was so easy. I think I am starting to understand how to use my powers a little more. At least for the easy stuff. It seems I still tend to need some heavy emotions for the bigger stuff especially if I don't' have the stones as a conduit."

It was in that moment that I had another bout of panic and froze. Cyprien could sense my change and he was on his feet in seconds and Séverin following his actions. "What is it?"

"Nothing, I think, but when we fell, I dropped the blanket covering y'all from the maps."

"Oh shit!" Séverin said. "Hurry, pack up. I thought I heard snuffling in the walls earlier but figured it was my imagination from hitting my head. Some kind of alarm must have gone off."

I put the blanket of stardust over them again for protection as we all packed up fast. I doused the fire, and we were once more trekking the cave systems following the symbols as we went. We had to stop at least three times and stand still as we heard noises. It was as if something was searching for us and I double checked each time that the blanket was covering both Cyprien and Sév. In fact, I was concentrating so hard that once more I made the blanket so strong both became invisible again and the only way I knew they were beside me was that I was still tied to them by the rope, and in this instant Cy was holding my hand.

When the snuffling was no longer heard, we started walking again. This time, as we were walking, the caverns started shifting and we had to run for the exit or we'd be squished inside. Séverin just made it out when the cavern sealed shut. "What the hell was that?"

"I guess that is the moving maze that Demetrius told us about." I pulled my paper map out that was crumpled from one of our run ins earlier. I tried smoothing it out on my thigh. "It looks like we are going to have to crawl through the next tunnels called the Dragons Back."

Cy breathed out heavily. "Let me see the map."

I handed it over to him. "Shit!"

"What?"

Cy turned to Sév, his lips tight. "I'm going first, Phin in the middle and you at the rear."

I turned to Cy. "What's going on? Why are you going first?"

"This isn't just a tunnel, it's a real dragons back. I thought I smelled sulfur. I'd been smelling it since we cooked earlier but I didn't think much of it. I should have known better when the scent started getting stronger rather than going away."

I took a deep inhale. "I don't smell anything different" and turned to Séverin. "Do you?"

He shook his head. "Are you sure, Cy?"

"I'm positive. When I was traveling the world, we stumbled upon a dragon's lair off the Coast of Slumber. I was one of only three shipmates who could smell it. They are very good at masking their scent. Anyway, to get across the cavern to get the dragons gold, we had to walk its back. The leader of our group had done this a million times, and he told me that all dragons have certain scales they cannot feel. Those are the ones that if walked on will not wake them from their slumber. If we touch any of the others, we will all be dead in moments because when the dragon wakes up the sulfur oozes from his scales like poison, and we will become immobile. Then they burrow in the small tunnel and their body will expand. We will die within seconds."

Séverin gestured to his brother. "Death by squashing? You first."

Chapter Nineteen

The moment we entered the dragons back I finally smelled the sulfur. It was strong and the small cavern was as hot and humid as a New Orleans summer and smelled almost as bad.

"Keep to the scales that have a dull point on them, watch my footing closely and we will only take one at a time so you can keep up. Dragons are long so this will probably take at least a half hour to cross. So please don't be impatient."

Cyprien turned to Séverin. "Do you understand?"

"What do you think I am— a fool? Of course I understand."

We started the uneven journey on the back of the dragon. "It's weird, the scales look like stone."

"What were you expecting?"

"I guess scales. Maybe shiny iridescent ones."

"I've never seen a dragon like that here in Nod."

"Hmph," was all I could say as we started the ascent up the dragon.

"This will be the hard part, we need to go up and there is nothing to hold on to so be extra careful that you don't place your hand anywhere."

As we started to move up a low growl came from behind Séverin. "Fuck, the wolves found us—hurry!"

Both Cy and I said shit at the same time, and he started hopping on different scales. One was so far away I didn't think I would be able to make it. Then he shouted, "Use the wind, Phin."

I called upon the element to help me have some height to jump and made it, but lost my balance and was flailing my arms trying to stabilize myself without touching the dragon.

The rope around my waist tightened. "Hold on to the rope." I'd did as Cy said, regained my balance and leapt to the next stone as Séverin landed on the one I'd just left.

"We're almost there, only three more to go."

I had just jumped on the last scale when the dragon started to move. I heard a yelp and the temperature that was already hot heated up. I jumped off the last scale to the edge of the cavern. "Hurry, Sév!" Just as he jumped on the last scale the dragon reared his head. The beast was enormous, and his eyes looked like burning coals. When he opened his mouth, it looked like Sév was about to fly into it and my instinct took over.

I yanked hard on the rope and Sév flew through the air towards us. I called upon all the water and I started shooting the stream at the dragon.

Cy screamed, "No!"

But he was too late. A loud explosion occurred and a

plume of sulfuric smoke filled the room. I felt Cy grab my hand. "Cover your mouth and nose with your shirt and run."

We ran until the air cooled and the walls shifted once more. We had no idea which tunnel we ran into or where we needed to go next. I collapsed to the ground coughing. "I am so sorry. I had no idea water could do that."

"You wouldn't have known that sulfur fires are different. Does anyone feel like they have any burns? Sév, you were almost dragon kibble how are you?"

He was sitting against the wall with his knees bent to his chest, his head laying on his arm that rested on his knees. He didn't lift his head or say anything only gave Cy a thumbs up.

I turned in Cy's direction after Sév confirmed he was ok. Cyprien had started pacing the cave. I was afraid to hear the answer, but I asked anyway. "Did the wolves die?" Even though they were chasing us, I felt bad that they died because of us. They were all related to Demetrius even if they didn't see eye to eye.

"I would imagine so. Rarely can any being survive the poison from dragon scales. One of them must of misstepped. We're really lucky we survived."

"We are lucky we had you guiding us," I told him.

Cyprien sat next to me. "Can I see the map? We need to figure out where we are. I tried to pay attention as we were running, but I'm not sure if I remember after one of the walls shifted."

I handed the map over to him and rested my head on his arm as he looked at the map. Séverin started snoring. "Do you think I should wake him up?"

"Nah, he needs to rest. He hit his head hard earlier and almost got eaten by a dragon."

"True. I snuggled into Cyprien and closed my eyes. "I am going to close my eyes for just a second, okay?"

He kissed the top of my head. "You need rest, too; you've used a lot of magic today."

I was lying on something so warm and comfy that when I rolled over and hit something hard, I let out an expletive. The warm soft body of Cyprien shifted beside me. "Phin?"

"Yeah, sorry about that."

"It's okay. Are you all right?"

"Yeah, just forgot where we were for a second."

Séverin's gruff voice spoke. "How can you forget we are in hell?"

"Whatever. I'm awake now. Were you able to figure out where we were on the map"?

"I think so. I don't think we are too far off course. While you were sleeping, I went a little ways away and noticed one of the symbols on the wall up ahead. It leads to the hardest part of our journey where we have to climb down a shaft. We won't be able to bring any of our supplies or our hats, Sév, because we may be too big, but Phin, you should be able to keep yours on."

"You shouldn't have gone off without us," I said.

"I didn't want to wake you. You both needed your rest especially if we run into Aza down there. We all have to be at our best."

"Ugh, you're right." I groaned.

"In that case let's eat now, because it may be our last meal until we can get back here to get our stuff."

I pulled out the can for the fire and started it. "I sure wish I could just teleport us there. It would have been so much easier."

"When Sév and I were gathering supplies, he asked Demetrius the same question. I am surprised you're only thinking of it now."

"Well don't leave me hanging. What did he say?"

"That it won't work because you don't know where she is. For all you know you could land on Mt. Olympus because that may be where she was last or gathering threads from the elves. That kinda would have been funny. Could you imagine if we landed in poor old Alfrock's bed. Poor old boy would have probably had a heart attack."

Séverin chuckled.

"That would have been horrible, but I guess that is true. I never thought about having to know where we needed to go. I wonder why I came the first time I landed in the grove and last time in the woods?"

"Well, the woods weren't that far from where Sév and I grew up and we were with you, so maybe that was, why and the first time you were searching for answers."

I looked up at Cyprien. "I swear you have a memory like an elephant. I forgot I told you all that stuff. That makes sense. Well, at least now I know where Vida lives and once we get the scissors I can teleport us back home."

I paused for a second when I said the word home. Vida's house felt like home; being here in Nod with Cyprien felt like home. I looked up at Cy then glanced at

Séverin. "When this is all over do y'all want to live back here in Nod or in the mortal realm in New Orleans?"

Sév looked at Cy then me. "I am going to stay here and try to see if our house is still standing and if it is still ours. If it is, I want to farm again and live the life I wanted before all this mess." He turned to me. "No offense. And before you start apologizing, I know this isn't your fault. I can still feel some of your emotions thru this damn connection and I really don't need your guilt right now."

"I'm sorry," I said anyway out of habit.

Séverin rolled his eyes at me. "What about you, little brother?"

Cyprien took my hand. "I guess that all depends on how Phin feels after your red thread has been severed. If she still feels the same, I will go wherever she wants to go."

I smiled up at him. "I think I want to go to New Orleans and explain things to Aurora. She has no clue about all of this and is probably wondering where I am. We've been gone for what four? Five days now? She is probably worried sick."

"Theo will probably let her know you are all right. He knew we wanted to come here for answers, and she was with him. He will think of something to tell her especially being he is keeping a huge secret from her as well."

"I didn't want this to be a secret; it just sort of turned out that way. But I will definitely clear the air when we get back. Then I think if you're up to it, come back here for a while. I'd like to get to know Vida more and learn more about my elementals."

He kissed me fully. "I love the sound of that."

Sév groaned again. "You love birds make me sick. I never want to be attached like this to anyone ever again. I give up on love, and fate. It is a trap."

Phin turned to him. "Aww, don't say that. You and I were just in the wrong place at the wrong time and Aza used us. I found Cy who was my destined fate even without the red thread connecting us. I think when you meet the right person it won't be as toxic as our relationship was."

"Well good for you, but I am still choosing not to ever fall in love again."

"That is your choice. All we have to do is get those scissors away from Aza and she will never be able to screw with anyone else like us again."

We finished eating our dinner and packed up all our belongings. Séverin was the first one standing. "You ready? I am ready to finish this."

Chapter Twenty

We started the descent down into the shaft. It was a tight squeeze for the guys. At one point, I had to pull out a knife from my bag and try to hand it to Cyprien so he could chisel out some of the rock. It took him an hour just to make enough space for his shoulder to pass. We were all sweating and dirty and as I reached for the next hand grip I screamed.

"What the hell, Phin!" Séverin shouted.

"I just held onto a skull going down."

Cy was below me. "Sorry, I was hoping you wouldn't notice. I didn't want to freak you out."

"Please freak me out the next time. I can't stop my heart from racing."

"In that case, the rest of the way down is no longer solid mountain. It is tortured bones melded into the rocky walls. This is a graveyard, and we have to crawl the rest of the way down in between them."

I breathed out. "Have mercy on their souls." I muttered as my foot landed on another skull.

"This is sacrilege," Séverin said from above me.

Cyprien agreed. The rest of the descent was solemn. My stomach churned and my heart raced with every move I made trying not to desecrate the bones of the deceased more than I already was. By the time we made it out into a small cavern, tear streaks were visible on Cyprien's dirty cheeks. I'm sure mine were tear streaked, too. Séverin landed into the pit.

"This better be the end of this journey. I don't think I can take much more."

I took the map out of Cyprien's back pocket.

"It looks like this last tunnel takes us to Tartarus where she keeps the scissors. All we have to do now is find the symbol again and it will open the rooms.

We only had to take about twenty steps and we found the symbol. I pressed my hand to it and said the word in a foreign language and a door appeared. We walked in and thankfully no one was in there. The room looked like a chemistry lab at the university. "Ok, split up and start searching. We need to find these black scissors."

I went to a desk and opened the drawer and there they were. I picked them up. "This was too easy?" Cy and Sév turned to me and before I could blink Séverin grabbed the scissors out of my hand and cut our thread. The black thread vanished, and he fell back into the desk and slid to the ground. "It's done. I don't feel you anymore." Then he passed out with a smile.

I smiled at Cyprien then jumped into his arms. "We did it!"

He spun me around. "We did!"

A loud laugh echoed through the room. "You didn't

think I'd let you just have my scissors now did you? I certainly hope you enjoyed your journey down. I've been waiting for you for days. However, I must admit I was hoping that the dragon would have killed you all and save me the trouble of getting my hands dirty. But now you all owe me the lives of three of my soul shifters."

Aza was just as beautiful as Vida and Goldie. It was so hard seeing her as being evil. I don't know what I was expecting, but I think it was something like the Wicked Witch of the West, not another Glenda. Cyprien shifted me behind him as Aza came closer.

"Isn't this sweet? Lover boy is trying to protect you and his brother."

She threw her hand out and blasted Cyprien and me back. She bent over Séverin's unconscious form and picked up the scissors and held them. I had to get them away from her. We couldn't let her keep them.

Cy must have been thinking the same thing and she blasted him to the roof with her magic as she laughed. "Oh, no one can help you now, lover boy."

While she was looking at Cy, I jumped on her back. I was small and lithe compared to her. She moved her hand, pulled my hair and a chunk of it came out. "Ow, you bitch, that hurt."

I dug my heels into her hipbones and wouldn't let go. I started pulling her hair too and as Cy fell to the ground I screamed and bit the top of her head as hard as I could until I tasted blood. She screeched and waved her hands. The room turned into a whirlwind, and I hung onto her as if I were riding a bronco at the rodeo. I never knew I had such strength but when I saw that the scissors in her pocket falling out, I moved my heel and kicked them down. Cy was watching me the entire time and he fought the flying objects in the room and grabbed them tucking them in the back of his pants.

The second my foot had moved, Aza bent forward, yanked my shoulders, and flipped me forward over her head. I landed on my back a little dizzy from my head rebounding off the hard floor.

Aza then said something in the same foreign words I had to use to open the lab. A portal of sorts opened. She started moving the wind around lifting both Cy and me up and towards the portal. I didn't know where it led but it couldn't be good. I called upon my own elements and fire was the first to come. The entire room was set ablaze. I made air circulate and protected Cy and Sév as best I could. I tried to make water to put out the fires, but I was trying too hard to protect the guys. Aza only laughed at my pitiful rescue attempt.

Cy was behind me, and she was herding us into the portal, or at least she was, until I noticed Séverin was standing behind her. I shouted, "NO!"

Aza thought I was talking to her and laughed at the same time as Séverin pushed her. Cy and I flew out of the way. Both Aza and Séverin were gone, the portal closed.

I was screaming and crying as Cy tried to hold me back. "No!! We have to find him! We can't just leave him there."

Cy pulled me into his arms. He was crying. "We can't, Phin. Aza was planning to send us into a cell in Tartarus. She never planned for any of us to get out. Séverin saved our lives."

"No," I whimpered in a small voice into his chest. "He just got free and now he will live in hell for eternity. How is that fair?"

"He knew what he was doing. If anyone is wrong, it is me for not trying to stop him and only saving you."

I placed my fingers over his lips. "Stop it! Don't say that! I don't want to be here anymore."

"Don't let his sacrifice be for nothing. We will start our forever, but for now, take us back to Vida's. Maybe she and Demetrius can help us find a way to free Séverin."

With teary eyes, I kissed him. "I love you."

"I love you too, always."

After our declarations, we didn't say another word, and within seconds I teleported us inside Vida's house, and I flew into her arms, crying.

"Séverin is gone."

She rubbed my back, trying to comfort me. "What happened?"

Cyprien told her and Demetrius what happened, and the only words spoken were from Demetrius. "The war has started. The wolves will be out for revenge. We must warn the others."

With nothing more we could do that night, Cyprien and I went to bed in the guest room of Vida's home.

I woke up crying and hugging Cy tight. He was soothing my back. I lifted my chin up off of his chest, "Bad dream."

His hand cupped my face and he wiped away my

tears with his thumbs. I kissed him lightly on the lips. "I was reliving the maze and Séverin saving us."

Cyprien rolled onto his back bringing me with him. I cuddled into his side as he spoke. "I miss him. I didn't have the gap in time that he had because of being in a frozen state of sleep, but knowing he lived so long here with no one and not knowing what happened or why he was banished here haunts me."

I straddled his waist, his hands settled on my hips. His eyes were glassy. I placed my hands on his shoulders and kissed his cheek, where a stray tear fell. "He fought so hard to understand why— and in the end, gave everything up for me," his words broke into a choked whisper, "us."

A rush of emotion filled me deep inside, the flame of my love burned within. I moved his hands from my hips and laced our fingers together. I closed my eyes and let the warmth of my love spread through my veins and radiate into Cyprien. The golden thread burned on my finger and a spark ignited, spreading out of me and into Cy's thread. I kissed our entwined fingers with the gold thread and gazed into his eyes. "Then let's not let his sacrifice be for nothing."

"Cyprien." I brought his golden thread hand to my heart and spread it for him to feel it's rapid beating. "Will you marry me and be my eternal love?"

The grin I loved so much showing all his teeth and squinted his eyes appeared. He sat up keeping me in position, moved his hands into my hair and kissed me until I was breathless.

Smiling happily, I asked, "Is that a yes?"

His grin returned. "It's a yes"

I kissed him, and as I did, the golden thread turned into solid gold bands resembling my parents' rings on the back of their wedding photo.

He wiggled his fingers. "Now, our bond will never be broken."

"Never. I am all yours, forever."

He rolled me onto my back and kissed me. "Our love is eternal, no matter the future, it will always burn as a flame lighting our way."

Epilogue

The cell was small and rough-hewn, except for one wall with two arms and a face. Firelight made its carved expression all the more eerie, but the woman standing in the cell just laughed and hung her cloak on an outstretched finger.

"Come," she called out in a cruel voice.

A smaller woman with short hair stood outside the cell. "I'm busy. What now?"

The first woman scoffed. "Busy? When is the goddess of retribution busy? Oh yes, my dear sister has fallen from the grace of the gods and has been hiding in the mortal realm playing human."

Nemesis smiled back. "I'd rather be playing human than imprisoned in Tartarus."

The first woman bared her teeth. "I'm not imprisoned here."

Nemesis rolled her eyes. The first woman shrugged; her expression tight. "A small miscalculation on my part."

Nemesis scanned the cell. It wasn't a typical cell in

Tartarus. Then she noticed the face and her stomach sank.

Nemesis turned to hide the expression on her face. "A purse rack? How thoughtful of you."

The first woman smiled. "The one good thing about this miscalculation."

Nemesis magicked a golden watch and fob, swinging it like a pendulum. "Tik. Tok," she said shortly. "Busy?" The last thing she wanted was for her sister to know the extent of her involvement.

The first woman yanked the watch out of her hands through the bars and smashed it. "I'm calling in my favor."

Nemesis moved closer to the cell. "What favor?"

"You owe me, and I know you remember. This time you will pay twofold, or I will make sure your master knows your hiding place. Her smile widened. "Bev."

Nemesis bent to pick up the broken watch, eyes hidden. "What do you need, Aza?"

A Moment of Your Time

Enjoyed this book? Please leave a review!

Reviews help indie authors like me reach new readers and help new readers decide if a book is for them.

Please take a moment to write a short review.

Thank you! Your support means the world to me, and I'm truly grateful for your time and feedback. Click HERE or scan the QR code to leave a sentence or two.

Book Extras!

Visit my website, where you can find extra goodies, such as images of the city, the cast, and merchandise for all my books and series.

https://kristentassin.com/tapestry

To stay in touch and be the first to find out about big news, book series, and giveaways, sign up for my newsletter at www.kristentassin.com. As an incentive, you will receive my first book ever written, a FREE Christmas in Cypressville ebook.

Acknowledgments

Always, my first thanks go to my two girls, Emily and Rachel, without whom I would be nothing. I love you always, and your ability to believe in me keeps me moving forward. I want to thank Megan for all our long nights at the cafe and bar, hanging out, talking, and dreaming of Nod. To Tina, thank you for endless hours of brainstorming together and listening to my ramblings of this incredible world. My mastermind group, Kathleen, Jenn, Holly, and Sarah, thank you for all the support and advice. A special thanks to Jodi Henly, my developmental editor, who helped me dig deep and discover not only Phin had magic, but I did too. Having a writing disability isn't always easy, but with a team of experts, life is easier, and in my opinion, the sentence structure of this book wouldn't be as read-worthy if it weren't for Patty MacFarlane, my editor. And last but not least, my appreciation goes out to Annette, a long-time client turned proofreader. You are the absolute best. Thank you all.

About the Author

Kristen Tassin is an independent author driven by a lifelong passion for storytelling. Overcoming the challenges of dysgraphia, she has dedicated more than two decades to refining her writing skills while working full-time and being a single mom to two amazing daughters and two fur babies.

With several sweet contemporary romances already under her belt, Kristen's journey of self-discovery and confidence-building has led her to a new frontier, writing books with mental health representation and fantasy romance. Her love for fantasy and her ability to draw inspiration from her thirty-year career as a cosmetologist. Her interactions with diverse individuals and ornery cats have enriched her narrative palette, allowing her to craft compelling characters and scenarios. Kristen's unique journey and rich life experiences infuse depth and authenticity into her storytelling.

Keep in touch, sign up for my newsletter at www.kristentassin.com

facebook.com/author.kristentassin

instagram.com/kristentassin.author

tiktok.com/@kristentassin.author

amazon.com/author/kristentassin

Also by Kristen Tassin

CONTEMPORARY ROMANCE

Cypressville Small Town Romance

Christmas in Cypressville

Love by Design

Love Under Construction

Christmas on Ice

FANTASY ROMANCE | SHORT READS

Neotropolis Bites

Fatal Grace

Small Town Short Reads: Alien Romance

Unexpected Destiny (Anthology)

Small Town Short Reads: Paranormal Matchmaker Romance

The Ghost in Apartment 99B

Tapestry of Fated Dreams

Land of Nod (Fairytales)

Woven in Dreams